MURDER AT THE LODGE

MURDER AT THE LODGE

J. M. Gregson

This first world edition published in Great Britain 2003 by
SEVERN HOUSE PUBLISHERS LTD of
9–15 High Street, Sutton, Surrey SM1 1DF.
This first world edition published in the USA 2003 by
SEVERN HOUSE PUBLISHERS INC of
595 Madison Avenue, New York, N.Y. 10022.

British Library Cataloguing in Publication Data

Gregson, J. M. (James Michael)
    Murder at the lodge
    1.   Peach, Detective Inspector (Fictitious character) - Fiction
    2.   Police - England - Fiction
    3.   Detective and mystery stories
    I.   Title
    823.9'14 [F]

    ISBN 0-7278-5813-0

Typeset by Palimpsest Book Production Ltd.,
Polmont, Stirlingshire, Scotland.
Printed and bound in Great Britain by
MPG Books Ltd., Bodmin, Cornwall.

*To John Cox, Keith Bedford, Mike Gizzey, Derek Briggs
and all the other policemen and ex-policemen who try to
keep me on the straight and narrow*

One

Detective Constable Brendan Murphy watched Detective Inspector Percy Peach out of the corner of his eye. It was marvellous how the man seemed to ooze aggression from every pore when he questioned suspects.

'You're in trouble, sunshine. Big trouble. Gives me a lot of pleasure, that does.' Peach smiled at his subject, his teeth looking very white and very sharp at the base of the round face.

The twenty-two-year-old on the other side of the small, square table, striving to appear indifferent, looked a little surprised despite himself at this open statement of satisfaction by a policeman: you could usually expect more caution from the pigs, nowadays. He looked meaningfully at the slowly turning cassette beside them and said, 'You could be sorry you said that, Inspector Peach.'

'Oh, I doubt that, Mr Afzaal. I doubt it very much. But I think *you* might regret what you did in Mr Alston's shop.'

The boy's fingers flicked automatically to the side of his head, caressing the glossy black hair where it was combed back over his temples. Thrown a little by Peach's confidence, he played the card he had intended to hold back for emergencies. 'This is racialist.'

'I'm glad you admit it, lad. We might get somewhere now.' Peach's smile was sudden and broad, like the crocodile's in *Peter Pan*. He turned briefly to the man at his side. 'Might be worth making a note of that, DC Murphy. Mr Afzaal admits his actions had a racialist motivation.'

Afzaal's brown eyes widened in consternation. 'Not what we

1

did – what you *say* we did – what you're trying to plant on us. What you're doing to us now, I mean. It's clearly racialist.'

Peach looked with distaste into the handsome, olive-skinned features. He was happier out-thinking white thugs with shaven heads and tattoos and limited IQs, but he was far too experienced to show it. You couldn't pick and choose your villains, these days. 'You mean questioning you about this assault with three of your friends on a defenceless man three times your age, with another officer present and a tape running? I doubt if you could make the racialist label stick, sunshine.'

Peach turned and grinned at DC Murphy, who took his cue, smiled broadly at the preposterous notion of Percy Peach being racialist, and said, 'Especially in view of what your friends have just been telling us.'

Fear flashed across the too-revealing young features. The others were a year younger than him, and he hadn't had time to brief them after their arrest last night. There was no knowing what they had been admitting to the police under pressure, especially if this little turkey-cock of an inspector had been at them. Afzaal licked his lips, tried to think, found it impossible under the mesmeric glare of the dark eyes on the other side of the table. He said weakly, 'It wasn't any more than a bit of fun.'

Even after years of experiencing it, it still gave Percy the occasional shock to hear a Lancashire accent issuing from an Asian face. He relaxed, gave the boy another grin, wondering if Afzaal realized that he had virtually admitted the incident in his last phrase. Then his face hardened. 'You tell the man whose shop you wrecked that it was just a bit of fun. See if that's how *he* sees it.'

'He was asking for it.'

Peach raised his black eyebrows as high as they would go beneath his shining bald pate. 'A man of sixty, with no history of violence? A man with a lot of respect in the community, trying to run a newspaper and general sundries shop? I doubt if the magistrate will see it that way.' He shook his head sadly at the obstinacy and unreality of the young man in front of him.

That young man had been very sure of himself when he swaggered into the interview room five minutes earlier. DC Murphy marvelled at the uncertainty Peach had induced in him without anything tangible to throw at him. A master in the art of bluff, was Percy.

Wasim Afzaal snarled, 'You can't frighten me with the bloody bench, Peach! This'll never come to court, and you know it. You'll never convince the CPS you've got a case!'

Peach beamed at him. 'You should be listening to your mates, sunshine. They've been singing like sweet English thrushes. Not racialist, that, is it?'

'They wouldn't do that!' Afzaal was shouting now, as though he hoped that the extra volume would convince them. But he could hear the doubt in his own voice.

Percy shrugged, without turning down the radiance of the beam on his face. 'Suit yourself, sunshine.' He turned to Brendan Murphy. 'Better make a note that Mr Afzaal refused to co-operate at this point. Said the case would never come to court. Won't please the judge, that.' Peach raised Afzaal's case effortlessly from local to Crown court. 'Won't even please Mr Afzaal's mum and dad, I shouldn't wonder.' He shook his head sadly again at the follies of youth.

It was always worth a mention of dad with these Asians. Your born and bred Lancashire ruffians had usually long since cut off the ties of home, but family values and pressures were still strong with Indians or Pakistanis, even when lads claimed to be brutally Anglicized. Sure enough, Afzaal's face clouded at the mention of his family. 'No call for you to go ratting to my dad,' he said sullenly.

'No. You've been an adult since you were eighteen, the law says. Responsible for your own actions, and likely to be put away for a year or two on a grievous bodily harm rap.'

There was no question of any charge as serious as that. Indeed, if Afzaal had but known it, there was no chance of old Harry Alston bringing any case to court: he'd be far too conscious of the retribution which might be visited upon his corner shop.

But Afzaal didn't know that. All he could see was Peach's grin growing wider as he felt panic coursing through his veins. He said hoarsely, 'It was a bit of fun that got out of hand, that's all.'

Percy sensed a collapse. His grin disappeared abruptly as he leaned forward. 'I can almost believe that, sunshine. Though my idea of fun wouldn't be the same as yours. And it's not how Mr Alston would see it, is it?'

Afzaal shut his eyes briefly, to shut out the inspector's toothsome grin. But in its stead, he could see only his father's thunderous brow, hear his harsh tones threatening to suspend the degree course he was enjoying. 'Is there no way out of this, then? Without going to court, I mean?'

Peach drew in a long breath, then let it out again slowly, in an astonished whistle. He looked at Brendan Murphy, shook his head sadly, then turned his attention back to the handsome, apprehensive young face on the other side of the table. Abruptly, he reached across and switched off the tape recorder. 'Can't promise anything. It would depend on the injured party, not me.'

'You mean Mr Alston? You think he might be persuaded to . . .'

Afzaal left his question hanging in the air, and Percy Peach regarded it curiously there for a few seconds, as if he was watching a smoke ring slowly disappear. He said doubtfully, 'You'd need to pay for all the damage. Mr Alston will need a new cash register: the old one's probably beyond repair after you flung it on the floor like that. And of course you'd have to pay for the cigarettes and the boxes of chocolates you stole.'

Afzaal gulped, then snatched hard at salvation. 'We could do that, I'm sure. If the four of us got together.'

Peach looked doubtfully at DC Murphy. 'We could ask Mr Alston, I suppose. In his place, I'd still want to bring charges, to see the ruffians who'd wrecked my shop put away safely for a stretch. But Mr Alston might be a more charitable chap than me.'

DC Murphy nodded slowly. 'He'd need some extra payment

for sundry damage to his stock when you smashed those bottles, and some compensation for the terror you brought into his life, I'm sure. But I think he's a kind chap, Mr Alston.' Old Harry would need some briefing to ask for enough, thought Brendan. The man had been anxious only that the police should forget about the damage to himself and his shop when they'd seen him that morning. Before this Peach magic.

The DI pursed his lips and added, 'And we'd need to make sure he had a public apology. As evidence of good faith. In front of police witnesses.'

For a moment, Brendan thought Percy had overplayed his hand. The young man bridled; this was surely more than his pride could take. 'No way!' he said harshly. 'Chanting out our sins to old Alston in front of a policeman? We'd be the laughing stock in—'

'I suppose your father would do as a witness, at a pinch,' said Percy thoughtfully. 'I know Mr Alston respects him as a fellow businessman.'

Afzaal glared at him. 'My father mustn't know anything about this. That's a condition for any—'

'You're not in a position to make conditions, lad!' snapped Peach, raising his voice for the first time in the interview. 'There'll be a police presence, then, when you make the apology. And you'd better name the sum you're offering in compensation for last night's little episode. I think two thousand would probably cover it. Five hundred each. But how you distribute the payment among the four of you is up to you. So long as Mr Alston gets his money and his full apology.'

Afzaal gulped. 'He'll get them. He can have the apology today, and the money within three days. Just make sure my father doesn't get to know anything about this, that's all.'

Percy gave him his blandest smile. 'Better tell the other lads what you've agreed. We'll get them up from the cells: I dare say they'll be a bit surprised. DC Murphy will run you down to Mr Alston's place when you've agreed the wording of your apology with him. All part of the service.'

*   *   *

5

Bricks made without straw. Old Harry Alston would be pleased, not to say astonished, to find these young thugs offering both compensation and apology. It had cheered up this Monday morning, when the drizzle fell in thin sheets over the drab old cotton town. Peach looked out over its greyness with a surprising affection as he climbed reluctantly up the stairs to see the superintendent in charge of the Brunton CID section.

An interview with Superintendent Thomas Bulstrode Tucker was the last thing he needed on a Monday morning. Probably another pep talk about the efficiency of the CID unit. You tended to get these when Tommy Bloody Tucker had no serious crime to divert his attentions. The pep talks tended to degenerate into bollockings when Percy refused to accept the aspersions cast upon the efficiency of his team.

But it was immediately apparent that this was not to be a bollocking morning. Tucker waved him expansively into one of the pair of deep armchairs which had just been delivered to his penthouse office, then came round his desk and sat uneasily in the other one himself. Within a minute, a tray arrived with a coffee pot, china cups, and chocolate digestive biscuits. The trimmings normally only afforded to civic dignitaries visiting the police station.

'I thought it was time we had a friendly chat,' said Thomas Bulstrode Tucker.

Bloody hell, thought Peach. You'll need to watch yourself here, Percy my lad.

'Help yourself, Percy,' said Tucker, proffering the plate of biscuits with a smile which seemed to be costing much facial effort.

'Thank you, sir,' said Peach, and filled his mouth with biscuit to prevent himself from meeting this charm onslaught with the wrong words. Everyone knew that Tommy Bloody Tucker hated his guts, that the superintendent only tolerated him because he produced results, that the high reputation of Tucker's CID section rested heavily on the back of Peach.

'We're a good team, you and I, Percy,' said Tucker, forcing his smile even wider to accommodate the thought.

That's two Percys already, thought Peach: watch your step here, lad, or you'll be in the dudah up to your knees. 'With the help of the rest of the lads and lasses who work for us in CID,' he said cautiously.

'With the assistance of the rest of the team, of course, Percy,' said Tucker expansively, throwing his arms wide for a moment to accommodate men and women whose names he mostly didn't know. 'Characteristically modest of you to share the credit like that, I must say.'

'An aspect of leadership I picked up from you, I'm sure, sir. Always give credit where credit's due, you taught me.' Peach sipped his coffee and nodded appreciatively.

Tucker looked thoroughly bewildered. He couldn't remember ever saying that. He had never failed to seize the credit for his unit's good results, never omitted to sidestep the brickbats when things went wrong. He cleared his throat. 'We've been together now for eight years, Percy.'

'Longer than most marriages nowadays, sir. Not everyone is as lucky as you in that respect.' Peach found that a mention of his chief's formidable Brunnhilde of a wife normally made Tucker uneasy.

The superintendent smiled wanly. 'And I think it's time that our efforts were recognized.'

Peach knew what was coming, now. Promotion. It had been hinted at before. The old fool was determined to get made up to chief super so that his salary would be raised for the last few years of service, which were all-important for his pension. He'd do anything to secure that – even take the hated Peach up a rung with him, if that was what it took.

And apparently it did. Tucker said, 'Of course, I wouldn't hear of promotion for myself unless they agreed to make you a chief inspector, Percy.'

'That's very generous of you, sir.'

'Not at all, not at all.' Tucker waved the plate of chocolate digestives at Peach so expansively that four of them fell in a semicircle round his inspector's feet.

Percy picked them up carefully and put them back in a neat arrangement on the plate. 'Rigging the evidence,' he explained cheerfully. 'The girl from the canteen will never know.'

Tucker pressed on desperately. 'The promotion board will be considering my case – our cases – in the near future, Percy. So it's important everything is shipshape and Bristol fashion within our empire.'

Peach looked suitably puzzled at this sudden switch to the nautical. Then he grinned conspiratorially. 'That a reference to our increasing number of female officers, sir?'

Tucker, in his bewilderment, returned for a moment to his normal tetchy self. 'No, it isn't. And how you can possibly—'

'Reference to Bristols, sir. Well understood between old sweats like you and me, sir, but there'd be some of the women who might take exception even to a bit of innocent fun like that!' He leered conspiratorially. 'Though I must say, one of the better aspects of increased female recruitment is the increasing presence of bouncing young Bristols around the station. I might have known a man of your taste and observation would have noticed that. But I wouldn't like you to be done for sexual harassment. Not with a promotion coming up. So the Bristols had better remain our secret.' Peach tapped the side of his nose and ventured the sort of conspiratorial wink which even he had never dared to visit upon Tommy Bloody Tucker before.

Tucker stood up abruptly. 'All I'm saying is that we have to behave carefully over the next few weeks if we want a promotion. Be aware of sensitive issues and treat them with proper consideration.' He sought desperately to divert himself from Peach's picture of abundant Bristols in the station below him. 'What have you been doing this morning, for instance?'

'Oh, nothing much, sir. Putting the fear of God into a couple of tearaways who were causing trouble last night.'

Tucker was immediately attentive, not to say apprehensive. Brunton, like most of the old cotton towns around it, had been suffering from racial tensions in the preceding weeks. 'National Front tearaways, were they?'

'No, sir. And they hadn't come into the town from outside to cause trouble, like some of the thugs who've assaulted our officers lately. Born and bred in Brunton, these lads. Causing trouble for the owner of a local corner shop.'

'And you've pinned them down. Charges pending, are they? Do us a bit of good in our relationships with the local Asian community, this will.'

'I doubt that, sir.'

'Don't underestimate the importance of public relations in modern police work, Peach. I've told you that often enough before.'

Percy noted that he had lapsed in his chief's address from 'Percy' to 'Peach' again. He was happier with that. He looked suitably puzzled. 'Yes, sir. But I don't quite see how pinning this crime on to young Afzaal and his gang is going to be a major PR coup.'

Tucker had gone rigid with his cup and saucer in his hand at the mention of the Pakistani name. The china rattled alarmingly in his fingers as he set it down upon his desk. He said faintly, 'Not the Afzaal who owns the chain of grocery shops in the north of Brunton?'

Peach nodded cheerfully. 'That's the chap, sir. Well, the family, I should say. It's his eldest son. I've been giving him the shits – sorry, causing him a certain degree of apprehension – this morning. Him and his nasty little mates.'

Tucker sat down heavily behind his desk, restoring the barrier between himself and his DI, resuming normal hostile relations. He attempted to assert himself. 'You can't do it, Peach!'

'I've done it, sir.'

'You can't bring charges against the eldest son of one of our most prominent Asian citizens. Not at a time like this.'

Peach didn't see any reason to tell his chief at this stage that no charges would be brought. 'Really, sir? Are you telling me that I have to ignore a cowardly assault on a sixty-year-old man who has run his own shop honestly and peacefully for thirty years, an assault which occasioned considerable damage to both his person and his stock?'

'Well, no, not ignore, exactly. But in the present sensitive climate of race relations in this area, we need—'

'Even when young Afzaal has confessed to me exactly what he did, in an interview room downstairs twenty minutes ago?'

Tucker looked as if such a confession was the last thing to be desired. 'We really shouldn't be bringing a case against the son of one of our most prominent Asian citizens, at a sensitive time like this.'

'I see, sir. Then you'll be glad to hear that we aren't.'

'We aren't?'

'Bringing a case, sir.' Peach enunciated his words carefully, as if talking to a retarded child.

'But you said—'

'I said he'd confessed, sir. Not that the case was going to court. Old Harry Alston doesn't want trouble. He won't support a prosecution.'

Tucker sighed his relief. 'Sensible man. Man with a sense of community, I dare say.'

'Man who fears he'll be beaten up and have his shop set on fire if he goes to court as a witness, sir. A man to whom we cannot offer adequate protection against such things.' Peach, who tried hard to be amused by the balloon of hot air who commanded him, was suddenly very angry.

'Well, anyway, I'm glad you've decided to let young Afzaal off with a caution. It shows a grasp of the wider issues involved here.'

'He's not exactly getting away scot-free, sir. He's agreed that he and his friends will pay compensation of two thousand pounds, and that they will make a public apology to Mr Alston with a police presence to witness it.'

Tucker's face clouded again. 'That seems highly irregular. I can't think that Mr Afzaal senior is going—'

'He won't know anything about it, sir.'

'But if his son—'

'Young Afzaal is most anxious that his father should remain in ignorance of what happened last night. That is why he has agreed to pay two thousand pounds and apologize.'

Belatedly, Tucker got the picture, or most of it. 'Well, it's highly irregular, but if you think—'

'It's the best we can do in the circumstances, sir. While people on our patch feel it's not safe to go to court as witnesses, we aren't going to be able to mount the cases against young thugs that we should.'

Peach spoke with real passion, but Tucker chose to ignore it. 'Well, keep me in the picture. And remember what I said about promotion. We shall need to watch our Ps and Qs in the next few weeks, you and I, Percy.' He produced his inspector's first name again, with difficulty, feeling he must close on a note of friendship, or at least mutual interest. 'We must show everyone around us, above and below, how well we operate together.'

Peach stood briefly to attention. 'I understand, sir. I shall maintain and demonstrate my normal degree of respect for you, of course.'

Then he was gone, seeming to leave a small, invisible column of disrespect where he had lately stood.

Superintendent Thomas Bulstrode Tucker mused for a moment on these exchanges. He'd have to take this odious little bantam-cock of a man up with him if he was to make chief super, he knew that. He decided the briefing of his senior inspector had gone as well as could be expected. Surely even someone as obstreperous as Peach couldn't ignore the carrot of promotion? Tucker shook his head uncertainly. That little sod would do anything to frustrate him.

It was only five minutes later that he realized he had forgotten to tell Peach about the man who had been threatened with violent death.

Two

'CARTWRIGHT'S FINANCIAL SERVICES', the words said in bold lettering over the door. The building also housed the branch office of a building society, which in public perception gave it the ultimate stamp of respectability.

Respectability was important to Darren Cartwright. His office was at the back of the building. His patrons passed into its quiet calm through a door to the right of the building society counter where two women in their early forties handled transactions with cheerful efficiency. Darren's centre of operations had the wide, expensive desk which was obligatory to implant the impression of financial stability and reliability, three deep armchairs which were replaced every three years, and an antique mahogany coffee table which was not. There were watercolours of Great Gable, Scafell Pike and Eskdale on the walls, with a nineteenth century print of Whymper on the Matterhorn to complete a wider climbing context.

It was many years since the slightly overweight Cartwright had climbed even a small hill, but most of his Brunton clients knew the Lake District, and mountaineering was a hobby which he found brought from them not only interest but respect – a respect of which they were usually scarcely conscious, which was the best kind of all. Nothing in this room, where he spent most of his working days, was introduced without consideration for the impact it might make on those who came into it only once or twice.

The business of financial advice he conducted here was efficient, lucrative, and highly respectable. His other business, conducted in the main in the afternoons and by telephone,

12

was less respectable but even more lucrative. And Darren Cartwright certainly did not publicize it.

Whilst Superintendent Tucker was attempting to beguile DI Peach with visions of promotion, Darren was advising a couple in their sixties on the investment of a hundred and twenty thousand pounds which would be available with the man's retirement. It was all carefully considered routine stuff. He made his suggestions, got his secretary to make a copy of them, sent the couple away with this to consider the different options available to them. They were to come back to him in three days with their decisions made.

In fact, he knew from experience that they would reappear on Thursday morning thoroughly confused, that they would ask him in effect to make the decisions for them, that he would advise them as he might well have advised them now. But the delay would fulfil both legal and ethical requirements: the couple would not have been rushed into any decision, would have had two days to consider their options, would retain the illusion that they and not he had made key decisions about their financial futures. It was all completely above board, pleasantly lucrative in terms of commission, and extremely dull.

Darren Cartwright didn't grumble about that. Financial services were supposed to be dull, because dullness meant reliability to the punters. And they never seemed dull to the clients on the other side of his big desk, as he had constantly to remind himself, because it was their money – very often their life savings – that was being deployed. Darren was proud of the concerned look he had cultivated for these occasions.

The business that excited him, the activity which gave him a higher return on his outlay than anything he could offer to his clients in pursuit of pensions and investments, was conducted mainly in the afternoons. He wasn't proud of it. It certainly wasn't the kind of enterprise which his Masonic friends would have approved of. So he kept very quiet about it.

It wasn't against the law, he told himself, in those increasingly rare moments when his conscience pricked him. Well, perhaps some of the methods he had to use to make sure he got his full returns stepped across that vague line between what the English law allowed and what it forbade, but that wasn't his fault. People who couldn't honour their obligations brought it upon themselves – asked for all they got, as his minions frequently announced to Darren's receptive ears.

He enjoyed a lengthy lunch with the Masonic friend who had introduced him to the West Brunton Lodge a few years previously. You could call it a working lunch, really, thought Darren as they finished the wine; the two pushed business each other's way when the occasion arose. As Jason Brown was a solicitor in a family firm, he was inevitably able to pass people with legacies to be invested in Darren's direction, whilst Darren invariably suggested Jason's name to anyone enquiring about a solicitor.

It was obvious, really, but quite productive for both of them. Of course, it was the kind of thing which people who were prejudiced against Freemasonry tut-tutted about, but that just showed how out of touch with real life such critics were. It was nothing more than jealousy, really.

As he came back into his office at quarter past two, Darren Cartwright checked the little wire tray in which the building society ladies put any incoming mail or communications for him. It was empty. He was surprised at how much relief surged through him when he saw that.

One of his staff rang in with a report at three twenty. The man was brief and direct, as fitted both his inclination and the orders he had received. 'Ridgeon didn't pay us. I knew last week he wouldn't.'

'Wouldn't, or couldn't?'

There was a pause. The man on the other end of the line wasn't used to having to give much thought to such distinctions. 'Couldn't, I should think. It's a slack time for gent's outfitting. And he owes others, as well as us.'

Darren Cartwright thought for a moment, staring unseeingly at the gold pen on the inkstand he never used. Ridgeon's was a sound enough business, even if it needed more dynamic management. A family business, one that owned its own premises, freehold. If the latest Ridgeon eventually couldn't handle the debt, Darren would be able to dispose of the high street site easily enough, at a handsome profit. Big clothing chains like Next would certainly be interested.

'No hard stuff. Not at the moment. I'll get one of my credit managers to call round. Give our Mr Ridgeon a bit of financial guidance. Show him the advantages of combining all his debts into one. We'll clear his other owings off for him, leave him with only us to worry about.'

'So no threats, Mr Cartwright? No final warnings?' The man on the other end of the line sounded disappointed.

'No. We'll see how well he co-operates. If he doesn't, you'll get your instructions.'

Darren contacted the man he called his 'credits manager' and gave him his instructions about Ridgeon. Usually people like him were quite ready to have their other debts cleared off, to have the simplicity of one large debt rather than a series of small ones. They didn't realize how completely they were putting themselves in one man's power, and surprisingly often they didn't even realize that the rates of interest they were accepting on the single large debt were sky-high. Thank heavens for suckers, Darren thought with a smile.

The building society counter was shut and the grille was down when he went out of his office at ten past five. He glanced automatically at the tray by his door and felt his heart flutter in his chest.

There was a single unstamped envelope in the tray. It bore his name, in bold letters, but no address. Though there was no one around now to see him, he took the envelope back into the privacy of his own office to open it.

He half-expected the message inside to be in letters cut from newspapers. Instead, it was from a computer-printer. It said simply:

YOUR TIME IS ALMOST UP. YOU WILL DIE QUITE SOON NOW.

*   *   *

15

Detective Sergeant Lucy Blake got quite a shock when she came into the living room of her mother's neat cottage.

This was the place where she had grown up, and she was not used to changes in it. And the last change she would have expected was for her father's picture to disappear from its pre-eminent position on the mantelpiece.

'Where's Dad gone?' she asked her mother indignantly.

'Never you mind, our Lucy! He'll be back soon enough, don't you fret. And he might have a companion with him. There are other good cricketers in the family now, you know. Or almost in the family.' She sniffed her disapproval of modern reluctance to tie the knot.

Lucy decided not to rise to the marriage bait. 'You're never going to put up a picture of Percy. I haven't even got one myself – he just refuses to be photographed. Anyway, you wouldn't be able to balance Dad's smile. You'd never get Percy smiling at a camera!'

Agnes grinned happily at such naivety. 'Nonsense! You just need to catch him when he's relaxed. Anyone named after Denis Compton is bound to have a sunny disposition. The "laughing cavalier of cricket", they called Denis, you know. "Denis Charles Scott", that's what the DCS stood for. I never thought I'd have a son-in-law named after Denis Compton.' Agnes gazed happily into a future full of smiling grandchildren.

Lucy tried desperately to divert her. 'Where will you get a picture? I told you, I can never get him to have his photograph taken.'

'I shall go to the *Lancashire Evening Telegraph*. Get them to look back in their files. I can remember a very good one, taken three years ago during his last season in the Lancashire League. Just after he'd made eighty-three not out when they won at Bacup. He looked very pleased with himself in that picture, if I remember rightly, and no wonder. He's only thirty-seven now – he retired from cricket much too early, you know.' She gazed into the distance, visualizing Percy's neat figure with bat and gloves as fondly as if he had been her own son.

Lucy said accusingly, 'You've moved Dad. His picture used to be here.'

'And it will be again,' said Agnes quickly. 'I'm cleaning his frame, that's all. He'll be back next time you come, and he might just have a cricketing companion.'

Lucy could remember every detail of the slightly fading picture of her father as clearly as if it had stood in its usual place. Nevertheless, in a gesture of loyalty to the father she had lost when she was seventeen, she went and found his picture in the kitchen, carefully removed from its silver frame to allow it to be polished. A veteran with a sweater thrown loosely round his neck smiled shyly as he led his team off the field and up the steps to the pavilion. 'Bill Blake after taking 6 for 44 against Blackpool', Agnes had printed carefully in Indian ink beneath the picture.

'Your dad can go back on the mantelpiece in due course,' Lucy's mother's voice said defensively behind her. 'Very likely he and your Percy will end up side by side. Bill would have liked that. Time you were thinking about settling down, our Lucy.' She thrust aside the thought of Percy's moustache and bald pate. 'You'd have lovely babies, I expect.'

'I've a career to make, Mum,' said Lucy firmly. She was twenty-seven, with her biological clock ticking steadily, and her thoughts ran sometimes towards a family. But it would be fatal to admit any such weaknesses to a mother who was now sixty-eight and yearning to be a grandmother.

Agnes ignored the mention of her daughter's career, as she always did. But she turned and looked without embarrassment into her daughter's fresh face, with its light freckling and its striking blue-green eyes beneath the even more remarkable auburn hair. 'You're a bonny lass, our Lucy,' she said quietly, 'and that Percy Peach thinks the world of you. I'm sure he'd like to see you safely out of that dangerous world where you insist on working.'

She was wrong there, thought Lucy. Percy had been out-raged to be allotted a woman for his DS at first, but they worked happily together now, and he relied on her a lot. They wouldn't be able to work together if they were married, or even if that doltish Superintendent Tucker realized that they were an item. She said, 'CID work isn't dangerous, you know, Mum. Not most of the time.'

She added the last phrase to cover how near she had come to death at the hands of the man the press had dubbed the 'Lancashire Leopard' only a few months earlier. Fortunately, her mother still did not know the full details of how close her daughter had come to death. Reassuring herself as much as her mother, she said, 'Anyway, it's very quiet in Brunton CID at the moment. Not a murder in sight!'

On that peaceful Monday evening in the old cottage, she had no idea of the lurid copy her mother would be reading in her newspaper by the end of the week.

Superintendent Thomas Bulstrode Tucker had lived long enough to know that nothing enjoyable in life comes without some downside. Or as his detested subordinate Inspector Peach expressed it, no silver lining comes without a bloody great cloud attached to it.

At this moment, the silver lining was his association with Freemasonry, which had over the years given him much pleasure, and a little professional advancement he did not care to acknowledge. And the bloody great cloud was Mrs Thomas Bulstrode Tucker. Or Barbara Tucker, as the feminists would have insisted, the driving force behind the CID figurehead that was Detective Superintendent Tucker.

They were in their bedroom, but it was only six thirty on a summer evening, so the place brought none of the feelings of inadequacy or blind panic which it could carry for him during the hours of darkness. His wife had never been one for sex in daylight, even in those earlier years which often seemed to Tucker to belong now to another life.

Barbara Tucker moved in front of the window, darkening the room for an instance by intruding her considerable physical presence between her husband and the light source. 'Do you think this colour suits me?' she asked.

It didn't. Not many women in their mid-fifties can get away with orange. When you tip the scales at a little under fourteen stones, and satin stretches over curves which are substantial rather than voluptuous, it becomes impossible. Tucker sought desperately for words which would convey the fact without insult. 'It's . . . it's perhaps a little daring for a Masonic Ladies' Night. They're a conservative lot, you know, and it's probably best you err on the side of—'

'You don't like it!'

'It's not that I don't like it.' Tucker shut his eyes and mentally crossed his fingers. 'You have a wonderful dress sense, dear, and look splendid in most things, to my mind – though I have to admit I'm biased, of course!' He forced a lover's smile, sidled up behind Barbara, and ran a finger round the patch of bare back at the top of the orange dress.

Mrs Tucker looked in the wardrobe mirror and saw only the sickly smile of a sycophant behind her. She turned irritably away from his touch and moved out of his sight into the dressing room. 'You're useless, as usual! I'll end up making the wrong decision and then being blamed for it.' She sighed at the injustice of it all.

Thomas Tucker sat down resignedly on the edge of the big bed and wondered if he dared to creep out of the bedroom during this interlude. He hesitated, and was duly lost. Barbara appeared like an avenging Valkyrie, framed in the doorway of the dressing room in bra and pants.

'They go for cleavage, your Masonic friends, don't they? Do you want me to see if I can still get into that low-cut turquoise number that used to get you so randy?'

Tucker remembered with mounting horror a drunken New Year's Eve when Bacchus had triumphed over his normal torpidity of recent years. He sought for diplomacy, looked at Barbara in all her opulent glory, and was lost. 'I don't think I'd advise that, dear. As I said, they're a nice bunch, but a rather conservative lot, and on this occasion discretion might be the better part of—'

'All right, you needn't say any more!' Barbara did the

outraged woman very well – and she composed an awful lot of outraged woman. She loomed over Thomas as he cowered on the edge of the bed. He caught a glimpse of the scene in the wardrobe mirror: it was reminiscent of one of the broadest of the seaside postcards of his increasingly distant youth.

Barbara pouted – which was considerably more frightening to her apprehensive spouse than her rage had been. 'You don't fancy me any more, do you, Thomas? You'd rather have the flighty young pieces you're importing into the police force nowadays. I expect you spend most of your days leering at them. It's no use expecting you to be content with what you've got at home.' She moved her bare thigh against her husband's leg and sighed dramatically.

Tucker controlled the urge to edge away from the contact, realizing that such a move could provoke real histrionics. Probably Barbara saw the scene as something out of *Antony and Cleopatra*, whereas he could think only of *Carry On* farce. He said unconvincingly, 'You know that's not true, dear. As the superintendent in charge of the CID section, I couldn't possibly be seen to be eyeing up young female officers at work.'

'But you'd like to, wouldn't you? That's what you mean, isn't it?' Barbara spoke the words in a rising whine, which was rather her speciality, then took his hand and placed it on her lower thigh, just above the knee. She said in a quieter, more intimate protest, 'Oh, Thomas, where has the magic gone? What has happened to the warmth we used to have?'

Tucker watched his hand as though it belonged to someone else. Barbara eased her ample thigh expertly, allowing the hand to drop between the white pillars of her legs, eased herself fractionally downwards on the bed, so that his nerveless fingers moved an inch higher. He wanted to move that hand, but knew he must not. He had a clear vision of impending disaster but no idea how to avoid it; he felt like a passenger in a plane spinning out of control.

He said unconvincingly, 'You're exaggerating, dear. You'll be the star of the show on Friday at the Ladies' Night, as you always are.' His reassuring chuckle rose into a high nervous giggle as the thighs closed like the jaws of a car-crusher upon his lifeless hand.

'I used to say you should have been not just Thomas but John Thomas, the way you used to be at it in the old days. Insatiable, you were. At it morning, noon and night!' Barbara closed her eyes and moaned softly in memory of that halcyon period. Then she slid a little lower on the edge of the bed and gripped the hand with surprising strength between the white vastness of her upper thighs.

Tucker's head swam briefly. He shook it sharply, knowing that one of his domestic panic attacks was imminent. He could see no way out of this. Barbara now had her eyes firmly shut. A smile of expectation was spreading across her broad features.

Violent, uninhibited sex was clearly called for, but Thomas knew that this solution was beyond his powers. He would have to offer to buy her a new dress for the Masonic Ladies' Night. That offer would be accepted and exploited, but Barbara would see it for the evasion it was. She would take his money and go on complaining about his libido.

Then, when he felt that all was lost, salvation rang like an angel's trumpet in his ears. Or rather, it chirruped. The sound of the phone came into this bad film he was living through like the sound of Hollywood cavalry. He started upright, snatching his lifeless hand violently from its imprisonment.

His precipitate movement shot his unfortunate wife from her perilous recumbence on the edge of the bed into a sitting position on the floor beside it. The noise and abruptness of her arrival there shook windows, light fittings, and every instrument upon the dressing table, but Tucker was oblivious to all in the delirium of his escape.

He ignored the phone on the bedside table, knowing that the scene in which he was such an unwilling player might be resumed rather than terminated if he used this extension. 'Important call from work! Better take it downstairs,' he flung over his shoulder tersely as he made for the door. Then, from the safety of the landing, he tried a regretful,

'You're never really away from this job, when you have my responsibilities.'

As he hurried down the stairs, he hoped the exultation had not been apparent in his voice.

Rather to his surprise, it really was a call connected with his work. The voice on the other end of the line was too agitated to announce itself. It said accusingly, 'None of your people came to see me.'

'Who is this, please?' Tucker had recognized his caller, but he was playing for time, gathering his shattered resources together.

'This is Darren Cartwright. You told me the matter would receive your most urgent attention.'

Tucker recognized one of his own phrases being quoted back at him. 'Yes. And it did, Darren, I can assure you,' he lied.

'Well, there's been neither sight nor sound of the senior police officer you promised me, either at home or at work.'

There wouldn't have been, no. As Tucker had done nothing about Cartwright's problem. He had meant to mention it to Percy Peach, to get the DI to go and see his Masonic friend about the threats he had been receiving, but he had been so glad to terminate his interview with Peach that morning that he had forgotten to mention it. He said, 'I'm sorry, Darren. We're under heavy pressure at the moment with these overnight disturbances among the Asian community. The officer I briefed must not have got around to it.'

'So death threats aren't a priority any more? Brunton is no longer subject to the rule of law?'

This was getting dangerously near to the kind of headlines which always loomed large in Tucker's nightmares. 'No, certainly not. The officer concerned should certainly have been in touch with you by now. I'll give him a hell of a bollocking in the morning, I can assure you, Darren. You can confidently expect him to contact you tomorrow.'

'He'd bloody better.' Darren was surprised to find himself speaking like this to a CID superintendent, an office which he had always treated with deferential awe in the past. It showed how shaken he must be. 'Otherwise you might have a murder on your hands, Superintendent Tucker.'

'Oh, that's a little melodramatic, Darren, I'm sure! I can assure you that, in my considerable experience, anonymous threats rarely result in anything more than—'

'I've had another one.'

'Another threat?' Tucker heard the sound of heavy, disgruntled movements above his head, of a lavatory cistern flushing violently, and rejoiced that his own ordeal was over.

'This afternoon. I've kept it, this time.' Darren Cartwright looked down at the sheet of paper he held between his trembling fingers. 'It says that my time is up. That I'm going to be killed quite soon now.'

Three

E ric Walsh was proud of his ringing baritone voice. 'Not
formally trained, but I've had a few compliments over
the years!' he would say, smiling with what he hoped was a
becoming modesty.

He had done Gilbert and Sullivan in his time, had been
complimented in the local press on his Pooh-bah. He had
made a convincing Offenbach gendarme as he 'ran them in'
with a reedy Welsh tenor from the church choir. Now, in his
mid-forties, he felt his days of singing glory were largely
behind him. It was not that his voice had gone, but rather
that he had noted a disturbing presence in his audience in the
last few years, a person who was definitely not there for the
music, but rather to unnerve the singer.

Eric had retired with secret reluctance into the chorus; in a
year or so, he would resign altogether from the Brunton Light
Operatic Society. In his philosophical moments, he envisaged
the glories of wine, women and song. He would cut down on
the song a little, enjoy the wine as he always had, and indulge
his passion for women to the fullest. He was not going to cut
down on that.

Meantime, he had one important solo left to sing. He was
to perform the song of welcome for the fair sex at the Ladies'
Night of his Masonic Lodge on the coming Friday. He was the
natural choice, they all said: he nodded a quiet acceptance of
this logic and was secretly delighted to be selected for the role.
The ladies would be surprised and delighted by the rich melody
of their welcome.

After eighteen holes of golf, Eric Walsh found that the

showers at the Brunton Golf Club were an excellent sounding board for his vocal health. He tried a scale, increasing the volume delightedly, then launched into vocal gems from *Oklahoma*. There was a bright golden haze on the meadow – the corn had just reached the height of the elephant's eye – and the tiles were ringing with that knowledge when the secretary of the golf club coughed discreetly behind him.

'Terribly sorry to interrupt such a splendid recital, Eric, but I'm afraid there's been a complaint – no, a request – from the ladies. Their changing room is on the other side of that wall, as you probably know, and they wonder if you could modulate the decibels a little. I didn't promise them anything, but I said I would relay the request.'

Eric Walsh's late companions on the golf course were doubled up with silent laughter in the changing room at this intervention. The secretary winked at them as he turned and went back to his office. He had a wry sense of humour and a capacity for keeping a very straight face. No one knew if there had been a genuine request from the invisible ladies, but Eric ceased his singing and fell into a low mutter of discontent about female golfers with his secretly delighted comrades.

He did not carry his resentment into the club lounge with him. Eric was a notable ladies' man, an old-fashioned term which was still instantly recognized in golf clubs, as were Eric's carefully preserved good looks. These were still some-times described as those of a matinée idol. Some younger men were not quite sure what the term meant, but Eric Walsh knew, and he had no doubt that it was meant as a compliment.

To the women he met in the lounge, who might or might not have been the complainants about his singing, Eric was all smiles. He moved among them with a grace and a gentle banter which he always thought of as part of his charm, managing to pass a light remark about the coarseness of most men even as he carried a tray of drinks past a group of ladies and returned to the men who had played with him on the golf course.

His golfing companions had taken the invitation of Eric's forename to nickname him 'Little by Little', after Dean Farrar's priggish hero, in recognition of the inordinate time he took to play his shots on the course. Moving now into the second round of drinks, they fell into tiresome jests about the slowness of his play and the remarkable volume and resonance of his voice. Eric smiled indulgently and retreated into a private consideration of his strategy for the Ladies' Night on Friday.

If these tiresome companions of his knew what success he had enjoyed with women, they wouldn't mock the stirring nature of his voice. If they knew the lady the vibrant baritone Eric Walsh had lately bedded, they would no doubt be even more impressed.

But as she was the wife of a prominent member of the Lodge, that, regrettably, must remain a secret.

Barbara Tucker was not the only woman wondering what to wear at the big night of the Masonic year.

Ros Whiteman, however, had several advantages over the superintendent's wife. She was ten years younger, for a start, and looked even younger than that. She was also tall and slim, with a way of holding her head that was unconsciously proud, which set her figure off to its very best advantage. Ros had been a county tennis player in her youth, and at forty-five she still moved with the grace and suppleness of an athlete.

They made a lovely couple – so everyone said – she and John Whiteman. He was the sort of man who was more handsome as he approached fifty than he had been as a young man. The tracery of lines around his eyes and mouth gave an interest to his regular features which had been absent in his youth. His hair was still plentiful, and its increasing greyness at the temples had brought distinction rather than any sense of ageing to his head.

He had been a grey man in a grey suit in his twenties, but nowadays his dignified appearance brought a sense of *gravitas* to his pronouncements, even when the actual words did not carry any great weight. People listened to John Whiteman when he spoke as Master of the Lodge, and he usually got his way on matters of policy. He was head of a family firm of solicitors which had operated in the old cotton town for over a hundred years, and the law always compelled a certain respect, particularly in those completely ignorant of its workings.

His wife was more nervous in the privacy of her own bedroom than those who saw her only in public would have believed possible. Ros Whiteman knew that she would be on show at the Masonic Ladies' Night, and she was human enough to want to be seen at her best. Other women would be eager to see what she wore, would dissect her outfit and the effects it had on the assembled company.

Ros claimed sometimes to be amused by the Masons. She teased her husband about little boys and their secret societies, about their absurd love for the rituals of membership, and she had genuine reservations about secrecy in a modern society.

But she didn't want to let either herself or her husband down on his big night. Not in the present circumstances.

Everything was in place. Her hair appointment was booked for Friday morning. The small presents which would be presented to every lady on the evening were ordered and ready at the shop: she would collect them on Thursday. The menu and the table placings had been settled long ago. It remained only for the Master's wife to decide what she would wear on his big evening.

In the empty house, Ros Whiteman got out the dark blue, low-cut dress she had planned for weeks to wear and prepared to inspect herself critically in the privacy of her bedroom. She laid the dress carefully on the bed and slipped off the jeans and shirt she had been wearing to clean the house. She could not find much fault with the shape she examined for a moment as she stood in bra and pants before the cheval mirror. The stomach was still flat. The breasts in the expensive bra might no longer qualify for that favourite trash novel description of 'pert', but they had certainly not slumped with the passing years.

The face. Ros had always said herself that you could not escape the face. The one which gazed back at her from the mirror was not without lines. The skin had no longer the

27

smoothness which would excite young men – but she had no interest in young men. The high cheekbones and straight nose of her youth were unimpaired, and a little skilfully applied make-up around the eyes would disguise the inevitable passing of the years. And Friday night's audience would surely not be too critical; there would not be many women there younger than she was.

The phone rang before she could pick up the dress. She had been expecting the call, yet it still made her start with surprise. Or was it excitement? she asked herself. She picked up the phone and sat half-naked on the edge of the bed.

Darren Cartwright had sent his personal assistant home. She was a married woman who appreciated being able to collect her two young children from school in the afternoons. She had offered her efficient secretarial services for a pittance to secure a post with hours which suited her. And Darren for his part didn't want anyone around when he dealt with the less savoury parts of his business life. The people he employed to ensure that this distasteful but highly productive section of his activities ran smoothly had strict instructions to ring him only at home or in the late afternoons at the office.

Since the threats had begun to arrive, he had taken to locking the door of his office whenever he was alone. He told himself that it was highly unlikely that anyone would attack him here, in broad daylight, with a busy building society branch conducting its business at the front of the building. But you couldn't be too careful, he thought: like many a man before him, Darren Cartwright found clichés a comfort in times of stress.

Darren was completing one of his more private calls when he was startled by a sharp rapping at the locked door of his premises. He concluded his instructions into the mouthpiece of the phone hastily, but a second, even louder knocking came as he set the receiver back into its cradle. His first thought when he opened the door a reluctant five inches was that his anonymous threatener had come in person to carry out his mission.

There stood a squat man, unsmiling, impatient, with a startlingly white bald head and a jet-black moustache, which seemed to add to his menace. Darren made to shut the door again, but the man thrust his fist and his foot forward into the narrowing aperture. Darren recoiled as he saw the fist raised, then realized that it held a photograph of his unsmiling visitor and the details of his name and rank beneath it. A police warrant card. Cartwright fell back in relief, and his caller was in the room as swiftly as a soldier storming a machine-gun post.

'Inspector Peach!' The intruder rapped out his introduction as brusquely as if he had been taking a prisoner. 'And this is Detective Sergeant Blake.'

Darren had not even noticed the woman at first, so precipitate had been Peach's entry. She was in her mid-twenties, with remarkable ultramarine eyes and red-brown hair that gleamed even in this sunless room at the back of the building. She was in plain clothes, and she filled her dark green sweater quite splendidly. Darren gave her a smile of welcome, which he would have amplified if the inspector in his immaculate dark suit had allowed it.

Without being asked, Peach sat down in the chair in front of the desk where Darren usually asked his visitors to sit, and said, 'Best make yourself comfortable. This may take a while.'

Darren sat as he was told, feeling immediately off balance as this visitor took the initiative in the chair where people normally waited for his advice. 'You must be the Cartwright of Cartwright Financial Services,' said Peach, scarcely bothering to register Darren's nod of acknowledgement. 'They say in Yorkshire that where there's muck there's brass. In Lancashire, we're more inclined to find that where there's brass there's usually muck. Us being policemen, of course, and muck meaning villainy.' He stared suspiciously round the walls, as if he expected villainy to leap out at him from Cartwright's tasteful prints of the Lake District.

Darren tried to recover his poise. 'Yes, that's as may be, but I wish you'd thought to make an appointment before you came!'

29

He made to shift the file he had been using for his phone call, then gave up the idea as the dark eyes opposite him fell like lasers upon the back of his hands.

'I was told it was urgent,' said Peach implacably, 'that you'd been complaining about the lack of police attention. So I came round here like a whippet out of its hutch.'

Darren wasn't sure that whippets were kept in hutches, but he had no direct experience of the animals. He said weakly, 'It's true that I had asked for some sort of police attention. I've been threatened, you see, and—'

'When did you first report this, sir?'

'Two days ago. I asked Superintendent Tucker to give it his attention. Not that I expected him to investigate personally, you understand, but . . .'

Percy Peach's sigh was heavy enough to stop him in mid-sentence. That old flatulence Tucker had forgotten to relay the message, as usual. Leaving others to pick up the pieces. Too interested in his talk of promotion to remember poor sods whose lives were in danger. Peach said heavily, 'You say you've been threatened, sir. When and in what way, exactly?'

'I've had notes, Inspector. Threatening my life. At first I didn't take them seriously, but when—'

'You've kept them, of course.'

This man seemed determined to throw him on to his back foot, as if he were a common criminal, instead of a member of the public entitled to police protection. But somehow Darren didn't fancy putting that thought into words. 'Afraid not, Inspector. I didn't take them seriously at first, as I say, and by the time—'

Peach turned to Lucy Blake and shook his head sadly at the omissions of the public. 'Evidence, they'd be, if they'd only been kept.'

'I've got the last one here, the one which came yesterday,' said Darren desperately. He slid open the top drawer of his desk with nervous fingers and produced the envelope with his own name but no address. 'I expect you might want to fingerprint it.'

'Probably won't produce much: I expect your own sweaty hands have been all over it,' said Peach accusingly. But he held the envelope by its bottom corner and picked up a paperknife from the desk to extract the sheet inside. He read the message aloud slowly, with every appearance of enjoyment. 'Your time is almost up. You will die quite soon now.'

As Darren studied the inspector's face expectantly, it relaxed into a broad smile, with the teeth looking very white against the blackness of the moustache above them. Darren found the smile more disturbing than the previous acerbity. Peach turned to Lucy Blake. 'Wonder what "quite soon" means in this context.'

'Difficult to say, sir. Different psychopaths have different agendas, don't they?'

Darren caught his breath at the word 'psychopath'. He had expected emollient words, a playing down of his fears, an assurance that the threats would be the work of some harmless crank whom the police would expose in due course. He licked his lips and said, 'You think these threats are serious?'

Peach smiled again, gently but complacently, as if rejoicing in the fact that he himself was certainly not in danger. 'Difficult to say, sir. Some are, some aren't. Still, you're still here, so far, so that's a good start. 'Course, if your anonymous correspondent is both serious and efficient, he might just be biding his time, planning the best opportunity for himself. Or herself, of course: we mustn't be prescriptive, in these days of equal opportunity.'

'So what do you propose to do about it?' Darren tried to be truculent, but his voice sounded too uncertain to carry conviction.

'How many of these notes have you had?'

'Four, altogether. That was the last one.'

'And it has no address. Delivered by hand to your home, was it?'

'No. It was left here. It was in my post tray outside. It must have been delivered about this time yesterday: I found it when I was going home.'

'What did the other notes say? The ones you unfortunately did not retain.'

'Much the same as the one you have. Simply that I was going to die.'

'No indications of when?'

'No. The one you have there is the first one which suggests that it's going to be soon.' Darren shuddered at the recollection.

'No phone calls?'

'No. Just the notes.'

'Pity. Voices often give people away, even when they try to disguise them.'

There was a pause before Darren said diffidently, 'I expect you get these things happening all the time.'

'Not all the time, no. Death threats are quite rare round here, wouldn't you say, DS Blake?'

'Very rare, sir.'

Darren smiled weakly. 'Still, I expect they're rarely carried through. Most of them come from disturbed minds, I should think.'

This time there was no answering smile from Peach. 'Couldn't really say that, Mr Cartwright. Only wish I could.' He leaned forward a little, as though about to impart a confidence. 'I think we need to take this seriously.'

'Yes. I see. Well, needless to say, I'm all in favour of that.' Darren gave a high, nervous giggle, which sounded ridiculous but was out before he could suppress it.

'We need to know your enemies, Mr Cartwright.'

'Enemies?'

Peach smiled patiently. 'People who dislike you. Hate you, even. I'm sure there are some.' He was interested that this man he had already decided he didn't like should play out this charade of surprise. Cartwright must have thought hard about just this question; you didn't get notes threatening your life and not wonder which of your enemies might have sent them.

'I suppose I must have a few people who dislike me.

32

Everyone has. But I can't think of anyone who'd be planning to kill me.'

Peach studied him closely, pursing his lips. 'Cartwright Financial Services. Where there's brass there's muck, as I said. You must have made some enemies in your business dealings, Mr Cartwright.'

Darren managed this time to produce his most urbane smile, as if the mention of the firm had restored the manner he usually produced automatically for his clients. 'You seem to have a misapprehension of how financial services work, Inspector. I offer people investment advice, I hope of an informed nature. People weigh the value of that, and choose whether or not to follow my suggestions. Where considerable sums of money are involved, I send them away to think about it before they put pen to paper. It's all very civilized, very cool.'

'So not the sort of business where people feel angry enough to kill you.' Peach seemed disappointed about that. 'But there must be occasions when your advice has gone wrong? When things have not turned out as people expected?'

Darren was relaxed enough now to allow himself another smile, this time of rueful acknowledgement. 'It's true that people often have expectations which are quite unrealistic. The financial press is partly responsible: advertisements quote the results of fat years in the markets to push their products. Not everyone realizes that there must be lean years as well.'

Sitting beside Peach, Lucy Blake sensed the rising irritation the inspector always felt when people went into well-rehearsed professional spiels. She said hastily, 'But there must surely be occasions when people blame you, Mr Cartwright, even if their expectations have been unrealistic.'

Darren welcomed the incursion of this pretty girl into the dialogue. It encouraged him into a smooth, 'No one has resented my advice enough to kill me, I'm sure, DS Blake.' He gave a little laugh at the absurdity of that thought, then bathed Lucy in his most dazzling professional smile.

'Right!' Percy Peach's hammering monosyllable removed the smile as effectively as detergent. 'So we'll write off the people who've had the benefits or otherwise of your financial advice, for the moment. What about your other business activities?'

'My other business activities?' Darren echoed the phrase stupidly, his brain reeling. He had no idea that the police knew anything about the other side of his working life. 'I don't know what you're talking about.' The denial sounded feeble, even in his own ears.

Peach's dark eyes stared at him until Darren's gaze dropped to the desk. 'Not much use calling us in if you're not prepared to be frank, Mr Cartwright. People who lend out money at high rates of interest to desperate people normally have enemies.'

'The loan side is a very minor part of my business.'

'I see. But a lucrative one, no doubt. The point is that people who lend money and have people to enforce repayments always have enemies. Sometimes among the people who borrow and cannot repay; sometimes among other loan sharks whose territory is threatened. What I suppose you would call fellow businessmen, though I might use a different term.'

'The loan side is only a very minor part of my business.' Darren repeated the lie stubbornly, anxious only to prevent himself from revealing more than this disturbing visitor might already know about him and the people he employed. He could not work out how these police people, whom he had called in to defend him against assault, seemed to have turned the spotlight upon the seamier side of his life.

Peach let the pause stretch until Darren raised his eyes from the desk again, as he knew he eventually must. 'We're here to talk about death threats, Mr Cartwright. You're not stupid: you know that the world of the loan shark contains violent people. I'm asking you if there is anyone in it who you suspect might have sent you these notes.'

'No.' Darren felt the silence beginning to stretch again. 'I'd tell you if there was.'

'I hope you would. Otherwise we're all wasting our time. Right, then: that leaves your private life. Is there anyone there who might be threatening you?'

34

'No.' The reply came promptly, perhaps too promptly.

'It might be someone who doesn't really intend to kill you. Whose warped idea of fun is to give you a scare. Who is wasting police time, incidentally: we take a dim view of that.'

Darren wondered why he should hear this last phrase as a warning to himself as much as to his anonymous tormentor. This time he gave his reply some thought. There was one name he could think of. But he was a fellow Mason, and the code in the Fraternity was strong. You didn't denounce a Brother to the police. He could end up with a lot of Masonic egg on his face if he wasn't right – and surely he couldn't be? He said slowly, 'I've thought about that, of course. When your life is threatened, you do. But I can't think of anyone I know who would want to kill me.'

Peach stood up. 'Keep your doors and windows locked. Only park your car in very public places. If there are any more threats, don't go to Superintendent Tucker. Get in touch with me at Brunton CID immediately.' Almost before Darren Cartwright realized what was happening, he was alone again in his office.

As she drove the police Rover back to the station, Lucy Blake said, 'You weren't very sympathetic to a man who fears for his life. Did you consider offering him police protection?'

Peach grinned beside her. 'Bloody expensive, police protection, as you know. Eat up our overtime budget for a month within a few days. Besides, I'd have more sympathy with someone who was completely honest with us.'

'You think Cartwright was holding something back?'

'I'm damned sure he was. He's into the loan shark business much more heavily than he admitted, for a start. And I'm certain he had someone as his candidate for those notes. Perhaps there's more than one possibility. But until he's scared enough to be completely frank with us, we can't help him.'

Lucy thought about this carefully as she negotiated the

town's notorious one-way system. She decided Percy was right; he usually was, in his snap judgements about people. But she hoped his words would not come back to haunt him in the weeks ahead.

Four

W asim Afzaal was a relieved young man. True, he had been forced to apologize to old Harry Alston in his crowded little shop, in front of a watchful DC Murphy and his cowed companions in the previous night's mayhem. That had meant some inevitable loss of face.

But the young thugs who had helped to smash up the shop were as scared of the police as he was, as anxious to get out of DC Peach's clutches without a criminal record and worse. They had accepted Afzaal's assurance that an apology and compensation to the offended shopkeeper represented the easiest way out, and when Wasim had provided the entire two thousand quid himself, they had been in no position to resist either the solution or Afzaal's continued status as leader of their little group. They needed to stick together to defend themselves against the white groups at the weekends.

Without it ever being stated, without any climb-down by their leader, they knew that any violence would be reserved for their contemporaries and natural enemies in the National Front. There would be no more attacks from them on Harry Alston or his like.

Which made Percy Peach into some kind of therapist, or social worker. It is not certain which of these labels would have most outraged the detective inspector. Or chief detective inspector: Superintendent Tucker was now resigned to pushing his subordinate's case for promotion.

Rather to Afzaal's surprise, he found that Peach had not spread the news of his disgrace around the town. The manager of the White Bull, where Wasim was serving his latest 'industrial placement' for his hotel and catering degree course, seemed totally unaware that his temporary employee had even been questioned by the police. The local paper reported that Harry Alston had been compensated for the damage to his shop, and that there would be no court case. But no names were printed beneath this short news item. The university would learn nothing of this undergraduate aberration in Brunton.

Even more important, Mr Afzaal senior appeared to know nothing of his son's latest escapade. Two thousand pounds was a hefty addition to a student loan which the father did not even know the son possessed, but that was a necessary evil in these circumstances.

Wasim determined to keep his head down and get on with his work at the White Bull. It was a surprise to himself as well as to some of his contemporaries that he seemed to be doing rather well there. His university tutor had said so when he came in to monitor his progress. Several patrons of the hotel had commented favourably upon his deft and assiduous service in the dining room. Although Wasim made due allowance as always for the liberal reactions which the colour of his skin could prompt in the more enlightened diners, he had to admit that his three-month spell in the White Bull seemed to be a success.

Confirmation came from an unlikely source. Like most people in the hotel industry, Charles Davies, the manager of the White Bull's restaurant, did not give praise easily. So when he told the slim, handsome Pakistani that he was doing well, Wasim knew that he had made an impression. And, contrary to his expectations when his father had directed rather than persuaded him to undertake the degree course, he found that he enjoyed the work. He was adept and swift in the manual processes of cooking and serving food, and when on duty in the dining room, he managed the difficult combination of being deferential to clients without seeming unduly servile.

Wasim Afzaal decided that he would stick with this. He would get his degree, obtain a job as a manager, serve his time. In due course, he would get his own hotel. It would be sooner rather than later: the old man would set him up, once Wasim showed him that he was serious and competent. The old man had a soft spot for him, beneath his paternal acerbity, and as the eldest son of the family it would be no more than his due. In time, he would make shrewd investments, having sized up the industry, and would in the end own a chain of hotels, passing among them like a regal presence to ensure that the appropriate standards were maintained. Wasim had not only ambition but also an excellent imagination.

His reverie was abruptly interrupted as he set out the cutlery on the spotless white table linen for the evening session in the restaurant. 'You know all staff are required this Friday?'

Wasim was not sure whether this was a statement or question from Mr Davies. But he displayed his usual alertness. 'Yes, sir. Saw the rota in the rest room. Whole of the dining room taken over for a special function.'

'That's right. And not just any function. The Ladies' Night of the North Brunton Masonic Lodge.' Davies rolled out the words clearly, as if introducing at least a duke. 'Our most important evening of the year. A booking we cannot afford to lose. And one which we shall not lose.' Like many a pompous man, Davies sought to increase his stature to match the weight of his pronouncements; he was now on the balls of his feet, seeking in vain to look down into the dark brown eyes of this latest addition to the staff of his empire.

'Yes, Mr Davies. I'll bear that in mind. It will be most instructive for me to see a fine hotel pulling out all the stops.'

Davies looked at him as if he suspected irony, but he could detect nothing in the smooth olive face. 'Yes. Well, tomorrow's a night when everyone will need to operate at full throttle,' he said, feeling that his own metaphor might give him more control over the pep talk he was rehearsing for the assembled staff on the morrow.

'Yes, Mr Davies. I'll make sure my suit is immaculately pressed before I present myself to the Lodge members and their ladies.

Davies looked hard into the smooth face, suspecting again that this fellow was enjoying himself. But Davies could see a way of deflating this confident young man. 'That won't be necessary. You won't be operating in the dining room tomorrow night. We need experienced hands for the serving. You'll be in the kitchen for this particular function, making sure the food is presented as it should be.'

It was a decision he had only just made, one motivated by his impulse to take young Afzaal down a peg or two. If there was a small part of him which said that the Lodge members were a conservative lot, that even now they would see an Asian in the dining room as a blemish on the standards of the establishment, Davies did not acknowledge it, even to himself.

But both men were conscious of the small hesitation he had made before his decision. Wasim Afzaal allowed himself the vestige of a smile as he said, 'Very good, Mr Davies. The kitchen it shall be.'

But the young Asian had an eye for the way a table should look, and Davies was shrewd enough to make the best use of the strengths of his team. It was when he was putting out the name-cards for the place settings that Wasim Afzaal found one name which interested him very much indeed.

At ten seventeen on Friday morning, Detective Inspector Peach looked out of the window of the CID section and saw Superintendent Tucker parking his car. Give the man his due, he thought: he's an immaculate parker.

It took Tucker a little time, because he had reversed in, but the superintendent eventually placed his car precisely between the white lines delineating the space labelled 'Head of CID'. He got out and looked at the alignment of his wheels with satisfaction before glancing up nervously towards the window from which Peach watched unseen. From above, his silvering hair looked even more immaculate than usual.

He's been to the barber's, thought Percy. Of course, it's the Lodge Ladies' Night tonight. Tommy Tucker will be parading himself at the White Bull, in best bib and tucker, under the watchful gaze of Brunnhilde Barbara.

Peach watched hopefully as three pigeons circled suggestively above the car park, but none of them bombed the immaculate coiffure below them. This remains an imperfect world, thought Percy. He gathered a sheaf of papers and went upstairs to the superintendent's office.

Thomas Bulstrode Tucker was in congenial humour. 'What can I do for you, Percy?' was his greeting.

He's like a bloody woman, thought Percy vituperatively; he finds a visit to the hairdresser's uplifting. Well, he's nothing but a bloody old woman anyway, Tommy Bloody Tucker. Bet he goes to that unisex Vidal Sassoon-style hairdresser's in Lord Street. Percy was of the old-fashioned school when it came to the admittedly limited attention his fringe of hair needed: if a barber didn't talk racing or football, preferably with a dog-end in the corner of his mouth, his sexual preferences were highly suspect. Even Percy's chosen barber, in the mean streets on the edge of the town, had now abandoned cigarettes while cutting, but you could still let your mind freewheel with him through the routine exchanges about the progress of the Rovers.

He caught Tucker raising his hand unconsciously to stroke the back of his newly coiffured head. 'Immaculate, sir!' he said with a reassuring smile. Then, as Tucker looked puzzled, he said, 'The old barnet, sir. Immaculate. I expect it costs a little to keep it like that, but it's worth it in your case. Wouldn't be in mine, more's the pity.' He passed his hand quickly over his smooth bald dome.

'I didn't bring you up here to talk about hair,' said Tucker sternly, forgetting already that he had not summoned the inspector at all. His brow furrowed for a moment as he wondered what had brought Peach here. Then he said with determined affability, 'Our promotions seem to be going ahead smoothly. Mustn't count our chickens too soon, of course, but I'm quietly hopeful. You'd have to move out of CID and into uniform for a year or so if they made you chief inspector. Standard practice, as you know, to give you more experience.'

41

He tried not to look too pleased at the prospect of sending Peach elsewhere.

Peach was human enough to welcome the idea of promotion for himself, but overcome with guilt that this old windbag should be rising with him. He knew that was the way the system worked, but it didn't make him feel any easier about it. He said abruptly, almost as though it were an accusation, 'Darren Cartwright, sir. Of Cartwright Financial Services.'

Tucker had been dwelling happily on the rosy prospect of promotion to chief superintendent. It took him a moment to refocus. Then he said, 'Ah, Darren, yes. Sorted him out, did you?'

'Not exactly, sir.'

'Not exactly? This isn't very good, you know. Darren Cartwright is a prominent businessman in the town, and entitled to our full . . . well, our full . . .'

'Full attention, sir? Yes, I agree with that. He was beginning to excite it anyway, before he made the official request to you that he should have it.'

Tucker tried to look approving, though his puzzlement eventually won the day in the ensuing silence. 'You were on to this already? Well, I must say, that's smart work. When he asked for protection, I had no idea that—'

'Not the threats, sir. First I heard of those was an hour or two before I saw him, though he maintained he'd reported them to you days before that.' Peach paused for a moment to allow an uncomfortable squirm in Tucker, then said, 'No, sir. I was referring to Mr Cartwright's rather unpleasant sideline to his main business, which he has been developing enthusiastically in recent months.'

'Sideline? Darren Cartwright runs Cartwright Financial Services, and provides a valuable and highly valued agency in the town.'

'Almost the very words he used to me himself, sir. Interesting to have it confirmed from the horse's mouth, if you'll pardon the vulgarity. But he does have another lucrative line,

42

which I'm afraid he doesn't publicize half as proudly. Doesn't publicize at all, in fact.'

'I can't believe Darren Cartwright would be involved in anything dubious.'

'Can't you, sir? You have a touching faith in human nature, which is quite admirable. And very unusual in a senior police officer: pity the public doesn't see more of this belief in the essential goodness of man.'

Tucker peered at him suspiciously from beneath the immaculately crinkled hair. 'You, Peach, on the other hand, have a taste for the grubby, it seems. What is it that you think you have raked out of Darren Cartwright's background?'

Percy noted that the first name approach had gone; he felt easier with that. 'Detected, sir. I prefer detected. That's our job, after all.' He gave the wall above his chief's head a wide, seraphic smile, then said abruptly, 'He's into loan-sharking, sir, is Mr Cartwright. And he's been increasing his business in that field. And employing pretty violent people as his enforcers. I know he's a Mason, sir, but in my opinion he's up to no good, your Mr Cartwright.'

'He's not *my* Mr Cartwright, Peach. And I've told you repeatedly that the fact that a man is a Mason has no bearing at all on whether—'

'Makes him four times as likely to commit financial crimes as an ordinary citizen, in this town,' said Peach evenly, his eyes still trained steadily on the wall above Tucker's head.

He derived this wholly delightful statistic from the fact that one of the local Brotherhood had been convicted in the previous year on seven charges of fraud, an event which had warped the statistics in a way that Peach had seized upon and Tucker had been unable to unravel.

'If you think Mr Cartwright is involved in anything dubious, you must take whatever action you consider appropriate,' said the superintendent stiffly. 'In the meantime, have you done anything about the far more serious matter of the threats which have been made upon his life?'

'Enquiries are proceeding, sir.' From one policeman to another, the enunciation of the official jargon was an insult.

'You mean you haven't a bloody clue.'

'You go to the heart of the matter with your usual trenchancy, sir. Cartwright hasn't kept any of the notes he's received, apart from the last one, and—'

'I don't want your excuses. I need action.' Tucker tapped the desk in front of him with an attempt at menace.

'I was going to say, sir, that even this limited trail was rather cold when we got there. Mr Cartwright claimed to have reported the matter to you some time before I was instructed to attend to it. There must have been a hiccup in our system, sir. I'm investigating where your earlier instruction to me got lost in the pipeline, and when I find—'

'Oh, don't bother with all that!' said Tucker hastily. 'I want you solving crimes, not getting bogged down with the workings of our bureaucracy.'

'Serious matter, sir. Man might have been dead before we even got to him.'

'Look, Percy, it may be that Darren Cartwright's request for our help slipped my mind.' Tucker tried not to register Peach's black eyebrows rising impossibly high in astonishment. 'As superintendent in charge of the whole CID section, I have a lot on my mind, you know.'

'Indeed I do, sir. I often have occasion to remind the lads and lasses who beaver away at the crime face of the amount your mind has to cope with.' Peach's eyes were back on the wall above his chief's head, his tone impeccably neutral.

'Did you offer Mr Cartwright protection?'

'No, sir. Considering your directive on overtime issued only last week, I thought it inadvisable.'

'So you don't think he's in any real danger?'

Peach pursed his lips, looked at the ceiling, enjoyed allowing the pause to stretch. 'Couldn't say that, sir. The last note – the only one we have, as I said – said, "Your time is almost up. You will die quite soon now." He enunciated the message

44

as tremulously as if it were the conclusion of a scene in an old-fashioned melodrama.

'And you gave the poor man no protection?'

'Cost us three officers a day, sir, on eight-hour shifts. With no guarantee of how long we should need to employ them. Knock a hell of a hole in the overtime budget. Couldn't sanction it without your express orders.'

As always, Tucker quailed before the responsibility of a decision. Then his face brightened. 'Well, I suppose he's in no immediate danger. I shall be able to keep an eye on him myself tonight. It's the Lodge's Ladies' Night. At the White Bull hotel. I expect Darren Cartwright will be attending that – it's one of our big functions, you know. And I can't see him coming to any harm there. Not with his friends all around him!'

'Yes, sir. Though as I say, it's four times as likely in this town that he'll come to grief among Masons than in ordinary company.' He nodded judiciously at the thought.

'If that's the best you can come up with, you'd better go and get on with your work, Peach! You know as well as I do that you couldn't have a safer gathering than the one I shall be attending tonight.'

Tucker's hand rose automatically to stroke his hair as the inspector disappeared, like a child reaching for its comfort blanket. He didn't think at that moment that his words might haunt him in the days to come.

Five

R os Whiteman's choice of the dark blue dress had been right. She knew that when she saw the way the other women looked at her as they came into the room. Men were not reliable guides: a little bare shoulder and a little cleavage would always get their attention and admiration. But she noticed very early that the women had that look of appreciation tinged with envy, which was the best assurance that you looked attractive.

She stood beside her husband; John was equally impressive in his new evening suit, confident in his office, with his beautifully cut hair given an appropriate distinction by the grey at his temples. The Master of the Lodge and his lady greeted each couple with a handshake as they were announced by the Toastmaster, who stood out dramatically among the dark-suited males in the vivid scarlet of his jacket.

Ros was glad of this garish assistant, for though her husband knew all the members of his Lodge and most of their ladies, she was happy to be reminded of the names of these people she had met for the most part but rarely. She heard someone whispering, 'They make a lovely couple,' and it took her a moment to realize that the woman was referring to her and John. If only the woman could appreciate the irony of her conventional phrase!

There were visiting couples from other Lodges as well as their own members, for this was one of the occasions when the Lodge put itself on show, returned hospitality, and generally relaxed on what was its premier social function of the year.

46

The spacious dining room of the White Bull was brilliantly lit, and as the room filled and the noise level rose, Ros was surprised how the gleam of glasses, the dark glint of bottles of wine and the glitter of cutlery on the snow-white linen added to the sense of occasion. She began to relax, even to enjoy this stuffy, rather formal function, which she had expected to be such an ordeal.

That was after she had acted out her little private charade, of course. She had rehearsed it a score of times in the days running up to the Ladies' Night, but when the real moment came, she found that she was surprisingly calm. The audience even helped her a little: she reacted with them as she played her part, conscious amid the cocoon of affability around her that they had noticed nothing, that she had greeted this couple with conventional formality, with no more and no less affection than all the others.

She did not dare catch his eye, and he helped her by exchanging a little joke with John rather than saying anything directly to her.

Ros greeted the lady on his arm with a brilliant smile. If there was a shaft of bitterness deep within her that this woman should be so partnered for the evening, it certainly did not surface. And indeed, Ros knew that she had no reason to be envious of this woman She was no more than a convenient ornament for the evening and a useful distraction for any chattering female tongues. He was good at deception, this man; she knew that now.

By the time the Toastmaster had announced the last of the couples as they entered through the wide double doors, there was a hum of anticipation in the long room, and John and Ros Whiteman made a stately progress through the smiling faces to the top table.

Each lady had a gift by her place at the table, and Ros was pleased to notice that the tiny but pretty bottles of perfume she had selected were being well received. She had deliberated over what to buy for several weeks, but finally decided that good perfume never went amiss. It might not be very original, but when you had to buy the same thing for fifty women, originality could easily be misplaced.

The Toastmaster announced that the Master would say grace, and John enunciated the words of thanks to the Lord in heaven clearly and simply, without any of the pomposity which in Ros's mind was always the danger when men got serious about their play.

The Beef Wellington, which was the main dish for all save the vegetarians, was both succulent and plentiful, the pastry encircling the meat surprisingly light and crisp. Charles Davies, a head waiter of much experience, ensured that his minions moved unobtrusively but assiduously among the assembled company, keeping the wine flowing freely as the conversational hubbub reached an ever higher pitch.

Ros, chatting animatedly to a woman who taught for the Open University, relaxed more than she would have thought possible. However, John was increasingly quiet as the meal proceeded, and she became aware that he was toying with his sweet, nervous of what lay ahead for the Master.

She watched the fingers of his right hand moving crab-like across the white linen to the base of his glass and then back again to his spoon. His hand moved in sudden, unpredictable bursts of energy, as if it was operating outside the control of the brain which should have directed it. It was only natural, she thought: all but the most practised of public speakers would have a little stage fright as they anticipated the moment when the room would fall silent and they would become the focus of everyone's expectant attention. Then she caught sight of her own twitching fingers, and allowed herself a rueful smile.

But when his moment came, John Whiteman was equal to it. He began his speech of welcome to the ladies a little nervously, but his first small joke went well, and he gathered confidence. The standard of speaking in North Brunton Lodge on occasions like this was in truth not brilliant, and John was well towards the top of the pile when measured against his predecessors of the previous few years. He managed to pay the ladies a few compliments without appearing completely smarmy, and interspersed his address with shafts of humour, mostly at the expense of his Brothers in the Lodge.

Above all, he did not speak for too long. He sat down to a generous round of applause, plucking nervously at his cuff links and trying hard not to look relieved that the most stressful part of the evening for him was over.

Ros, despite her own nervousness at what was to come, felt a sharp pang of relief for John as he sat down again beside her. Relief and a little guilt, perhaps, that she should be playing out her charade of fidelity so adeptly and successfully.

But there was no time for reflection, as the Toastmaster announced the song for the ladies and Eric Walsh drew himself to his full height and thrust out his chest. His ringing baritone, surprising in its sudden volume in the cramped acoustics of the long, low-ceilinged room, boomed out the words of the familiar song:

I'll sing a song to praise the ladies,
Our partners in all that we do.
Without them our lives would be empty,
And cheerless as morning's cold dew.
They readily shoulder our burdens,
And cheerfully help us along.
Providing, consoling, inspiring,
And here's to their health in a song.
And here's to their health, and here's to their health,
And here's to their health in a song.

There were two more verses in the same vein, with all the men joining in the choruses, each time more confidently and stridently. The waiters and kitchen staff, in safe anonymity behind their double doors, grinned at each other in wide-eyed wonderment at this rowdy carousing from men they knew as pillars of the local establishment.

In the dining room, there was tumultuous applause at the end, mainly polite from the ladies, mainly raucous from the men, some of whom felt that Eric Walsh took his singing too seriously and had pretensions which were beyond his vocal calibre.

Ros Whiteman, with senses heightened by tension, was aware of both strains in the reception of Eric Walsh. Then the Toastmaster announced that Mrs Rosemary Whiteman would reply on behalf of the ladies and she rose to begin her speech.

It was here at last, the moment which she had anticipated for weeks, and even as the applause for the Toastmaster's announcement rang round the room, Ros Whiteman, county tennis player and confident athlete over many years, felt a wholly unaccustomed trembling at the back of her knees.

But her opening remarks were well received, and she sensed a sympathetic audience, well primed by this time with food and wine. The men were immediately responsive to this erect and elegant woman in the striking blue dress; the women accorded her the gender support which was natural in what was still the overwhelmingly male ambience of a Masonic Lodge, where women were allowed in on sufferance on this one strictly social occasion of the year.

She knew she had to compliment the singer on his song, and she began with a carefully prepared comparison of herself with Lady Macbeth, chanting revealingly in her mad scene, 'Who would have thought the old man to have had so much blood in him?' Her sentiments, she said, having listened with much pleasure to Mr Walsh's song of welcome to the ladies, were rather, 'Who could have thought the young man to have so much voice in him?'

Mixed among the general bonhomie, this met with some ribaldry among the men at the idea of Eric's youth. Ros gathered confidence and rode on the support she now sensed in her audience. She made a graceful, humorous speech about how the women saw the activities of the menfolk, carefully avoiding any reference to the Masonic rituals about which some of the men were notoriously sensitive. This was not an occasion for controversy, and she contented herself with a little gentle irony.

At the fringe of her vision, Superintendent Thomas Bulstrode Tucker smiled indulgently and tapped the table politely in response to Ros's humorous sallies. He was careful not to show too much enthusiasm for the speaker. Barbara Tucker had eventually insisted on wearing her orange satin for the occasion, so Thomas could hardly fail to remark his spouse's every reaction. Tucker tried to pitch his response to the only female speech of the evening on that delicate tightrope between the enthusiasm which would be right for his fellow members of the Lodge and the zeal which Barbara would consider inappropriate and which might provoke her domestic retribution in the privacy of the Tucker home.

It was a delicate balance to strike, but Tucker, who prided himself upon his skill in public relations, had had much practice over the years in assessing what his reaction should be in a variety of situations, and he thought he brought it off. By the end of Mrs Whiteman's speech, he was confident enough to engage in eye contact with the other males at his table to emphasize his appreciation.

He didn't dare to catch Barbara's eye, not wishing to endure the dent to his confidence which her censure would bring. But he did not really think his wife would disapprove of the animation he was showing: after all, he had held out to her the heady prospect of his being Master of this Lodge in the years to come. With an eye to this glorious future, even Barbara could scarcely disapprove of a little Masonic bonding on Ladies' Night.

Ros Whiteman sat down to an excellent reception as the women applauded and the men moved on from clapping to that thumping of the tables which was their ultimate sign of bucolic male approval. Not all women in their forties can blush prettily. Ros, who had expected no such reaction in herself, reddened spontaneously and splendidly. She snatched up the glass she had eschewed before her speech, downed its contents in a half-comic toast to the smiling faces around her, and flushed most attractively above the dark blue of her dress.

She was aware of John's hand, now wholly under his brain's

control, stealing softly over the tablecloth to cover hers and squeeze it in congratulation. For the first time in weeks, she accepted his touch without any feeling of hypocrisy. She had enough of human vanity in her to want this moment to stretch indefinitely, to feel herself cocooned for long hours in this convivial congratulation, with the harshness of the larger world wholly excluded.

It was several minutes before she looked for the approval of one other pair of eyes in that large and busy room.

Her speech was the last formal moment of the evening, and she came down gradually from her exhilaration in the next hour or so as the noise level rose to its highest of the night and the hilarity rang in noisy bursts around the room, whilst the Master and his lady circulated among members and guests.

Superintendent Tucker stayed until the end, well aware that his profile among the longer-standing members of the Lodge might be enhanced by diminishing numbers. Silver-haired and trim in his evening suit, he offered little beyond his praise of the evening's events; he gave a detailed account of his approbation to the Master as John and Ros Whiteman paused at his table. Tucker knew from long years amidst the police hierarchy that praise never went amiss, that however banal and conventional his eulogies might be, people were never very discriminating about things they wanted to hear.

As the numbers of Lodge members remaining grew smaller, he took the opportunity to move around the room in the Master's wake. Much to his relief, Barbara had decided that she was enjoying her evening, and her Wagnerian presence cruised happily at his side, trilling the chorus to his paeans of praise as he sowed seeds that he hoped would bear fruit in his Mastership of the North Brunton Lodge. Barbara did her best to help his cause by dropping the hint that they might expect Superintendent Tucker to be chief superintendent before very long.

Tucker had stressed the need for secrecy when he had revealed his hopes for a final promotion to her, and he laid a finger across his lips in mock admonition. But it was the stage of the evening when no one was entirely sure what was serious, and the thinning company around them, mellowed by drink and conviviality, smiled upon Barbara's indiscretion.

Tucker had a sudden dismal thought: he had not yet revealed to Barbara the necessary condition of his proposed elevation, that he must take the detested Inspector Peach up the ranks with him. His wife, who had decided on her more limited acquaintance that she detested DI Peach even more deeply than her husband, would be aghast at the thought that Percy would have to be elevated to the title of Chief Inspector Peach.

The Tuckers were amongst the last dozen people in the room at the end of the evening. Tucker was concluding an extended goodnight to the Master when the head waiter, Charles Davies, appeared and drew the superintendent discreetly to one side. 'We have a problem, Superintendent,' he announced, in what was little more than a whisper.

'What sort of a problem?' Tucker, who was nerving himself to be driven home by Barbara, was immediately cautious.

'A police problem. In the car park.'

'If someone has had a bump, it's not the sort of thing a superintendent gets himself involved in,' warned Tucker portentously. He drew himself up to his full height and smiled indulgently at Davies; he did not want the Master of the Lodge to see him being impatient.

'It's nothing like that. You'd better come and look, Mr Tucker,' said Davies. He then pre-empted any further argument by turning on his heel and walking away, as smooth and erect on his head waiter's feet as if he were drawn on castors.

Tucker hesitated for a moment, then shrugged his shoulders towards the Master and his lady and moved after Davies with what he hoped was an air of command. There was something at least in being in demand on such an occasion, he told himself. An emergency emphasized one's professional standing in front of the Master, rather as if one was a doctor able to save a life.

Davies did not look back. He led the way through a car park that was now almost deserted. The smell of petrol from recently started engines hung heavily in the still night air. The head waiter moved smoothly but surprisingly swiftly to a distinctive car at the far end of the car park.

It was not he but Thomas Bulstrode Tucker who stopped abruptly as they neared the handsome Triumph Stag. As the shaft of light from the door forty yards behind them fell palely upon the windscreen of the car, the head of Brunton CID saw a figure slumped forward over the steering wheel.

Some dim memory from long ago, from the years when he had been used to attending the scenes of crimes, told Tucker that this was not a living figure.

A series of memories flashed across the superintendent's suddenly active imagination. He saw Darren Cartwright's frightened face; heard his voice on the phone, full of apprehension at the threats to his life; remembered his own omissions in the matter; recalled Peach's view that Cartwright should not have protection; recollected with horror his own assurance that Cartwright would be safe tonight at least at the Lodge's Ladies' Night. All these things flashed with surprising clarity through the mind of Superintendent Thomas Bulstrode Tucker.

'Don't touch anything!' he said automatically to Davies. He summoned an air of authority. 'I'll have a scene-of-crime team along as soon as I can muster one. There'll be a fingerprint expert, a photographer, and a whole team of people to gather forensic evidence.' Even in this crisis, Thomas Bulstrode Tucker could not refrain from adding a little vicarious importance to his office.

He took a deep breath and bent to peer inside the vehicle. Then he recoiled, not in revulsion, but in sheer surprise.

He had seen the bulging eyes and contorted features of asphyxiation victims often enough before. As a young policeman, he had had to contemplate many more distressing deaths than this.

What surprised Tucker was the identity of the man who was so indisputably dead behind the wheel of this car. This was not the repeatedly threatened and duly apprehensive Darren Cartwright at all.

The eyes which stared so unseeingly past Tucker's head were those of the late singer of the song to honour the ladies, Eric Walsh.

Six

Superintendent Tucker was rather out of touch with modern criminal investigations. He was indeed widely regarded as an anachronism at Brunton Police Station, though his rank ensured that few displayed such contempt to his face. But he remembered the basic procedures for confronting a serious crime.

As soon as he was made aware of Eric Walsh's body, Tucker asserted himself. He announced firmly that the few members of the North Brunton Masonic Lodge who remained in the White Bull and the entire staff of the hotel would not be allowed to leave. He bustled in and out of the main rooms of the hotel and made a series of phone calls with a growing air of authority, secretly pleased by the way people looked to him for a lead in this crisis. He remembered the form for these occasions clearly enough, and that gave him confidence. He was implacable in the face of the growing displeasure amongst those who had thought to be comfortably in bed by now.

By the time DI Peach and DS Blake arrived, it was nearing one in the morning, and irritation was mounting towards unpleasantness among those most anxious to be away. Superintendent Tucker was relieved to announce that what he called the 'details of the investigation' would now pass into the hands of his inspector whilst he withdrew from the front line, assuring the thunderous faces that he would be maintaining a 'continuous overview of the case'.

Percy Peach was not best pleased himself. He had been in bed with Lucy Blake, getting very near the point of no return, when the phone had rung so insistently. He had spent most of

56

his time in the car on the way to the White Bull grumbling that he had given up coitus interruptus when he had renounced the Roman Catholicism of his boyhood.

He found that Tucker was too relieved by his arrival to think it suspicious that he and Lucy came into the White Bull together. Percy brought a brisk despatch to the practical details of the case. He announced that a proper scene-of-crime team could not be assembled until the morning, and instructed the two uniformed constables already at the scene to cordon off the area around Walsh's white Triumph Stag at the end of the hotel car park.

The police surgeon had arrived minutes before Peach and Blake. He went through the formality of confirming the death they all knew had happened at least an hour earlier, and even went so far as to venture the view that it looked to him like murder by person or persons unknown.

As the man in the driving seat had plainly been garrotted savagely from the rear with some sort of cord which was no longer here, this did not seem unduly speculative. But the doctor was young and eager, so Peach accorded him the privilege of a couple of routine questions.

'How long since this happened?'

A shrug of the young shoulders. A venture at an answer where in a year or two he would be professionally cautious. 'He's still warm. Not more than an hour and a half ago, I should think.'

'Any great strength needed for this?'

The police surgeon smiled, thinking he saw where the inspector was going. 'No. Anyone could have done it. Especially if he was taken by surprise from behind. It could have been a woman. Even a child.' He couldn't help a small smile. This was almost like being on the telly. Much better than the routine deaths he had to certify in hospitals and suburban homes. Much better than the drunken drivers from whom he had had to extract blood samples earlier in the evening.

Peach nodded sourly. 'We don't get many children garrotting

drivers at midnight in Brunton. Not yet, anyway. Perhaps you're on to the first.'

The young doctor looked crestfallen. He tried not to sound piqued as he said, 'I'm only saying it was possible. I didn't say that's what happened.'

Peach grinned. 'Of course you're not. And it's good to have the assurance that it might be a woman. Isn't it, Detective Sergeant Blake?'

Lucy didn't see the need for a reaction to this. She looked at the handsome car and said to the police surgeon, 'It looks as though he had no warning of this. As though someone waited in the back seat for him to come to his car and crouched down as he arrived. As if he was taken completely by surprise as he settled into the driving seat. As if he probably never even saw who did this.'

The doctor nodded, then looked apprehensively at the impassive Peach. He was a quick learner. 'It's your job to decide about these things, of course. But the little I can see without disturbing his clothes would indicate that that is entirely possible. The pathologist will be able to tell you more after a full post-mortem examination, of course.'

'I'm not sure he will, in this case,' said Percy Peach grimly. 'The simplest murders are always the worst. The buggers leave less of themselves behind.'

It was a crude summary, but an accurate one. Forensic science always looks for an 'exchange' at the scene of a serious crime, the idea being that the criminal, however careful he might be, always leaves something of himself at the place of his crime, and usually takes away something from it, such as blood from his victim or fibres from the dead person's clothing.

This already looked like one of the least rewarding murder spots, with the victim despatched swiftly and silently and the killer away without detection. Enquiries among the hotel staff and the Lodge members might reveal some suspicious presence around this car, but Percy was not optimistic. He had already noted that the seats of the Triumph were covered in leather, the most unhelpful of materials so far as the collection of fibres went. He summoned up a cheery politeness he did not feel to dismiss the doctor; no detective wanted to make an enemy of the official police surgeon.

Peach's dark eyes blinked a little at the suddenness of the light as he went back into the brightly lit dining room of the hotel. It was now one twenty in the morning, and those members of the Lodge who had been unfortunate enough to be still on the premises when Walsh's body was discovered sat in a rough semicircle, white-faced and emotionally drained.

The men here were part of a Masonic Brotherhood, and they wanted to support each other now, but they were so fatigued and the situation was so beyond their previous experiences that they did not know how. They gave each other occasional glances, sometimes of sympathy, sometimes of speculation about this sensational end to their evening. But mostly they looked at the floor and said nothing, having long since exhausted the few conventional phrases which suggested themselves.

The women said even less and looked even worse. Shock flatters no one's looks, and coming as it had at the end of the evening it had cut through the make-up which was already tired and left the women looking frail as well as old. Lucy Blake, who was thirty years younger than most of the women who sat tight-lipped and bewildered here, felt sharply for them as she glanced around.

There was much finery in the dresses and the jewellery on display, but like the make-up on the ageing faces, the effects seemed damaged beyond recall by the knowledge of what had happened in the car park outside. She was reminded of the hospital casualty departments she knew so well, where women with parchment faces waited for the news of their injured men, at the end of evenings which had started out full of excitement and glamour.

Barbara Tucker, garish in the orange dress which made her look even bigger, was dispensing coffee from a large jug and talking in muted tones to the people who held out their cups.

'It's better than letting the staff do it,' she explained to Lucy. 'You want to be private at a time like this.' The big woman seemed glad to speak to someone who would not be shocked by the situation, and Lucy guessed that she had been getting little more than monosyllables as she took on the unaccustomed role of comforter and circulated among the stricken group.

There were a few tears and much smudged eyeshadow among the other women, but the predominant impressions were of exhaustion and bewilderment. John Whiteman, whose evening as Master of the Lodge had been so suddenly disrupted by the discovery in the car park, was in a corner of the room, talking quietly to Superintendent Tucker. His wife, the star of that part of the evening which now seemed days behind them, sat on her own, weeping quietly, wiping her eyes from time to time with a handkerchief which seemed already sodden.

Tucker noticed Peach's entry and came over to speak to him, trying to convey an air of authority to an audience which had long since ceased to care. 'Time we sent these people home,' he said. 'They've convinced me they have nothing useful to tell us.'

He waited for Peach to challenge him on this, but as usual when he wanted his inspector to speak, Peach remained obstinately silent, his only reaction a slight raising of his expressive black eyebrows. Tucker said nervously, 'They're respectable people, known to me personally.'

'Yes, sir. Of course, one of them is quite possibly a murderer.' Peach permitted himself a small smile at that thought. Then he turned and addressed the ragged semicircle of people. 'We shall need statements from all of you, as you might expect. It's far too late to begin that tonight. Is there anyone here who has any information, any previous knowledge, any suspicion which might help to throw some light on what happened out there tonight?'

There was a moment of absolute silence. Lucy Blake looked round the exhausted faces with what she hoped was an encouraging smile, but no one spoke.

Peach said, 'In that case, I suggest you go home and get

whatever sleep you can. I or a member of my team will be along to see each of you tomorrow. I trust no one is planning to be away from their home or their normal place of work?'

No one took up what sounded like a challenge. John Whiteman said with an attempt at a smile, 'I suppose this means that we're all suspects at the moment.'

'No more than forty others who left before the body was found. No more than anyone on the hotel staff who had previous dealings with the late Mr Eric Walsh.' Peach sighed at the enormity of the field confronting him.

The remnants of what had begun as a glittering concourse shuffled wearily out of the room. Peach watched their departure keenly, observant for any signs of excessive relief. Then he nodded to Lucy Blake and the duo went into the kitchen of the White Bull.

It was still warm in here, though the central heating in the main rooms of the hotel had been off for over an hour. And the atmosphere, though far from noisy, was less muted than among the group they had just left. The kitchen staff in their white overalls had mingled with the waiters in evening dress. The only real division was that between a small group who were smoking at one end of the big room and the rest.

Peach looked round both groups in the silence which had fallen upon them with his entry. He acknowledged the presence of Charles Davies, whom he had known since long before he became head waiter here. He registered the apprehensive face of Wasim Afzaal with no more than a minimal raising of his right eyebrow.

Davies took it upon himself to speak for the staff around him. 'Your constables have already been questioning us, Inspector Peach. No one has been able to offer anything useful. Everyone here is exhausted. Almost all of us will be working tomorrow. We need our rest.'

Percy nodded. 'Even policemen need their rest. But there is someone here – perhaps more than one person – who knows something, who has seen things which may be vital in the detection of a murder.'

An absolute hush fell on the line of white faces with the first mention of the word 'murder'. Even though they had been discussing the thing in the car park in exactly those terms for the last hour, the official voicing of the word brought its own grisly glamour into the lives of people who had never met it before.

Davies cleared his throat. 'I'm sure no one here is withholding information, Inspector.'

Peach allowed the disturbing effect of his smile to run along the line of hotel staff. His gaze seemed to assess each of them in rapid succession. 'I wish I could be as sure of that as you, Mr Davies. I repeat my view that someone here knows things of value to us. He or she may as yet be quite unaware of the importance of some chance sighting, some overheard remark which will have an important bearing on bringing a murderer to justice. Or he or she may of course be deliberately withholding valuable information, which would be most unwise.'

His smile disappeared abruptly with this last thought. 'Mr Davies, I shall need the name of anyone who was working here during the evening but is not here now. The rest of you should give your names to Constable Curtis as you leave this room.' There was a slight, involuntary start from Curtis, who had not known that the local legend Percy Peach knew his name. The inspector said solemnly, 'I advise you to think carefully overnight, and to try to recall any small detail which may be significant in this case.'

It was a dismissal, and with a collective murmur of relief they moved hastily towards PC Curtis and then on to the taxis which Davies had laid on to take them home.

Wasim Afzaal was careful not to be the first through the door. He placed himself in the middle of the ragged line of staff, stifled a yawn as he waited to give his details to Constable Curtis, exchanged a few words with one of his companions in the corridor outside before he went out into the cover of the night.

Peach hadn't fastened upon him in there, as he had half-expected he would. But even Peach couldn't know everything. And no one else on the hotel staff knew enough to give him away.

Seven

Two hours after Peach had dismissed both the staff and the patrons of the White Bull, a car eased softly into a quiet suburban road four miles from the centre of Brunton.

It was a cold night for early November, but it was apprehension, not the cold, which made the driver shiver as he sat for a moment and looked at the dark outlines of the silent houses ahead of him. There was not a light to be seen, but he still parked here, at the end of the road, rather than outside the building which interested him; some insomniac, drawing curtains silently aside, might see the dark shape of an unfamiliar vehicle.

His overwrought imagination pictured that very thing happening, even now. But those prying eyes would not be able to pinpoint his whereabouts from the position of his vehicle. Not if he left it here. He steeled himself to open the door, slipped quietly into the cold velvet of the darkness, and pressed rather than slammed the door shut behind him.

He removed the keys, but did not lock the door. There would surely be no danger of car thieves in this quiet place at three thirty in the morning. And he might need to get away very quickly, if he was disturbed.

That thought set him trembling anew, and he hurried down the road beneath the sheltering trees, finding a release from his tension in the movement. The temperature was low, but there would be no frost tonight. The cloud cover would ensure that. And the clouds cut out any light from the stars and the thin crescent of the new moon. That suited his purpose. He had to struggle with the catch of the familiar gate when he reached the house.

He hesitated for a moment. What he proposed to do was foreign to him, totally outside his previous experience. He had no moral scruples about it, but the danger which always attends the unfamiliar pressed hard upon him, pounding the blood in his ears as he loped swiftly up the drive.

He was surprised how much his fingers shook as he tried to get the key into the lock. He had to use both hands, finding the seating for the key in the Yale lock with the index finger of his left, then sliding it home at the second attempt with the fingers of his right. The kid gloves he wore made it a little more difficult, but he knew that nerves were the things which slowed him down.

For an awful moment, he thought the key was not going to turn the lock, that the catch had been applied from the inside. But he knew that could not be so, and in a moment the heavy door fell back and he was inside, shutting the door carefully behind him, leaning against the inside of it for an instant's respite, feeling the coldness of the single small pane of glass against his forehead.

He was safe now, for the moment. He turned and shone the torch he had not dared to use outside around the line of doors in the silent hall. He knew that there could be no one here, that he was alone in the house. Yet he had to force himself to turn the handle of the door he knew he needed to open, as if some inhuman presence was waiting patiently for him behind it.

There was nothing, of course. He flashed the beam of his torch round the room, finding the familiar objects more dramatic in the sudden shaft of harsh light. Then he switched on the room light at the door. This room was at the rear of the house. And who was to know that this was not the normal occupant of the house, unable to sleep and come down to search out a book? They said you only attracted attention to yourself if you behaved like a guilty person. Boldness be my friend, then. Who said that? The question rattled inconsequentially and irritatingly round his fevered brain.

Now that he was here, he realized that he did not know exactly what he was looking for, and the task suddenly seemed for the first time impossible. At least the filing cabinet wasn't locked. He went hastily through it, fumbling over the sheets of paper with his gloved hands. He snatched out a couple of sheets, cramming them hurriedly into the pocket of his leather jacket. But he hadn't time to inspect everything, and he couldn't carry everything away with him.

In a rising panic, he went out into the hall, careless where he had lately been so careful, switching on lights in the hall and landing, taking the stairs two at a time, as if swiftness could compensate for the knowledge he did not have. In the bedrooms, he turned out drawer after drawer, swearing aloud as he found only clothes, heaping obscenities upon the absent owner when he could not find the things he wanted.

He went downstairs again, almost falling headlong in his haste, back into the study, shouting at the desk and the bookshelves, which seemed to mock him with their solemn, watchful silence.

It was when he went into the dining room that the full futility of his errand struck him like a blow in the face. A laptop computer was on the big table, with the chair in front of it drawn back at an angle, as if the user had just risen from his work. Of course! This is where the records would be. This is where the details of his involvement would be preserved.

Even with that realisation, the hopelessness of his mission crashed about his ears, and his head turned dizzy with the knowledge. He sat down heavily on the chair, shooting a sharp spasm through his back with the abruptness of his descent. How had he ever thought he could outwit a damned computer? You needed passwords to get into the stuff he wanted.

'You bastard!' He shouted the word uselessly at the room at large, heedless now of the noise as well as the light. Then he snatched off his shoe and crashed the heel into the monitor screen of the instrument, seeing the glass shatter an instant before the noise beat back at him from the walls. He raised the laptop above his head and smashed it as hard as he could against the parquet floor of the room. Putting his shoe back on his foot, he made ready to jump upon the instrument, seeking at least to vent his fury and frustration upon its blandness.

Then at last caution reasserted itself. They could do things with what you left behind – take prints of your shoes, or something like that. He looked helplessly at the shattered screen of the monitor, on which he had used the heel of his shoe like a hammer. But they surely couldn't learn anything from those scattered fragments, could they?

But the caution which had surfaced so belatedly now took him over like a powerful drug, coursing through his veins, turning the desire to be away from here into a panic. He banged off the lights violently, as if the switches had caused him some personal hurt.

He had thought when he came here that he would search carefully and methodically, removing all traces of himself meticulously from the house. Now he left drawers open and chaos in every room he had visited, anxious only to be out of the place as the impossibility of what he had wanted to do washed over him.

He slammed the front door behind him, the very door which he had taken such pains to open quietly on his entry. Then he fell flat with a cry of fear when his foot caught wet leaves on the lower of the two steps in front of the door. He picked himself up without checking the damage and raced through the darkness, flinging himself with a huge gasp of relief into the seat of his car.

He started the engine, revved it more than he had meant to, careless now of the noise. He was a good mile away from the place before he saw that his gloves were torn and blood was seeping from his fingers.

Superintendent Tucker very rarely appeared in the station on Saturday mornings. In the wholly exceptional circumstances of a murder in his own North Brunton Masonic Lodge, he felt he had no option but to present himself this Saturday. It did not improve his temper.

He had been in his office at the top of the new police

building – 'Tommy Tucker's piss-packed penthouse', as Peach sometimes called it – for over half an hour before his inspector appeared. As head of the Brunton CID section, Tucker was convinced he should be doing something, but he was not quite sure what. He found that Peach had already put together a murder team. The members of it were even now deployed about the town, so there was no one in the station for Tucker to bollock or galvanize into action. He wasn't much good at anything else, and he knew it as well as anyone, even if he could never admit it.

It was a relief when Peach rapped smartly on the door of his office. Tucker relished a rare opportunity to put one over on his junior officer. He said sniffily, 'I've been here for nearly an hour. In the circumstances, I should have thought you could have got out of your bed rather earlier, even if it is Saturday.'

'Sorry, sir.'

'If I can make the effort when I recognize a serious crime, it should surely not be too much for a younger man to show willing.'

'Yes, sir. I mean no, sir.' Peach stood like a schoolboy before the big desk, his hands behind his back as the toe of his right foot rubbed against the heel of his left and his gaze focussed on the floor in front of him. He thought, I shouldn't really take the piss out of the pompous old bugger, but I'd hit him if I didn't, and that would be much worse.

As usual, Tucker didn't see the warning signs. 'It's not the behaviour of a man I'm proposing to promote to the rank of chief inspector, a man whom I have supported through thick and thin in his career.'

The effrontery of this, from a man who would have consigned him cheerfully to hell had it been possible, was too much for Percy Peach. 'Yes, sir. Can you tell me what you have turned up about this case which is so significant?'

'Significant?' Tucker looked like a retarded goldfish.

'Yes, sir. I mistakenly thought I'd be better employed at the scene of the crime. Sorry, sir.'

'You've been round at the White Bull?'

'Since seven o'clock, sir. Scene-of-crime team's working hard there in the car park. DC Murphy and DC Clay are questioning the staff of the hotel about anything they may have seen or heard last night. And the uniformed officers are—'

'And has all this activity produced any results yet?' Tucker tried desperately to stem the tide of information from his inspector.

'There have been certain sightings, sir, which may or may not be significant. I shall be following them up myself when we have completed preliminary questioning. Unless of course you would like to take this over yourself, sir? First day is always crucial in a case like this, and it would be advantageous to have the sharpest minds operating at the crime face.'

'No, no. I don't want to interfere with your enquiries.' Tucker recoiled as always from the prospect of direct involvement. 'So long as you can assure me that maximum energy and resources are being properly applied. It's my job to keep an overview of the case, you know.'

'Yes, sir. Exactly what I told the lads and lasses when I was ringing them at six thirty on a Saturday morning. "Superintendent Tucker will be keeping an overview," I said. I thought they'd find that reassuring when they were losing their weekends to form a murder team.'

Tucker glared at him suspiciously, but Peach's expression was earnest, his gaze fixed resolutely upon the wall above his chief's head. Tucker, who had thought that his very presence here on a Saturday morning would be enough to awe his staff, was left wondering what to say next. He opted for a portentous, 'This will be a very high-profile case, you know. Eric Walsh was a well-known and highly respected citizen of this town.'

Peach nodded. 'A member of the North Brunton Masonic Lodge. A singing member.'

Tucker frowned. 'The fact that Mr Walsh sang the song of welcome to the ladies last night has surely nothing to do with this case.'

Peach pursed his lips. 'Good singer, was he?'

'Quite good, yes. He had a considerable local reputation.'

'We can probably rule out tortured musicians, then. But I wouldn't like to rule out a musical connection completely at this point, sir. Not until we have more of the facts. Unless your overview has already provided us with a leading suspect, of course?' His dark pupils fastened for the first time on Tucker's face, bright with an innocent hope.

'Don't be ridiculous, Peach!' Tucker leaned forward confidentially. 'I want you to give this case your utmost attention. The press will make a lot of it once they get on to it.'

'Yes, sir. Do you think we should use the media to help us find the culprit?'

Tucker was immediately suspicious. 'How on earth could we do that?'

'Well, I thought if I let old Alf Houldsworth know the details of the killing, and pointed out that it was probably a Masonic crime, the Masons in this area being four times as likely to commit serious crimes as ordinary citizens, we might frighten whoever—'

'Peach! You will do no such thing. I don't know where on earth you got this statistic about the Brotherhood from anyway, and I certainly forbid you to go promulgating any such ideas through that old soak Houldsworth!'

The one-eyed Alf Houldsworth, retired for his final working years from a national daily to the cosier pages of the local *Evening Dispatch*, was an occasional drinking companion of Percy's, with a similar well-honed contempt for Superintendent Thomas Bulstrode Tucker.

'You don't think Masons should be investigated, sir? Even when one of their number is killed in their midst? Well, that will cut down on the work and the overtime budget very considerably, I must say. The benefits of your overview will be demonstrated in very practical terms. I dare say the media will be curious about why we're laying off the Masons, but—'

'Peach, I didn't say that! Why do you wilfully misunderstand me in these things? Of course you must investigate the members of my Lodge. It's my belief that you won't find the

70

killer among them, but you must treat them exactly the same as everyone else.'

'Exactly the same, sir?'

'Exactly. There must be no allowances made.'

'And no exceptions, sir?'

'Certainly not.'

'Very well, sir.' Peach nodded several times, as if he might thus embed a difficult concept into his memory. 'So where were you between eleven twenty and midnight last night, sir?'

'Where was I between—? You're not seriously suggesting that *I* might have killed the wretched man?'

'No exceptions, you said, sir. Just trying to eliminate you from the enquiry, cut the number of suspects down. You know the form. And did I hear you call the victim "the wretched man", sir? I don't like that. Most unfortunate expression, from your point of view. You don't want your solicitor present for this, do you?'

'No I damned well don't! And you just be bloody careful, DI Peach. You can go too far, you know.'

'Yes, sir. Sorry, sir. So are you refusing to tell me where you were between eleven twenty and midnight, then?'

Tucker longed to tear a real strip off this odious tormentor. But he knew that his own reputation rested on the broad shoulders of this squat little Torquemado. And being intensely media-conscious, he saw everything in terms of headlines. 'Head of CID Keeps Mum in Murder Probe' is the one which sprang to mind, if Peach leaked this exchange to that old rogue Houldsworth. Tucker said through gritted teeth, 'I was in the main dining room with the rest of our group, I suppose.'

Peach recorded this eagerly in the small leather-backed book he produced from his inside pocket, mouthing the words 'I suppose' with silent satisfaction as he wrote them. 'You didn't leave the room for anything during this forty-minute period, sir? No calls of nature or other unspecified absences?'

'Of course I didn't! Well, I may just have gone out to the gents in that period, I suppose. The meal and the speeches had

71

gone on for quite a long time, and we'd drunk a fair amount. Yes, I think I did go to the men's cloakroom during that period. I couldn't be sure exactly when.'

Peach nodded thoughtfully over his notebook. 'Pity about that. But understandable, I suppose. Can anyone vouch for your movements?'

'Vouch for my movements?'

'Yes, sir. To put it bluntly, as we're in the business, is there anyone who can confirm that you went to the bog and only to the bog, rather than nipping out to garrotte the Irish nightingale in the car park?'

'No. I don't remember anyone being in the cloakroom when I was.'

Peach shook his head sadly, looking at his notes. 'Can't eliminate you from suspicion, can we, sir? Not at the moment. But I should assure you that as far as I'm concerned, it's just a formality.'

'I'm glad to hear it.'

Tucker tried to weight his words with a heavy irony, but Peach did not seem to notice it. 'You've no reason to dislike the deceased, have you, sir?'

'Eric? No. No reason whatsoever.'

'Only you did refer to him as "the wretched man", if you remember. You didn't owe him any large sums of money?'

'Of course I didn't. Look here, Peach—'

'And he hadn't been paying unwelcome attentions to your desirable wife?'

The adjective threw Tucker. For a moment he wasn't certain that his inspector was referring to the formidable Barbara. Then he said, 'No, of course he wasn't. This is preposterous!'

'But it was you who pointed out to us in your address to the CID section last month that sex and money were overwhelmingly the most common motives in crimes of violence, sir.' Percy didn't see any reason why Tommy Bloody Tucker's inclination for stating the blindin' bleedin' obvious should not be invoked against him.

'Look, Peach, I didn't kill Eric Walsh, and both of us know

that. He hadn't lent me money and he wasn't bedding my wife.' Tucker decided it was time he went on the offensive. 'Now, I suggest you get on with finding who did kill him. Why were you sniffing round the scene-of-crime team when Jack Chadwick is a perfectly competent officer who has been doing the job for years?'

'Because Sergeant Chadwick isn't at the White Bull, sir.'

'Well why the hell not? He's our most experienced scene-of-crime officer.'

'Indeed he is, sir. And he was at the White Bull with his team. But he transferred it, sir. Left a couple of his constables in charge of the car park site at the White Bull. That's why I thought I ought to go down and check on them, sir. Maintain an oversight of their activities, as you might say.'

Tucker chose to ignore the insolence of the phrase. 'Why the hell did you move Chadwick away from there? I told you, this is a high-profile crime, and Chadwick should be where he's needed most.'

'Yes, sir. That's why he transferred the team. He's attending the scene of a burglary.'

'A burglary! When there's murder been done?'

Peach tired of the game. There was work to be done. 'A burglary at Eric Walsh's house, sir. During the night. By person or persons as yet unknown.'

He decided as he went back down the stairs that he had seen goldfish who looked more alert than his flabbergasted chief.

Eight

The woman was now called Mrs Pearson. She was probably in her late forties, but very well preserved. To Lucy Blake she did not appear to be much affected by grief.

The widow of the late Eric Walsh looked out of the window of the Edwardian house as if assessing the state of the lawn, which was green and neatly edged even at this time of the year. It stretched away for eighty yards towards mature laburnums and cherries, and Lucy wondered if it was a condition of residence in the plush suburb of Alderley Edge that you kept your own patch of Cheshire in prime horticultural condition.

Then the former Mrs Walsh said, 'I'm not going to pretend to be devastated by Eric's death. But the manner of his death was certainly a shock.'

'It must have been. And I'm sorry we have to intrude at a time like this. But in the case of a violent death there are . . . well, there are certain things we need to know, as quickly as possible.'

'Like whether his ex-wife killed him or not, I suppose. I'm happy to say that I didn't.'

Lucy smiled. She felt she could get on well with this woman, in happier circumstances. She liked people who talked straight, who cut out the fripperies which surround so much of human conversation. 'No one is suggesting that you did. But since you've raised it, you'd better tell me where you were last night.'

The grey eyes looked at her with a hint of mockery. 'We – that is to say, my second husband and I – were at a dinner party. So I have seven witnesses until around midnight. After that I was with my husband alone. Fortunately we occupy the same bed.'

'You can account for the period up to midnight. That is quite sufficient.' Lucy was already thinking that Eric Walsh must have been a fool to abandon this bright and attractive partner.

The correction to that thought came as promptly as if the widow had read her mind. 'I tired of Eric and his way of life many years ago now. I haven't seen him for the last ten of them. No doubt I wouldn't have seen him for the next ten either. You can see why I'm not pretending to a grief I don't feel. When the woman police officer came round with the news this morning I was shocked, as you'd expect, by the suddenness of it. But not anguished.' She sounded as if she was analysing her own reactions and finding them of interest to her.

Lucy said quietly, 'Do you know of anyone who will benefit from his death?'

The woman who had once been Deborah Walsh smiled into the young, earnest face beneath the aureole of red-brown hair. 'You mean was it worth my while employing a contract killer to see Eric off? I don't imagine he was worth very much, Detective Sergeant Blake, unless he'd altered his habits considerably. And I'm sure he wouldn't have been leaving anything to an estranged wife he hadn't seen for ten years. Nor would I be interested: my present husband is on the board of his company and it's doing well.' She glanced around, taking in the softly gleaming antique furniture, the house and its grounds. She was comfortable rather than apologetic about the opulence in which she lived.

'I wasn't suggesting a motive for you. We need to build up a picture of a murder victim about whom we know almost nothing at present. I thought you might be able to tell us something about his way of life.'

The pause stretched for so long that Lucy thought the older woman was refusing her any response. Then the widow said quietly, 'I haven't seen him for ten years, but I don't expect the leopard changes its spots. You persuade yourself a relationship is deeper than it is for the sake of your own vanity, I think. When I look back, although our marriage lasted nine years, there was never much more than sex between Eric and me.'

It was spoken with a measured regret, and coming from this attractive, intelligent woman, it gave Lucy a sudden chill. Would she be talking about her own relationship with Percy Peach in the same terms in twenty years' time? She said, 'I don't want to pry into why you split up. But is there anything you can tell us about Eric Walsh which might help us in the search for his killer?'

There was another pause, not quite so long this time. Then the woman who had been married for nine years to Walsh said, 'He could never resist a bit of skirt, Eric. I don't think for a moment that he would have changed in that.'

Superintendent Tucker was not the only one to make an unscheduled visit to work on this bright winter Saturday. John Whiteman also chose to go into his office on the morning after the murder of Eric Walsh. Moreover, unlike the egregious Tucker, Whiteman chose to spend the whole day in the labyrinthine Victorian building which housed the offices of JS Whiteman and Son, Family Solicitors.

Percy Peach wondered why.

Whiteman offered a breezy explanation. 'I couldn't settle to anything at home – not after last night's events. And I had a particularly tricky bit of conveyancing to work my way through. It seemed like a good opportunity to get the office to myself.'

Peach didn't find the explanation convincing. In his experience, solicitors rarely showed such a sense of urgency, and certainly not about conveyancing. He wasn't going to say so, not yet anyway. But he didn't see why the man he had come to interview shouldn't be ruffled; indeed, ruffling people was so much a habit to him that he scarcely needed to think about it. He nodded towards the big, fresh-faced officer at his side. 'This is Detective Constable Brendan Murphy. He's a Roman Catholic: that's not going to make it difficult for you to talk, is it?'

John Whiteman looked puzzled. 'No. Why should it?'

'You being a Mason, sir. Master of a Masonic Lodge, indeed. There's no love lost between you and the Roman Catholics, is there? The Pope condemned Freemasonry, I seem to remember.' Peach remembered it in fact very clearly: it had been reiterated to him many times by the Irish Christian Brothers, in what now seemed another life.

John looked carefully at the impassive round face beneath the shining bald pate. It didn't look as if the man was joking. So John smiled his most urbane smile. He was good at urbanity, and he knew it. 'You're very much out of date, I'm afraid, Inspector. It's true that well back in the past there was a certain animosity between us and the Catholic Church, but that is long gone. We make no distinctions on the grounds of race or creed. Indeed, I think the North Brunton Lodge has several Catholic members.'

'I'm glad to hear it. I'm sure that's an excellent thing.' Peach nodded thoughtfully; whether he thought it a excellent thing for the Order of the Free and Accepted Masons or the One Holy Roman Catholic Church was not clear. His voice hardened. 'Because we need complete frankness here, Mr Whiteman. Yours may be a secret society, with its own arcane rituals, but we are here to investigate a cold-blooded and brutal murder. We want nothing held back on account of loyalty to the Brotherhood.'

John Whiteman wondered if those dark eyes which studied his reactions so unwaveringly ever blinked. He had not detected a blink so far. He was more disconcerted than he would have thought possible by this thickset figure, with his strange prejudices and warnings. John was nothing like as suave as he wished to be as he said, 'Of course. As a matter of fact, the secrecy of our Masonic dealings and rituals is nothing like what it was. And speaking for myself, I can only say that I welcome that. Now that we are in the twenty-first century, we—'

'I'm glad you feel like that. Because it's very possible that one of your fellow Masons, a member of your own Lodge, killed Mr Walsh last night.' Peach paused, assessing the man opposite him, whose plentiful, well-groomed hair with its becoming grey at the temples was such a contrast to his own pate with its mere fringe of black hair. He waited for Whiteman to protest, as Tucker had, that he could scarcely contemplate a Mason as the perpetrator of this crime, but the man said nothing. So Percy said, 'There is no room for any withholding of information. Still less for any deception.'

John Whiteman was planning to do both of these things. He wondered if he looked as flustered as he felt to hear them now voiced so specifically. His tone sounded weak in his own ears as he said with a weak smile, 'Of course. I understand that. This is murder. But I'm afraid you'll find that I'm able to offer you very little that will be useful. I was as shocked as anyone by what happened last night. I still find it difficult to believe that Eric is dead.'

Peach, without taking his eyes off the man behind the huge old desk, gave a tiny nod to Detective Constable Murphy, who said, 'As far as we can determine, Mr Walsh was still alive at eleven twenty last night: he was seen then by a member of the hotel staff. His body was discovered at one minute before midnight. Could you tell us where you were between eleven twenty and midnight last night, Mr Whiteman?'

'You think I might have killed him?' It didn't sound as preposterous as John had hoped when he had rehearsed it.

'No, I think it's unlikely. But we're asking everyone the same question. In the absence of anything more positive, we have to work by eliminating as many people as possible.'

John Whiteman nodded. It was logical enough, of course. Indeed, it was what he had expected. And it was surely a good sign that they had, as the young DC said, nothing more positive to help them as yet. He wondered why he had to lick his lips before he said, 'I was in the bar next to the dining room, with a lot of friends, relaxing after the meal and the formal part of the evening. When you're making a speech, it's nice to have it over and done with. And you feel a certain responsibility for everyone enjoying their evening when you're the Master of the Lodge.'

He faltered to a halt, feeling he was saying too much. He had expected to be interrupted, but this disconcerting man let him ramble on when he had nothing much to say. Peach nodded, 'And do you think the evening was a success, sir? Until the discovery of Eric Walsh's body, that is.'

'It seemed to have gone quite well. People gathered round me and said so. Not least your own colleague, Superintendent Tucker.'

'Yes, sir. You must have been relieved to have an experienced officer on the spot when the murder took place.' He kept any tendency towards irony carefully out of his voice.

'Yes, it was. He took charge of things, knew what to do immediately.'

'Yes, he would, sir. And you're telling us that you were in the bar with other members of the Lodge and their ladies throughout the forty minutes DC Murphy mentioned?'

John didn't like that phrase 'telling us'. It made it sound as if they were already setting a trap for him. He said pointedly, 'That is what I said, and that is the truth. There are at least a dozen people who can bear me out. Not least, as I said, your own superior officer.'

Percy always liked it when they threw rank at him: he took it as a sign of weakness. 'Ah, but I have already questioned Superintendent Tucker about this period. We have to eliminate people, as DC Murphy explained. And it emerges that Mr Tucker was himself absent for part of this period. So he cannot vouch for you, you see. Not for the whole of the forty minutes.'

John could not see why Peach appeared to find this so satisfactory. He forced a smile. 'Well, I'm sure there'll be lots of people who will confirm my presence in the bar during that period. The Master of the Lodge does tend to be the centre of a little group on an occasion like this. It's nothing personal, of course; it's the office which makes it so.'

'I see. Well, we shall be asking other people about this, in due course. In the meantime, can you confirm which members of the Lodge were with you for the whole of this time? That would clear them, you see. And enable them to vouch for you, no doubt, when we see them.'

John Whiteman furrowed his brow. 'I'm sure some of the people were there all the time. But I wasn't checking that, of course. And I talked to a variety of people. I'll go on thinking about it, but at this moment I don't think I could say for certain that any of the people who were there when the body was found had been there for the whole of that period.'

'A pity, that. But understandable, I suppose.' Peach sounded as though he was reluctant to admit it.

John Whiteman leaned forward and put his hands on the scarred leather top of the desk which had sat in this room for a hundred years. 'Inspector, please don't think I'm telling you how to do your job. But isn't it probable that whoever killed Eric wasn't in that group at all? If I'd waited for a man in his car and then killed him like that, I wouldn't have had the nerve to go back into the hotel and fraternize with other people. I'd have driven off in a hurry.'

'Would you, sir? That's interesting, isn't it, DC Murphy? And entirely possible, of course. That's why the team has been busy all morning taking statements from the people who weren't in your group in the bar but left after eleven twenty. They make up a distressingly large group. Or a pleasingly large group for the person who did this, of course.'

'And isn't it entirely possible that someone came in from outside and waited in the car for him? Someone who was quite unconnected with the Masonic Ladies' Night?'

'Entirely possible, as you say. You should have been a detective, Mr Whiteman. Must be your legal background. We haven't turned up any outsider like that yet. He would need a lot of nerve to go into a closed car park and wait like that. Most professionals don't like going into areas with only one exit: it makes them feel like rats in a trap. And he'd have to have known exactly what Mr Walsh was about that evening and when he was likely to leave the gathering and come out to his car. Do you know of any such person?'

The abruptness of the question caught John off guard. He had thought he was steering the discussion into safer waters. 'Well, no, I don't. I was just speculating about how this might have happened. But there must be such people.'

'With a grievance fierce enough to make Walsh a murder victim? How well did you know Eric Walsh, Mr Whiteman?'

Again the suddenness with which the focus had been switched back to himself shook John. The answer he had prepared for this question wouldn't come to him, and he stumbled over the words a little as he said, 'Fairly well, I suppose. We'd been fellow members of the Lodge for fifteen years or so. But Eric wasn't an intimate friend.'

'He wouldn't have visited your house, for instance? Or you his?'

'No. Is this relevant?'

Peach shrugged the broad inspectorial shoulders. 'Who knows, Mr Whiteman? I'm just trying to build up a picture in my mind. Eventually we shall arrive at some fairly clear impression of the network of relationships which surrounded Mr Walsh. Later still we shall know which of them were the significant ones. Only then will I be able to tell you what is relevant. Most of it won't be, of course, but at this time we need to be like a sponge, absorbing all the information we can. Had you any reason to dislike Mr Walsh?'

Again that abrupt, aggressive question, at the end of a passage where he had seemed to be merely explaining the workings of the system. John forced himself to think before he replied. 'No. He was a pleasant man, Eric. A good singer, you know.'

'So I've heard. Does that make him a pleasant man? I've known some pretty dodgy tenors in my time.'

John managed a smile at what he took to be a small joke. 'Singing in public wins you a certain admiration, because most of us can't do it. Eric was a rich baritone, of course, not a tenor.'

'Buggers they are, in opera, you know. Most of them villains, if you believe Verdi and Puccini and that lot. Was Eric Walsh a villain?'

John smiled, forcing himself to take his time. What he said now might be important in the future. 'No. Not a villain, in my view. Some people would say it depends how you define a villain. I think I once heard Eric referred to as a likeable rogue.'

This time he had delivered almost exactly the words he had prepared. But it sounded curiously stilted. He had thought it would have been drawn from him phrase by phrase, as if he was reluctant to speak even so much that was derogatory of a dead man. But Peach had let him go on, all the while studying him carefully, as if he was more interested in him than the words he was delivering about Walsh.

Peach paused for what seemed a long time after John had delivered himself of this, as if he wanted to be sure that he was not going to commit himself further. Then he said, 'And which of these terms would you use yourself, Mr Whiteman?'

John took a long breath. 'I'm not sure I'd want to commit myself. I didn't know Eric that well.'

'Fifteen years in the same Masonic Lodge? Fifteen years of looking out for each other's interests? Fifteen years of interchange between your wife and whatever partners Mr Walsh had in that time? You must have some opinion of him. I wouldn't like to go away thinking you were withholding information from policemen investigating a murder case.'

The two men glared at each other and DC Murphy looked up from his notes to emphasize, 'This is the most serious crime of all, Mr Whiteman. It is no time for social niceties or respecting confidences.'

John glanced at the large fresh face beneath the tousled hair for a moment. In the intensity of his concentration upon those mesmeric black eyes of Peach's, he had almost forgotten the man who was quietly recording his replies. He said, 'You're right to remind me of that. I was trying to be discreet about a dead man, to protect his reputation in the normal way. I can only say that I've never had to speak about a murder victim before.'

Peach didn't trouble to acknowledge the apology. 'So was Eric Walsh a rogue, then? Likeable or otherwise.'

John said, 'He wasn't a rogue at all, not in your sense. He didn't steal money or beat people up. Not as far as I know, anyway.' He smiled, but the feebleness of his joke was emphasized by his interlocutor's stony face. He went on hastily, 'His only crime, if you could call it that, was that he was rather too fond of the ladies.'

'Randy bugger, you mean.'

'Yes, I suppose I do.'

'And he didn't control it, I suppose. Made his decisions with his dick rather than his head.' Peach nodded sadly. 'We see a lot of that in this job.'

John managed a smile. 'I think Eric would have preferred to say that his heart ruled his head, but broadly speaking, you're right.'

'So there'll be a few jealous husbands in the North Brunton Lodge who won't be bemoaning his death today.'

'Inside and outside the Lodge, I'd say.'

Peach nodded. 'Dicks aren't exclusive in their tastes, that's true. More's the pity.' He shook his head sadly, contemplating the serried ranks of cuckolds who stretched before him as suspects. 'So who was Eric Walsh knocking off at the time of his demise, then?'

'I don't know! I've really no idea!' The denial had come a little too promptly, but John was thrown by the methods of this odious little inspector. 'I told you. I wasn't an intimate friend of Eric's. I didn't know what he was up to from day to day, and I didn't wish to know.'

Peach looked at him in mock astonishment. 'Didn't want to know what this fellow member of your Lodge was up to? Didn't have the natural curiosity to wonder who was the latest conquest of a man who must have been the talk of the Lodge? Not to say the envy of the Lodge! You're not telling me that there wasn't a healthy interest in the doings – if you'll pardon the expression – of the Lodge lecher. Wouldn't be natural, that.'

John Whiteman summoned his starchiest legal demeanour. 'I have better things to pursue than petty gossip, Inspector Peach.'

'But you invited him to sing at the Lodge Ladies' Night. Surely you would want to know who was the latest of your ladies to drop her drawers before the Lodge Lothario? It would only be prudent.'

It made a weird sort of sense. John said haughtily, 'These things are arranged months in advance. And you seem to have the impression that Eric Walsh was knocking . . . *pursuing* all the married women in the Lodge. May I remind you that I have already told you that his interests were not confined to the Lodge? Nor was he exclusively interested in married women. He divorced many years ago, and was a free agent in these things.'

Peach looked for a moment at the flustered Master of the North Brunton Lodge, then sighed with the air of a man who had had his fun and must return to business. 'This is a murder enquiry, Mr Whiteman. I need hardly remind you that it's your duty to provide us with any information which we may think relevant. I'm not asking you to tell me who killed Eric Walsh; I'm assuming you don't know that. But it's time you told me about anyone who had a grievance against him.'

'I'm sure no one hated Eric enough to kill him. Not like that.' He gave a little shudder of recollected horror at the memory of how the man had died.

Brendan Murphy said, 'We'll be the judges of that, Mr Whiteman. It's our job.'

No it's not, thought John. It's your job to uphold the law, not to be judge and jury of who's guilty. Give you a good suspect and you won't look any further. He looked into Peach's unblinking eyes and decided not to argue that point. 'I'm afraid I can't help you with anything more specific, Inspector. I know that Eric had, well, a certain reputation as a ladies' man. No doubt other people will be able to provide you with more detail, if you decide it's relevant to his death. I would remind you that I am helping you in an entirely voluntary capacity, acting—'

'Acting as a good citizen should. Yes, I'm well aware of that, Mr Whiteman. We'd have to arrest you and take you to the station if we wanted to question you and you appeared to be obstructing us.' He looked wistful for a moment, as if the arrest of the Master of a Lodge would be the stuff of his dreams. 'But of course, as a representative of the noble profession of the law, you are anxious to give us all the help you can.'

This time he didn't disguise the irony. John tried not to show how rattled he felt. 'There are other people who can tell you a lot more about Eric Walsh than I can, I'm sure.'

Peach stood up abruptly. The conclusion of the interview was as startling as the way he had acted throughout it. 'We'd better go off and talk to them then, hadn't we, DC Murphy? And when we've got a fuller picture of who dropped her drawers and when, we'll be back to compare notes. In the meantime, Mr Whiteman, when you remember anything which might have a bearing on this death, we'll expect to hear from you. Good afternoon.'

He was gone almost before John had concluded a formal goodbye. He was left flustered and not a little confused. But as he went over the uneven course of the exchanges in his mind, he decided that he had kept his nerve under fire. He hadn't revealed anything he hadn't intended to reveal.

And he had certainly kept quiet about the one thing he was determined to conceal.

Nine

W asim Afzaal had a nervous Saturday.

After the discovery of the murder at the White Bull, he had given his statement to a constable with a round white face and startled eyes who had seemed scarcely older than himself and much less versed in the evil ways of the world. It had apparently been accepted at face value: no one had asked him any questions about his account or sought for other witnesses to verify it. But then at between one and two in the morning, they hadn't been probing anyone's account. They had been anxious to get what they called 'preliminary statements' from everyone. The police had seemed to want to get whatever they could quickly and get everyone off home to bed, now he came to think about it.

And Wasim Afzaal did think about it, for most of that long Saturday. He wasn't working again until the evening shift, and he had little else to do but think as he sat alone in his flat. He had seen that bugger Peach coming into the White Bull last night, had been relieved that the man hadn't made a beeline for him. Compared with Peach, that moon-faced constable hardly seemed like police at all.

Wasim wondered what the police were doing as the hours dragged by. They'd have put quite a big team on a murder enquiry, he knew that much. Would they have found themselves a chief suspect, be harrying him even at this moment? Would they be checking out his own statement against those of other employees? Would someone be denying even now that what he had told that constable was true, thus throwing him into the spotlight, like a moth fluttering hopelessly against the odds?

86

He thought hard about his own situation without finding anything that he could do to alleviate it. He would just have to brazen it out, to defy them to turn up anything which could prove him a liar. What he needed was someone to bear out his statement, but he hadn't got anyone. As the hours dragged by, he found himself looking out of the wide window of his sitting room at the car park of the flats and the road which led into it, but throughout the day there was no advent of the garish police car that he feared.

He was due in at the White Bull at six o'clock. At five to six he was parked in the staff section of the car park, wishing for once that his green MG two-seater looked a little less distinctive. At two minutes to six, the man he was waiting for arrived. Afzaal slid quietly from behind the wheel of his car and followed him into the cloakroom.

They were alone in the basement room, with its uneven, tiled floor and the hisses of trickling water in high, ageing cisterns. This was the oldest part of the building, far removed from the eyes of the paying public. Wasim noted the nervous young face above the white overalls the man was donning for his evening's toil in the kitchen and took heart from it.

'Fancy a spliff, Tom?' he asked casually.

Tom Cook darted an anxious glance towards the door. 'Not in here. You never know who's around.'

Wasim smiled a superior smile which said that he knew far more about this dangerous world than his young friend. He slid his slender arms into the jacket of the evening suit he would wear in the dining room, as if to emphasize his superior status in their working environment. 'You could be right there. Take one for later, then.' He slid his hand inside the white overalls, found the breast pocket in the shirt beneath, and left the spliff there.

Tom Cook's hand rose automatically to his chest, checking that the spliff of cannabis was safely stowed, wanting to refuse the gift but not knowing how. He said uncertainly, striving hard to bolster himself, 'They don't bother about recreational use now, the police.'

'That's right, Tom. It's me, as a supplier, who would be taking the risk.' Wasim smiled a thin smile which was meant to be reassuring. He failed in that; to Tom Cook the handsome olive face looked predatory. Tom knew that there was something behind this exchange, that Afzaal was striving to put him under some kind of obligation.

Sure enough, there was a veiled menace in Wasim's tone as he said, 'All the same, I don't think the management of this place would like to know that you indulged. Against their rules, isn't it? I believe that they tell everyone about that at the time of hiring. Of course, I'm just here on a university placement, so I'm not an employee.'

Tom didn't respond to the question, except to say, 'I don't smoke pot on the premises. It would be more than my job's worth.'

Wasim smiled again and nodded. 'Very wise, that. Gives you a kick though, doesn't it, the odd spliff? Plenty more where that came from.' He nodded at Tom's chest, reminding him that he had provided such comforts not only now but in the past, and that this young white-faced man with his acne and his inexperience was under an obligation to him.

Tom wished now that someone would come into the basement changing room, that someone would interrupt this colloquy before Afzaal could say anything more. But no one came, and there was no sound of movement outside, only the trickle of that unseen leaking cistern, unnaturally loud in the silence. He said, 'Well, I must get up to the kitchen or that chef will be having my guts for garters!'

Wasim smiled at the cliché, as if it was an evidence of weakness in this man he must use. He said, 'There was something I wanted to discuss with you, Tom. Only a little thing.'

Tom Cook had known it: there was a bleak comfort to him that he had spotted this coming. How oddly the Lancashire accent sat upon the soft Asian lilt of Afzaal's delivery. Tom tried to be firm as he said, 'I'm not interested in drugs, Wasim. I don't want to become a pusher, not even for soft drugs. I'm not planning to use them myself for much—'

Wasim's laugh interrupted him, killing the words in his throat and the thought in his brain. 'It's nothing to do with drugs, soft or otherwise, Tom. Surprising as it may seem, you're in a position to do me a favour. A very small favour. One which would cost you nothing at all.'

Cook's relief made him incautious. 'A favour? Of course, Wasim. Anything I can do. We're friends, after all, aren't we?'

'Indeed we are, Tom. And it's something and nothing, really. Just what you might call a precautionary measure.' He smiled, as if savouring a phrase which suited his purpose well.

'Sure. Though I can't quite think how—'

'Last night, Tom. That poor bugger who bought it in the car park. The police took statements from us. Said they'd be back in due course. And I expect they will. Suspicious lot, the pigs.' He sighed and shook his head sadly, taking in the injustice of the world at large and the police in particular.

'You don't mean you told them a . . . a . . .'

'A lie? Oh, no, nothing like that, Tom. I wouldn't get you involved in anything like that, would I? No, it's just that they're suspicious bastards, the police, and I've had a little minor trouble with them recently.'

'Trouble?' Cook repeated the word foolishly. This exchange seemed to have robbed him of the capacity for independent thought.

'Only a few days ago, actually. And the pig involved was that bugger Peach. The one who seems to be taking charge of this investigation.'

'The little bald chap with the moustache who was here last night?'

'That's the one.'

'But he didn't even question us.'

'No. He left that to the poor sods in uniform. Peach is CID, though, and he's in charge.' Wasim tried not to show his impatience with the naivety of this young innocent.

'You covering something up, then?'

'No! Of course I'm not. It's just that in the circumstances,

Peach already having a down on me and all that, I'd like someone to back up my story.'

'And how am I going to do that?' Tom Cook was cautious, suddenly and belatedly.

'Simply say I was with you in the kitchen for the whole of the period between eleven twenty last night and midnight. That I didn't go out into the car park during that time.'

Horror flooded into the long, pale face. 'What were you doing? You're not telling me—'

'I'm not telling you anything, Tom.' There was a sudden steel in the soft voice. 'I was in the kitchen for all of that time. We'd cleared the tables. I was doing nothing. Chatting to you and the others. Waiting for those Masonic geriatrics to go home so that we could tidy the place.'

Tom nodded. 'That's what I thought. But why—'

'Why do I want you to say just that? That you were with me for all of those forty minutes? Good question, Tom. Well, as an insurance, I suppose. I know enough about Peach to know that he'll pin anything on me if he can, like the rest of the pigs. Even murder, if he gets the chance.'

'And all you want me to say is that you were in the kitchen with me for the whole of that time?'

'That's it. Just as an insurance, as I say. You can't be too careful with the fuzz.'

Tom felt a surge of relief. It wasn't much, after all. 'All right. It's the truth, anyway, isn't it?'

'Of course it is, Tom. I know that and you know that. I just need someone to repeat it to the police. Just to be on the safe side.'

'Yes. All right. If they ask me, I'll say you were with me for all of that time. I'll only be telling them the truth. It's their own fault: they shouldn't be such suspicious sods.'

'That's just it, isn't it? Thanks, Tom. Fancy another spliff, for later?'

Before Cook could answer, he found those slim fingers beneath the white cotton of his overalls again, slipping another twist of cannabis into the pocket of his shirt.

Wasim Afzaal watched his alibi leave. Then he walked over to the urinals and gave himself the relief he suddenly needed. He put his forehead for a moment against the cool dampness of the tiles.

Tom Cook wouldn't be the most reliable of supporters if they pressed him hard. But Wasim couldn't see any reason why they should do that. Still, it was, as he had said himself, an insurance.

Ten

J ohn Whiteman had told DI Peach that modern Freemasonry
embraced all creeds, that there were even a few Roman
Catholics among the membership of the North Brunton Lodge.
One of them was Adrian O'Connor.

Adrian had not been called upon for a statement about his
whereabouts in those crucial forty minutes on Friday night,
for he had not been among that group around the Master who
had remained to relish the success of the evening. He had left
the main body of the company at around a quarter past eleven
and driven quietly home. He had only attended this function
at the Master's request, accompanying the widow of a former
Worshipful Master of the Lodge.

Adrian was a man who generally kept himself to himself,
so this behaviour was what might have been expected of him.
He was not nowadays a heavy drinker, so he had not needed
the taxis which many of his companions had arranged to avoid
having to drive home.

At eight thirty the next morning, he received an excited
phone call from one of his fellow Lodge members, telling him
the sensational news about Eric Walsh. He expressed appropriate shock and surprise. But no police arrival troubled Adrian
O'Connor during the Saturday which passed so anxiously for
John Whiteman and Wasim Afzaal.

Now, on Sunday morning, he attended nine o'clock mass
at the Church of the Sacred Heart. Like many Catholics in the
new century, Adrian did not treat the 'obligation' the church
put upon him to attend Sunday mass as seriously as he once
had. In his youth, he would have felt the stain of mortal sin

upon his soul if he had missed Sunday mass, would have feared eternal damnation until he had confessed this heinous sin of omission. Not that he had ever put that to the test, in those days: the direction to attend Sunday mass had been one of the easier directions of the One Holy Catholic Church to fulfil.

He wasn't the only one who had lapsed. The pews were nothing like so crowded as they had been in the old days, when the nine o'clock mass on Sunday mornings had always been the most popular of the five Sunday masses available. The parish priest, Father Hanlon, came out to talk amiably with his flock as they left the church – for all the world like a Church of England vicar anxious to preserve his declining congregation, thought Adrian uncharitably.

'Good to see you, Adrian,' said Father Hanlon. He was a red-faced, professionally cheerful, shrewd man of around sixty. Adrian wondered if this was to be a reminder of his erratic Sunday attendance. But then if you had been brought up a Catholic, priests usually induced a feeling of guilt, even when their intentions were wholly innocent.

'It's good to see you, Father,' Adrian responded, 'and to join in the service the way we do nowadays. The mass is a comfort in trying times.' He reiterated the conventional sentiment the priest must have heard a hundred times – and was surprised to find that he meant it.

'Bad business on Friday night at the White Bull,' said Father Hanlon.

Adrian realized that the priest not only knew about Eric Walsh, which wasn't surprising, but knew also about his own Masonic membership, which was. But priests seemed to have their own ecclesiastical grapevine, mysterious and efficient. He said rather foolishly, 'A very bad business, Father. Not the kind of thing you expect in a town like Brunton, even in these violent days.'

'The devil is all around us, showing himself when we least expect him,' said Father Hanlon.

Adrian was surprised at this, even from a priest. It was a long time since he had moved in circles where the devil got a mention. 'Yes, it was quite a shock. I didn't know Eric well, of course.' He wondered why he had said that; the words had sprung automatically to his lips.

Father Hanlon raised his grey, humorous eyebrows as he said, 'But you were both Irishmen, weren't you?'

And both Masons. That's what you mean, though you're too clever to voice it, thought Adrian. He pointed out cautiously, 'But Eric was not of the faith, Father.' What a curious expression that was, thought Adrian. You would only use it to a priest nowadays, in England. But in Ireland, everyone would still recognize immediately what you meant. 'It's a barrier, you know, still, between people of our background.'

'Indeed it is. More's the pity. Well. I must let you get along now. Though I think there's someone else here to speak to you.'

Adrian saw the priest's eyes looking past him, turned quickly, and tried to repress a start of alarm.

The man was short and powerful, with a black leather coat above sharply creased dark trousers and shining black shoes. The whiteness of his round face was accentuated by the jet of his eyebrows and the fringe of black hair around the bald pate. Everything about this man seemed black, and his darkness was somehow more intense, more threatening, than that of the priest before him. And the blackest things of all seemed to be the pupils of the eyes, which assessed Adrian without a hint of apology.

The man's smile did not extend to those eyes. He said, 'I'm Detective Inspector Peach, Mr O'Connor. I'd like a few words with you.'

It took them a little time to find the house they wanted. The road had once been a country lane, and though it had been widened a little, there was only just room for cars to pass each other, and the sharpness of the bends made for cautious progress. The substantial houses here still had no numbers, and they had to pause frequently to read the names on the gates.

Ravenscroft, when they finally arrived at it, was identified quite clearly by a sign on the high gatepost which depicted a plump black bird over the bold lettering on a white background. It was a solid 1930s house, rambling comfortably across the breadth of its one-acre plot. The double garage ten yards to the right of the house had a studio above it, and the greenhouse beyond that was large enough to house sizeable camellias in large pots.

The police Mondeo eased into the curved drive and circled the small roundabout in front of the garage before stopping outside the porch, which shielded a heavy oak front door. Lucy Blake was in the front passenger seat; she took a last look at DC Brendan Murphy's account of his and Peach's meeting with John Whiteman on the previous afternoon before she slid out of the car and looked up appreciatively at the gables of the house. It was unpretentious: it looked more like a home than a castle. But it was grander than anything Lucy had ever aspired to live in.

The door opened quickly when she rang; as the drive ran past the front of the house, it must be difficult for anyone to drive in and park without being seen. And they were expected. John Whiteman smiled a greeting from the doorstep and said, 'You must be Detective Sergeant Blake.'

'And this is Detective Constable Pickering. We're sorry to have to disturb you with this on a Sunday morning.'

'That's all right. We realize that the circumstances are quite exceptional. I haven't really come to terms with Eric's death myself, and my wife is still very upset by it. I'm no medical expert, but I should think it's the shock.' He was curiously stiff and formal, as though reciting a prepared statement. Lucy, who had not spoken to him before, wondered if that was his normal manner. In her as yet limited experience, solicitors tended to be cautious men.

He took them into a comfortable sitting room, warm after the cold outside. There were windows in three of its walls, and the bright morning light brought the best out of the vase of chrysanthemums which filled most of the fireplace. Mahogany gleamed from the antique bureau and bookcase in the alcoves on each side of it. The woman who rose as they entered the room looked much more confident than he had implied she would.

She said, 'I'm Rosemary Whiteman. Everyone calls me Ros. You were at the White Bull on Friday night, weren't you?'

'Yes. Detective Sergeant Blake. And this is Detective Constable Pickering.'

Gordon Pickering, who had worked hard for a transfer from uniform to CID, was a tall, rather gangling young man whose lack of social ease concealed a talent for sharp observation and lateral thinking, qualities which Percy Peach had noted in selecting him, though he affected to deride them. Pickering stepped forward and reddened, almost held his hand out on the introduction, then contented himself with excessive nodding.

John Whiteman said, 'Would you like coffee? I thought we could do whatever we have to do in here, if—'

'We'd like to see Mrs Whiteman alone, please,' said Lucy. 'It's standard procedure. I know that DI Peach has already spoken at some length to you, and now we'd like to check your wife's recall of events.' She was firm but courteous, trying not to notice Pickering's enthusiastic supportive nodding on her right.

John Whiteman hesitated. 'I see. But as I said, Ros is still very disturbed by what happened on Friday night.'

'I appreciate that. Murder *is* disturbing. And you will know better than most people that you are helping us with this inquiry quite voluntarily. But we'd still like to speak to Mrs Whiteman alone.'

'But I told you, she's—'

'That's all right, John.' Ros Whiteman cut in quietly, but her tone brooked no argument. 'Either go off to your study and leave us to it, or we'll remove ourselves and leave you here.'

Though plainly not happy, her husband acknowledged defeat. 'All right. You stay here with the officers, and I'll go.' He turned resentfully to Lucy Blake. 'But bear in mind what I said: Ros is more shaken than she might appear on the surface. Please don't take longer than you have to over this.'

There was an awkward silence as he removed himself and they listened to the diminishing sounds of his footsteps in the hall. Then Ros Whiteman sat down in the chair her husband had been about to use and motioned to the two armchairs opposite it. 'I'm sorry about that. He means well, and I suppose that I should be pleased that he still feels the need to protect me.'

Despite the smile and her apparent composure, as the light from the window beside her fell upon her face, Lucy realized that Ros Whiteman had been crying. There was a puffiness around the eyes and a redness on their lids which make-up could not wholly conceal. Was it just shock at this death and the brutal manner of it? From her lithe body movements and her air of command in her own house, this did not look like a woman who would be convulsed to the point of tears by shock, not thirty-six hours after the initial bombshell of the event.

Lucy said, 'How well did you know Eric Walsh, Mrs Whiteman?'

Ros Whiteman paused, assembling her thoughts and picking her words carefully, reinforcing the impression of composure she had given throughout. 'We'd known him for years, of course. I'm sure John told your inspector for just how long: he's much more precise about these things than I am. I'd say Eric was a friend, but not a close friend.'

'Forgive me, but I need to clarify what you mean by that, because we're trying to build up a picture of a man who can give us no account of himself. Did he visit this house? Did you go to his house?'

'Eric lived in a flat.' As if she thought she had made a mistake with this prompt correction, she gave a small, involuntary grin and stroked her dark hair above the temple. 'And no, we weren't on regular visiting terms. He's been here a few times over the years, and I think John and I called at his flat once. These were social occasions, with other people. Other people in the Lodge. We might meet for a drink before going off to something like Friday night's dinner, but there were always other people there.'

'So you'd say you were friends, but not intimate friends.'

She looked quickly into DS Blake's unlined face beneath the frame of reddish hair, as if she suspected some kind of trickery. Seemingly reassured, she said, 'I'd say that was a fair summary. Eric never came here for a meal, for instance, and nor did we visit him in that way.'

'And you feel that despite the Lodge connection, your husband was not much closer than you were to Mr Walsh.'

Again that quick, appraising look, which this time took in DC Pickering as well as the questioner. Gordon Pickering retreated into his notebook; nothing in the training courses had prepared him for formidable middle-class women like Mrs Ros Whiteman. She watched his busy ballpoint pen for a moment before she said, 'I think John would say he was friendly with Eric, but less friendly than with ten or a dozen other people in the Lodge. No doubt he will have given Inspector Peach his own assessment of that friendship.'

There were the first signs of irritation in her words. Pickering was uncomfortable, but Lucy Blake had worked long enough with Peach to feel lifted by anything which ruffled an interviewee. She said, 'And your own friendship? Did you know Mr Walsh entirely through your husband?'

'Entirely. I don't think I ever saw Eric without John being in the company at the same time. I knew him as one of a group of pleasant friends, brought together by a common interest in the Lodge.'

The reply had come promptly and precisely, and this time Lucy was sure that the woman had had the words ready. She wondered why, and decided to see what she could tease out. 'But no doubt you knew Eric Walsh well enough to know that he had a certain reputation.'

'Reputation?'

You know damn well what I mean, I'm sure, but you're going to make me state it, thought Lucy. All right. 'Eric Walsh was a ladies' man. He had an eye for a pretty face. And it didn't stop at the face, we're told.'

This time Ros Whiteman was not merely ruffled but positively rattled. She flushed. Lucy, as someone with freckles and fair skin who had suffered for years from blushing, was an expert on flushing. She was sure that this tall athletic woman with dark hair didn't flush easily. She seemed to be struggling to control anger as she said, 'You shouldn't listen to gossip, DS Blake.'

Lucy smiled, taking a little of the sting out of her words as she said, 'On the contrary, in a murder investigation, where the victim cannot speak up for himself, it is a positive duty to listen to gossip. We have to weigh it, and set it against facts and other people's views, of course, before we can decide how much to rely upon it. That is what I am doing now. Are you telling me that Mr Walsh had no interest in the opposite sex? That he lived a life of monastic seclusion?'

Ros Whiteman smiled, but Lucy was certain that it was a forced smile. 'Put like that, I have to agree with you. Eric was a lively, heterosexual man. And he did not have a wife: I understand he was divorced several years ago. You would no doubt expect him to have liaisons. What I was rejecting was the idea that he was irresponsible or promiscuous. That seems hardly fair to a man who, as you say, can no longer defend himself.'

It was logical enough, and as she outlined the argument, she recovered her composure. Yet for some reason her voice quavered on the last phrase. She reached across to the small table beside her, took a tissue from the box there and blew her nose. Lucy Blake watched her dispassionately whilst the silence stretched. It was DC Pickering, looking up from his notes and feeling a need to break the tension, who said clumsily, 'So could you tell us who were the women involved in these liaisons, Mrs Whiteman?'

'No I couldn't. I didn't know him that well. And I don't see why you're wasting your time prying into these things, with the man lying dead.'

Lucy Blake glanced sideways at the too-revealing face of DC Pickering. She had enough to do without nursemaiding new DCs. But she knew that the thought was unworthy even as it flashed into her mind. Gordon Pickering was shrewd enough;

he just needed time and experience. She said, 'I think you must see that this is relevant to the investigation, Mrs Whiteman. Sex and money are the chief motivators in violent crimes. If Eric Walsh was conducting an affair which made someone – man or woman – insanely jealous, we would have to investigate that person.'

'All right!' She looked down at the carpet, struggling to control her petulance. 'You're talking about what the French call a crime of passion, I suppose. And I can see the logic of your argument. It's just that I don't like the life of a dead man being raked over like this.'

'Not even if it leads us to the man or woman who killed him?'

'Of course, if it does that, it justifies itself. I suppose I'm just not used to murder cases.'

'No. We understand that. So tell us, who was Eric Walsh sleeping with at the time of his death?'

Lucy would never have been so direct, so unapologetic, before working with Percy Peach. But she had learned what a valuable tactic brusqueness could be with those who were used to the polite oiling of conversational wheels.

Ros Whiteman flashed her an unguarded look of hostility that was itself revealing. Then she said, 'Neither John nor I knew Eric well enough to be able to tell you that. I'm not even sure that there was anyone.'

'Indeed? From what other people have told us, that seems unlikely. Not a man to restrain his sexual appetites, Mr Walsh, from what we've been told.'

'Who told you that?' The words were out before she could contain them, and this time she did not check her hostility.

Lucy let that enmity hang between them for a moment in the quiet room before she said, 'I'm sure you'll understand that I couldn't tell you that, Mrs Whiteman. We respect confidences. We shall respect yours, when you tell us things about this murder victim. Whatever the nature of your friendship, you will surely wish to see his killer or killers arrested.'

'Of course I do. I don't know about any partner of his, that's all. I can see why you have to pry into these things. But I'm glad I haven't got your job. I wouldn't enjoy it.'

Lucy wasn't going to react to that. She watched Gordon Pickering making a note on her left, waiting until he had finished writing before she said abruptly, 'Where were you between eleven twenty and midnight on Friday night?'

Ros Whiteman fought for control for a moment at the suddenness of the challenge. 'I was in the main bar at the White Bull. As other people have no doubt told you. Relaxing after the main part of the evening, receiving compliments on the speech I had made. And for your records, I didn't speak to Eric at any time during the evening, apart from when I greeted him formally as the Master's wife.'

Lucy ignored this gratuitous information. 'Did you leave the room and the rest of the company at any time during those forty minutes?'

'No. I'd already been to the ladies' cloakroom to repair my face. That would have been at some time around eleven.'

'And was your husband present with you throughout the forty minutes?'

'John went out to the gents' cloakroom, I think, briefly. Otherwise he was there.'

'Thank you. You didn't see anyone acting suspiciously when you went to the ladies' cloakroom at about eleven?'

'No.'

'You didn't go out into the car park?'

'No! What the hell would I—? I'm sorry. No, I didn't go into the car park. Nor did I see anyone else go into the car park.' She was tight-lipped now, staring ahead of her, only occasionally glancing at her questioner.

'All right. Now, before my last question, perhaps I should warn you formally that it is your duty to give us all possible help. And to remind you that nothing you say will affect the fate of anyone you name. We are asking other people the same question and we shall investigate any suggestions without prejudice. Can you think of anyone who had a reason to kill Eric Walsh?'

'No. Eric was a good man. A friendly man. I can't think why anyone would want to kill him.'

She seemed near to tears, and Lucy allowed a few seconds to elapse before she spoke, in case emotion should lure this contradictory woman into any revelation. Then she said, 'Some significant thought may occur to you at any time. Please get in touch with Brunton CID immediately if it does. Ask for Detective Inspector Peach.'

Ros Whiteman nodded bleakly, seemingly anxious now only to have this over, her initial politeness long since forgotten. A few minutes later, she stood with her husband on the step of the handsome house, presenting a picture of marital unity as they saw these visitors off their property.

Lucy Blake was sure that there was much more to come yet, from both of the Whitemans. And Ros had already contradicted a key statement of her husband's.

Eleven

A drian O'Connor decided not to take Detective Inspector Peach back to his flat. His neighbours were not particularly curious, but something told him they would not miss this police presence accompanying him into the quiet house, and he did not want that.

He opted instead to accompany Peach to the Brunton police station, making it as clear as he could that this was a voluntary visit. Within five minutes, he was wondering if he had made a wise decision.

Although there was a choice of interview rooms available on a Sunday morning, Peach chose the smallest and the oldest. The green paint had bubbled a little towards the top of the walls. In the lowest two feet of the room, the colour was scarcely visible at all beneath the multiple dark scuffs of chairs and feet. When a big man who Peach introduced as DC Murphy sat down beside the broad-shouldered inspector, they appeared to present a wall in themselves, for Adrian could see nothing beyond them. The warm, claustrophobic room smelt strongly of disinfectant.

He glanced up at the single harsh light in this windowless cube, and said with a nervous smile, 'I heard police funds were short. This is hardly the Ritz, is it?'

Peach glanced around him, as though registering his surroundings for the first time. 'Seen some action, this place has!' he said with a nostalgic grin. Then he looked back at its latest occupant and said, 'We'll have the tape on, I think. Just so that we can all recall what's said, if we need to go back over any of it. Not that you've been charged with anything, of course.'

His round, eager face seemed to imply that it was only a matter of time.

He looked interrogatively at Adrian, as though he expected him to begin the conversation. The Irishman was disconcerted enough to say, 'I want to help you, as you'd expect. But I'm sure that there's nothing I can tell you which will be of any help to you.'

Percy Peach liked that; it put his man on the back foot to start with. 'Been involved in many police investigations, have you, Mr O'Connor?'

Adrian found himself licking his lips, wondering just how much this bothersome, powerful man knew about his background. He had thought he would be a good deal cooler than this, but he realized now that it was a long time since he had been questioned by policemen of any kind. The cloak of respectability he had gathered around him had ensured that people treated him with respect; it had also made him softer than he used to be. He said stiffly, 'This is the first time I've been involved in anything like this.'

Peach grinned wolfishly. 'What we need to clarify is the exact nature of your involvement.'

Adrian had meant involvement in the investigation, not in the murder itself. He said tersely, 'That's easy. I had nothing to do with this killing. I wasn't around at the time Eric died. And I've no idea who might have done it. I'd like to know why I'm here.'

Peach's dark eyes assessed him coolly for a moment. 'How do you know when Eric Walsh died?'

Adrian felt the colour rising to his face. 'I don't. I meant I'd left the place before he died.'

'You see, even we don't know exactly when he was killed. We know when he was last seen, but not when someone tightened a cord round his neck and nearly took his head off.' A little exaggeration never did any harm when pressurizing a suspect, Percy believed.

'And when was he last seen?'

Peach smiled as a man might have done with an impetuous

child. 'When did you leave the White Bull on Friday night, Mr O'Connor?'

'Eleven fifteen.'

A pause stretched like taut elastic across the three feet which separated the eyes of the two men whilst Peach allowed the notion that answering with such precision had been a mistake to take root in the other man. 'Thank you. That's very exact. Did you think at the time that such accuracy might be important?'

'No. I . . . I remember looking at the clock in my car, that's all. Sometimes these things stick. I should have thought it was useful that it had, from your point of view.'

'And from yours, Mr O'Connor. Eric Walsh was last seen alive at eleven twenty. His body was discovered at midnight. We're asking people to account for their movements between those times.'

'Including me, I suppose. Well, I've already told you that I left the place at eleven fifteen.'

'Which your partner of the evening can no doubt confirm.'

O'Connor smiled. 'As a matter of fact, she can't, though she will confirm that I took my leave of her just after eleven. I was partnered at the Ladies' Night by the widow of a former Worshipful Master. The present Master suggested it to me: we try to ensure that widows are not left out of things. But the arrangement was that someone else would take her home after the event. So I left the White Bull on my own. I hadn't drunk very much, so I was quite fit to drive.' He smiled at this reassurance to the guardians of the law.

'But you say you were away by quarter past eleven.'

'Yes. I drove quietly home, had a hot drink, and went to bed.'

'And is there anyone who can confirm this?'

Adrian smiled, feeling on firm ground now, despite the fact that he had to say, 'No. I live alone, Inspector. I don't for a moment think that any of my neighbours saw me coming in at that hour of the night, or that they could give you the exact moment if they had. If your questioning of the White Bull staff is as comprehensive as you claim, I suppose it's possible you may find that one or more of them saw me drive away.'

Peach watched the tape turning silently in the cassette recorder for a moment. Then he said quietly, 'Fond of Eric Walsh, were you, Mr O'Connor?'

'We weren't bosom pals, no.'

'But you went back a long way, didn't you?'

'We'd known each other for years, yes. But that doesn't mean—'

'Right back to the days when you were both in Belfast, indeed. You certainly weren't bosom pals then, were you?'

'No.' Adrian hadn't been prepared for this. Now he wondered exactly how much this disconcerting man did know about those days. He found himself licking his lips. 'It was a long time ago.' As soon as he'd said that, he regretted the words. They sounded so feeble.

'1988. Not so very long, in terms of the Irish memory. They've treasured the memories of Cromwell's excesses for three and a half centuries.'

'And the Orangemen have shot their mouths off about the Battle of the Boyne for almost as long.' Adrian knew he shouldn't have risen to the bait, but the words had come shooting out before he could abort them.

'Indeed they have.' Peach shook his head sadly, without taking his eyes off his man. 'Eric Walsh was an Orangeman, wasn't he?'

'I believe he was.'

Peach smiled, relishing a small victory. 'You *know* he was, Mr O'Connor. I expect he'd call you a Papist, if he were here now.' He pronounced the two syllables carefully, savouring the old-fashioned word.

'I don't see how these old Irish enmities can have any relevance to this investigation.'

'Don't you now? Well, that's interesting, I must say. And you may well be right. But that remains to be seen. Remains to be investigated, as you would no doubt say.' Peach nodded thoughtfully. Then he rapped out suddenly, 'Knew each other well in Belfast, you and Eric, didn't you? Knew all about these old Irish enmities.' He threw the phrase back in the face of his quarry like an accusation.

Adrian made himself pause, forced himself to frame the words as carefully as he could. 'I wouldn't say we knew each other well, no. We certainly knew about each other, but we weren't friends. Not then.'

'And not ever, perhaps.' Peach waited for a denial which did not come. 'You were on opposite sides of the great Irish divide, weren't you?'

'I was a Republican, if that's what you mean. A believer in a united Ireland. I still am. It's an honestly held opinion. In a democracy, you're not allowed to harass me for my opinions.'

Peach smiled a smile that Adrian did not like at all and nodded to the man at his side. 'DC Brendan Murphy. There's an Irish name for you to conjure with – but he's spent all his life in Brunton. I'll let him fill you in on what we know. Save a lot of time, that will.'

DC Murphy leaned forward, replicating Peach's position but not his smile. 'You were questioned by the RUC in Belfast about a violent incident in Belfast in 1988.'

It was a statement, not a question; Adrian didn't like that. 'Lots of people were questioned. There was a lot of violence around the Shankill area at that time. The RUC were bastards. If you were a Catholic, you were a suspect. They took in whoever they fancied for questioning.'

'And they fancied you, Mr O'Connor. As a suspect, that is.' Peach's smile was back again.

'That didn't mean anything. I told you, they—'

'Oh, but I think it did, Mr O'Connor. Because they suspected you of an attack on a certain Dennis Walsh, didn't they? Brother of Eric Walsh, businessman and singer of this parish. Now the late Eric Walsh.'

'They couldn't pin anything on me. I wasn't even charged with anything in 1988.'

'Interesting way of putting things, Mr O'Connor. I notice you don't say you didn't do anything.'

107

'I didn't. Nothing happened to Dennis Walsh.'

Brendan Murphy said quietly, 'No. But it certainly would have, if a British Army patrol hadn't arrived at the right moment.'

'Or the wrong moment, for you,' said Peach just as quietly.

'I wasn't there!' The voice was harsh. The sudden noise bounced around the cell-like room.

Peach studied the face which Adrian was struggling to keep impassive, noting with satisfaction the nerve which twitched in the right temple. 'Maybe not. Possibly you weren't at the scene of the crime. But you were certainly involved in the threats of GBH. Reading the record, it looks to me as if you were lucky to get off with an official caution.'

Adrian stared at the small square of table between him and the CID men. His face set into the rigidity of a fanatic who states his case and listens to no other argument. 'Dennis Walsh had it coming. He was going out with a Catholic girl. Trying to make it serious. You didn't do that, not in Belfast.'

'Apparently not. Especially when the girl was your sister, eh? You've hated the family ever since. Hated Dennis's elder brother, Eric.'

'Eric was the man who put his brother on to Kathleen. Eric was the head of that Loyalist gang. He thought he could do whatever he wanted, just because he could sing a bit.' Adrian was careless of his own situation as the old bitterness came leaping back down the years. The brogue he thought he had lost long ago came out with his anger.

'So you followed him to Brunton.'

'No. He disappeared from my life. I got myself a job with Shell Oil. I worked abroad for a few years, and then in Southampton and London. I lost touch completely with people in Ireland.'

Peach doubted that, in view of the passion that had sprung out of him when he described events in Belfast. 'How long have you been working in this area, Mr O'Connor?'

'About four years now.'

108

'And when did you discover that your old enemy Eric Walsh was working and living in Brunton?'

O'Connor pursed his lips. 'A few months after I'd been posted here, I suppose. I found out quite by chance. I wasn't even sure it was the same Eric Walsh at first.'

'But it didn't take you long to find that out.'

Adrian smiled, feeling himself on firmer ground. 'Brunton is a smallish town, Inspector.'

'How long have you been a member of the North Brunton Masonic Lodge, Mr O'Connor?'

'Three years.'

'And why did you join?'

Adrian managed what he hoped was a condescending smile. 'That's my business, surely.'

'Not in a murder enquiry it isn't.' Peach's answering smile was much more savage. Adrian thought he had never seen teeth which looked so white and so sharp.

'I . . . well, I suppose I found I was in sympathy with the philosophy and the aims of Freemasonry. We do a lot of good things, you know.'

'So I understand,' said Peach dryly. 'But wasn't it to get nearer to Eric Walsh that you joined?'

'No!' The monosyllable came too promptly and too loudly, and all three of them knew it. 'I joined for the reasons I said, and for the social side of the Lodge. We have some good evenings, you know.'

'I see. And the fact that Eric Walsh was present in the same company didn't in any way impede your enjoyment.'

Adrian shrugged his shoulders and strove hard for a dismissive tone. 'You have a rather melodramatic view of things, Inspector. Eric and I weren't bosom pals, as I said earlier. But the days when we were bitter enemies were long behind us. We were young men then. We had both acquired a little more balance since those days back in the eighties.'

But you didn't sound very balanced a moment ago when you spoke of a united Ireland, thought Percy Peach. He studied O'Connor for a moment, watching the smile fade from the

Irishman's lips. Then he said slowly, 'Had you anything to do with this death?'

'Nothing whatsoever. I told you, I wasn't even around at the time Eric Walsh died.'

'So you did. But if I'd been in your position and wanted to kill him, I wouldn't have done it myself.'

Adrian looked puzzled, then almost amused. 'A contract killer, you mean? That's what you call them, isn't it? What a preposterous idea! I wouldn't even know how to go about hiring such a man.'

Peach leaned forward, looked earnestly into the long face opposite him until the smile drained once again from its lines. 'You won't be shedding any tears over this death, despite what you say about old scars healing. But it's your duty to tell us about anyone whom you think might have been involved in it.'

Adrian felt easier now. The worst was over, if they were moving to a consideration of other suspects. He resisted the temptation to overplay his hand, to point them in other directions too obviously. 'He had enemies, did Eric. But I wasn't a member of his intimate circle, as you can well imagine, so I can't give you names.'

Peach sighed theatrically. 'But no doubt you can give us certain pointers.'

'He was fond of women, Eric Walsh. Too fond, some-times. And he didn't care much about the areas he fished in.'

Peach nodded. 'Took it where he could get it, did he? Didn't worry too much where the drawers dropped, if there was an attractive woman inside them?'

'You have a delicate way with words, Inspector. But I wouldn't disagree with the line of your argument. I was going to say that Walsh didn't worry if his women belonged to someone else, but the feminists wouldn't like that way of putting it, would they? Let's just say that he was careless of whether women had other commitments. I'm told that his conquests included married women and long-term partners as well as ladies who were free agents. Eric must have made a lot of enemies.'

Peach nodded as he pursed his lips. 'The kind of enemies his brother made all those years ago, I expect. Dangerous ones.'

Adrian knew he was being insulted, but didn't know how to react. He had become accustomed over his years in England to being a middle-class citizen, one to whom the police were carefully polite, sometimes even deferential. It seemed to be part of this man's technique to put people's backs up. Perhaps he would mention that to Superintendent Tucker from the Lodge. In the meantime, he said stiffly, 'I don't know who they were. I don't know if anyone felt strongly enough to kill him.'

Peach nodded. 'If you decide you've anything more to tell us, ask for me in the CID section. If anything else occurs to you which may be of relevance to this case, it is your public duty to relay it to us immediately.'

It took Adrian O'Connor a few seconds to realize that he was free to go at last.

Even with a juicy murder case in progress, a detective must have his relaxation. A man concerned with the sordid side of humanity must take care to develop his spiritual side.

To this end, Percy Peach had a game of golf on Sunday afternoon and Lucy Blake on Sunday night. Both were admirable avenues of relaxation for a busy detective inspector. He won his four-ball at golf. He liked winning. But Sunday evening proved that there were better things even than that.

Lucy shivered in the big bedroom at the back of Percy's semi-detached house. 'You haven't done anything about that central heating boiler,' she grumbled. 'How the hell do you get yourself into bed so quickly?'

'Long practice,' said Percy happily. 'That and a generous nature. I'm warming the sheets up for you. With your icy feet, I'm a hero. Probably get a George medal for it, if you'd only recommend me.'

His dark eyes sparkled happily above the duvet; they were

all that could be seen of his face as he snuggled deeply and studied his sergeant and bed-mate avidly. She paused for a moment in her dark blue slip, glancing at herself in the wardrobe's full-length mirror, nerving herself to disrobe further in the chilly room. Percy said, 'Shouldn't you ask, "Does my bum look big in this?" I've always wanted to hear a woman say that.'

'I wouldn't give you the satisfaction. I know all about my backside, thank you. And you know far too much about it for your own good.'

Percy moaned softly. 'They're one of the things that makes you think there's still a heaven, female backsides. That's a vulgar word, for peasants like you. Posteriors, we gentlemen call them. Derrières, the French say.'

Lucy Blake knew from previous experience that she should not linger over her undressing. She took a deep breath, whipped her slip up, her pants down and the light off in what to Percy's entranced eyes seemed a single graceful movement. He allowed himself a small yelp of pure pleasure as she arrived in the darkness.

'Now this,' he said appreciatively, 'is definitely not what I'd call a derrière. This is more of an arse, I'd have to say. But a very nice arse indeed!' He explored the phenomenon with both hands, whilst Lucy wondered again how a man of his considerable bulk had slipped so deftly beneath her.

'You talk too much!' she whispered into his surprisingly delicate ear.

'Aaaaaaaargh!' said Percy as he entered her with practised ease. A single syllable could surely not count as talking too much.

A little while later, he spoke to the dimly visible face above him. 'I like where you're putting it, but it's still an arse, Lucy! That's what you peasants have, you see. But it's a totally splendid arse. Sitting pretty, as you might say. In view of that, I've decided to waive protocol and let you have your way with me. Oooooh!'

This last was provoked by his voluptuous rider's prompt

acceptance of his invitation. Other, similar sounds, just as inarticulate but increasingly intense, followed as he disappeared into paradise.

In that miraculous suspension of time, DI Peach lost all thought of the murder of Eric Walsh.

Twelve

Darren Cartwright found DI Peach waiting for him when he arrived at his office on Monday morning. It was a disconcerting start to the week.

The fact that Peach had his buxom detective sergeant with the dark red hair at his side should have mitigated the shock for Darren. But Peach had such threatening, baleful charisma that the financial adviser was for once not diverted by a pretty face. 'You'd better come through to my office,' Darren said, trying not to let his hand shake as he withdrew his keys from the door.

'Sorry to disturb you so early,' said Peach. He did not look sorry; on the contrary, he seemed extremely pleased with himself to have surprised his prey at eight twenty-five on a frosty morning. 'We thought you might like to get this out of the way before other people arrived. Some people don't like to be seen being questioned by the police. It's peculiar, but there's no accounting for tastes.'

'Can't think why you're here,' said Darren grumpily. It was a thoughtless thing to say, but the words were out before he could stop himself.

Peach raised his expressive eyebrows to show the man how silly he'd been. 'When we were last here, you were in fear for your life. Anonymous threats. You wanted all the police attention you could get.'

'Yes. I must seem ungrateful. I'm sorry. But I had rather a heavy night last night and it was rather a shock to—'

'Out celebrating, were you, sir?'

'Well, I don't mind admitting I had rather a lot to drink. Rather too much, if I'm to be completely—'

'Not upset, then. Certainly not devastated.' Peach nodded at his detective sergeant, as if confirming something she had said before they arrived here. It was disconcerting.

'Upset?'

Percy was pleased with the effect he had created. Cartwright's face reminded him for a moment of Tommy Bloody Tucker at his most baffled. 'Yes, sir. I thought the murder of a friend under your very nose might have spoiled your weekend a little.'

'I wasn't there when Eric Walsh was killed, Inspector.'

'If you had been, Mr Cartwright, I'd be thinking about arresting you for murder.'

Darren tried to summon up a patient smile. 'I mean I wasn't in the vicinity, Inspector Peach. I didn't attend the Lodge Ladies' Night. So I'm not able to help you with your enquiries.'

He tried to smile equably, but the attempt fell away in the face of Peach's delighted beam of response. The small white teeth flashed brilliantly as the round face lit up the small room. 'Not strictly true, is it, Mr Cartwright? That you weren't in the vicinity, I mean.'

'I didn't go to the Ladies' Night. Ask anyone who was there.'

Lucy Blake tapped a small gold ballpoint pen against teeth which were almost as white as Peach's. 'We know that, Mr Cartwright. We've taken statements from all the Lodge members who attended the Ladies' Night. Also from all the staff of the White Bull who were working on Friday night. That is how we know that you were on the premises at the time when Eric Walsh died.'

Darren almost denied that outright. Then he realized that he would be admitting he knew the time of the murder. You needed to be careful, with these buggers. 'I see. I'm sorry.' He turned back to Peach and found the beam full upon him. 'I suppose I should have told you that at the start.'

'Indeed you should have, Mr Cartwright. But don't be sorry that you didn't. The fact that you attempted to conceal your

115

presence in the White Bull is of immense interest to us. We have to ask ourselves why you chose to do it.'

Darren looked from Lucy Blake's alert, unlined face to Peach's more experienced one, from the sergeant's remarkable aquamarine eyes to the inspector's unblinking black pupils. They were very different in appearance, these two, but he found comfort in neither. He said slowly, 'You don't know what it's like, to be involved in a murder hunt from the other side. Even when you're innocent, you try to hide things.'

Peach's smile did not disappear. 'Really? That would be most unwise. If you are innocent, that is. We find it's usually people with something nasty to hide who try to deceive us.'

'I've nothing to hide.'

'Really? You would be most unusual, if you hadn't. Of course, you may have nothing to hide in connection with the murder of Eric Walsh. If you haven't, you've made a very bad beginning.'

'I don't know anything about this death.'

'Why were you at the White Bull on Friday night?'

'Partly just because it was Friday night. The week's work was over and I was at a loose end. I went out for a couple of drinks. Nothing sinister in that, is there?'

'Remains to be seen, Mr Cartwright. Your choice of drinking venue is most interesting. So is the fact that you lied about it.'

'I told you, the natural inclination of an innocent member of the public is to put himself as far as possible from the scene of the crime.'

'Wrong, Mr Cartwright! In our experience, the natural inclination of an innocent member of the public is to tell us the truth. Had you arranged to meet someone in the White Bull?'

'No. I told you, I was at a loose end and I went out for a couple of drinks.'

'Hardly your local is it, the White Bull? Over four miles from your house.'

Apparently they knew already just where he lived. Darren tried to be calm. 'No.'

'Go there often, do you? Favourite drinking hole of yours, perhaps?'

Darren almost fell into the trap of claiming it was. But if the filth had questioned the staff in enough detail to establish that he'd been there, they probably knew he wasn't a regular. 'No, not really.'

'So how often do you drop in there for a casual drink? The way you say you did last Friday night.'

Peach was calling him a liar without putting it into words. Darren felt himself rattled. 'Once or twice a year, I suppose.'

'So why were you there on Friday night?' The question came like a checkmate at the end of a series of chess moves.

Darren made himself take his time. 'I'm not sure I can tell you why, not exactly. I knew the Lodge was holding their Ladies' Night there, and I suppose I thought the meal would be finishing about that time and I might meet a few friendly faces in the bar.'

It was almost convincing. Except that the Masonic function was a private one in the upper rooms of the hotel, and he must have known that Lodge members in evening dress were unlikely to leave those private rooms and roam into the public bar downstairs. Peach contented himself with a rise of those expressive black eyebrows beneath the bald pate. 'Friend of yours, was he, Eric Walsh?'

Darren had known that this must come, sooner or later. He said, 'Yes, in a general sort of way. We weren't particularly close, but I enjoyed his singing and his company. I would like to have had the chance to get to know him better. Now I never shall.'

The attempt at pathos did not sit happily on the anxious face beneath the thick brown hair. Peach studied him for a moment, as though he was waiting for him to squirm, before he said, 'So who do you think might have killed him?'

'I don't know. I've thought about it ever since I heard the news on Saturday, but I've really no idea.'

Peach nodded as if he had expected no help here. 'What time did you leave the White Bull, Mr Cartwright?'

'Didn't look at my watch at the time. But I can probably tell you fairly accurately.' Darren nodded to himself, frowning with concentration, showing how hard he was trying to help them. 'It must have been around ten when I got in there, as I said, and I only had a couple of whiskeys – can't be too careful, with the breathalyser about!' His nervous giggle died quickly when there were no answering smiles from the other side of the desk. 'But I was there when they called time at eleven o'clock. I hadn't found anyone I knew to talk to, so I drank up pretty promptly and left. I must have been away by ten past eleven.'

Percy Peach and Lucy Blake took their leave then, noting Darren Cartwright's evident relief as they left his office. Once outside, they looked at each other for a moment, as easy with their professional relationship as they were with their private one. 'Don't like him much, that one,' said Lucy. 'Natural liar, I'd say. He started off with a big one when he claimed he'd been nowhere near the White Bull on Friday night.'

Peach nodded. 'Did you notice that he didn't want to talk about those threatening notes he'd been receiving? Last time we saw him, he claimed to be in fear for his life. You'd think with a fellow member of the Lodge murdered, he might have been wetting his pants.'

'The fact that he may be a habitual liar doesn't necessarily make him a murderer,' said Lucy Blake rather regretfully.

'No, but it gives us the right to go on harassing him,' said Percy happily. 'Especially as he not only began with a big lie but ended with an even bigger one. He said he left when the White Bull closed and was away by eleven ten, putting himself comfortably outside the murder period. But the pub doesn't close until eleven thirty on Friday nights, which means that he would be away at about twenty to twelve. Which puts him bang in the frame.'

'And also suggests that he knows the time when Walsh died, though we haven't released anything about that yet.'

'We shall need to have further words with Darren Cart-wright, in due course,' said Percy Peach. He spoke with deep satisfaction.

'Have you arrested our murderer yet?' said Superintendent Tucker when they returned to the Brunton police station.

'Whimsical, that, sir.' Percy Peach smiled appreciatively. 'As the man in charge, you'd know if we had, wouldn't you? Good to see a senior officer with a sense of humour on a Monday morning, I say. Shows a sense of perspective, that. I often tell the team that a sense of perspective—'

'This is no time for a sense of perspective,' thundered Tucker. He wondered if that had come out quite right, and went on hastily, 'This is a high-profile murder. Perhaps you don't realize quite how high-profile.' He picked up a tabloid newspaper from the pile on top of his desk and thrust the front page towards his inspector. 'Singing Star Cut Down at Masonic Dinner,' the headline stated. A ten-year-old picture of Eric Walsh smiling broadly at the camera occupied most of the page.

'Good likeness,' said Peach. 'Flatters him a bit, perhaps. Course, I've only seen him dead.'

'This is not about what Eric Walsh looked like. It's about *detection*, Peach! You need to wake your ideas up. Don't forget I've put you forward as chief inspector material.'

'Yes, sir. I expect they'll treat your recommendation with the consideration which your standing deserves.'

Tucker peered suspiciously at the inscrutable face of his detective inspector. You could quell most of your subordinates with the mention of promotion, but this irritating man seemed proof against blandishments as well as threats. 'Time to get your finger out, Peach, if you wish to retain my support! Turned up much over the weekend, did you?'

'Several interesting facts, sir. Nothing conclusive.'

'I thought as much.'

'No one's been able to clear you, sir, as yet. Not absolutely. Not for the whole of those forty minutes. But between the two of us, sir, I shouldn't worry. I think it's fair to reveal that you're not high on my list of suspects.' He ventured a conspiratorial grin and tapped his forefinger against the right side of his nose.

'Don't be ridiculous, Peach. And don't make that absurd gesture again, please.'

'Sorry, sir. I don't know the appropriate Masonic gesture to convey a confidence, sir. Not being a member of the Brotherhood, of course.'

'You're obsessed with Freemasonry! I've told you until I'm sick of telling you that it has nothing to do with the job. Nothing whatsoever!'

Peach pursed his lips and shook his head doubtfully. 'Looks like it was a Mason who did this, sir.'

'I very much doubt that, Peach. I think you need to keep a more open mind than you appear to—'

'Reinforce my statistical survey, that would, you know. "A Freemason is four times as likely to commit a serious crime in the Brunton area than an ordinary member of the public." Remarkable, that.' He mouthed the words like a piece of well-established religious dogma, then shrugged sadly at the mystery of it.

'Just because a member of the Lodge was the victim, you shouldn't assume that his killer was a member of the Fraternity. I hear you've already been bothering the Master of the Lodge and his lady. I trust this was absolutely necessary?'

'Absolutely, sir. You'd have done it yourself, in my place, I'm sure.' Peach leaned forward confidentially, feeling the leap in his spirits as he saw Tommy Bloody Tucker recoil. 'Both of the buggers telling porkies, if you ask me!'

The Superintendent's heart leapt to his throat on the other side of the big modern desk. He saw his dreams of the Mastership vanishing into thin, Peach-polluted air. 'I'm sure that can't be true. What grounds could a man like John Whiteman have for lying to the police? A respected local solicitor of many years' standing! And still less his good lady. Why, Ros Whiteman gave us a wonderful speech on

Friday night. An impeccable lady. She's positively . . . well, positively . . .'

'Fragrant, sir? Like Lady Archer once was, in an eminent judge's view? We mustn't forget that that fragrant lady's testimony in court was subsequently shown up as highly suspect. It's my belief that the fragrant Mrs Ros Whiteman will eventually prove to be telling us porkies.' He smiled, happy in both his confidence and his chief's distress.

'And what possible reason could a lady like Ros Whiteman have for killing Eric Walsh?'

'Don't know yet, sir. Not for certain. Just intrigued that she wouldn't be completely honest with us. An inspector's hunch, if you like. But I think I'd still have it, even if I were a chief inspector.'

'And John Whiteman? You saw him both in the office and his home. An unwarranted interference with his privacy, unless you had very clear grounds. He's the Master of the Lodge, you know.'

'Yes, sir. You said so earlier.' No doubt the Masonic grapevine had informed Tommy Bloody Tucker of all his inspector's movements over the weekend; scarcely any point in him coming up here to report, really.

'Mr Whiteman is a man of considerable influence in this town. He might even be in a position to block your promotion.'

And yours, thought Percy. And up yours, too, Tommy Bloody Tucker. He produced his most innocent smile, topping it with a small frown of bewilderment. 'Even if he proves to be a murderer, sir?'

Tucker's jaw dropped for a moment. Was all his diligent preparation work on the Master, all his months of what others might have seen as creeping, to be made suddenly and cruelly worthless? 'Are you telling me that the Master of the Lodge murdered one of its valued members?'

'Oh no, sir. Not at present. Just that he's behaving suspiciously. And so's his wife. I don't like people who hold things back when we're engaged in a murder inquiry.'

121

Tucker glowered at the round, open face. Peach's piercing dark eyes, which so often seemed to be trained on a spot just over his head, were now staring into his face with a frankness which infuriated him almost as much. He wanted to repudiate what the man was saying, but he could find no immediate flaw in the logic of his statement. He tried the only diversion he could think of. 'Well, at least Darren Cartwright is alive and well, despite the threats to his life you were supposed to be investigating. When I was taken out into that car park to see a body on Friday night, I thought at first it might have been Darren who'd been killed.'

'No, sir. He's gone very quiet about the threats to his life now, your Mr Cartwright. Doesn't seem to be worried any more.'

'No? Well, at least he wasn't in danger on Friday night. I thought he'd be at the Ladies' Night, but he wasn't.'

'No, sir. Except that he was, in a manner of speaking.'

Got the little bugger! thought Tucker triumphantly. Correct him on a matter of fact, take the cocky little sod down a peg or two. 'No, Peach. Darren Cartwright wasn't at the White Bull on Friday. He didn't attend the function. Perhaps I should remind you that I was there and you weren't.'

Peach allowed himself a small snigger. 'Very good, that, sir! Of course you were! And of course I wasn't! Not until there was police work to be done, anyway. Nevertheless, Darren Cartwright was at the White Bull on Friday evening.'

Tucker frowned hard, struggling to take this in, like a child confronting an impossible riddle. 'I didn't see him.'

'No, sir. Nor he you, very likely. He wasn't at the Masonic function, as you say, but he admits he was in the hotel. Claims he went down there for a drink.'

Tucker digested this, then leaned forward himself. 'I find it difficult to believe that a man like Darren Cartwright could be involved in anything like murder. But this could be suspicious, you know.'

'Yes, sir. I thought that.' This man will never lose his talent for the blindin' bleedin' obvious, thought Percy.

'I think you should question him.'

'Already have done, sir. This morning. He didn't go to the White Bull by arrangement, he says. Just on impulse. Claims he didn't meet anyone who can bear out his story. And we haven't turned up anyone yet who can confirm his account of when he arrived and left.'

'Then, however unlikely it seems, you have a suspect. You'd be far better employed investigating him rather than harassing the Master and his good lady, if you want my opinion.'

'Yes, sir. You wouldn't like to take over yourself, would you? In case I get a little out of my depth in the murky waters of Masonry?'

For a moment, Tucker was sorely tempted. It would be wonderful to claim all the credit for a high-profile murder case. But his suspicion of Peach and his awareness of his own incompetence rang simultaneous bells of warning in his smoothly coiffured head. 'No. It wouldn't be right to take the credit away from you, Percy. But do tread carefully, won't you? Of course, if I can be of any assistance, I'll be only too ready to—'

'Thank you, sir. What can you tell me about Adrian O'Connor?'

Tucker gaped for a moment at this prompt response to his offer. 'He's a fairly recent member of the Lodge, I think.'

'Three years, sir. Wasn't even a Mason before that.'

'He's a Catholic, I think.' Tucker's brow wrinkled with distaste for a moment; he was a man who wore his prejudices on his sleeve. 'But I don't really know anything against him. He was there on Friday night, though. Accompanying the widow of a Worshipful Master.'

'But he left quite early, sir. Eric Walsh was seen alive after he'd gone.'

'Why are you pestering me for information about him, then?'

Peach noted that after an offer to help wherever he could, Tommy Bloody Tucker was now accusing him of pestering. Par for the course, that. 'He goes back a long way with Eric

Walsh, sir. To 1988, in Ireland, sir. When they were sworn enemies.'

Tucker adopted his elderly statesman expression whilst he paused to digest this. 'Better investigate him, then. They can be strange people, these Catholics.'

'Yes, sir. I was one myself, once.'

'Well, there you are then!' Tucker laughed uninhibitedly at a joke he seemed to have made by accident. 'Seriously, though, you'd better look into Mr Adrian O'Connor. Though I find it difficult to believe that this murder could have been done by a Mason. A fellow member of Eric Walsh's Lodge.' He shook his head. 'Most unlikely. What about the staff of the White Bull? Aren't there any suspicious characters there?'

'Not really, sir. There is an Asian chap who has given us trouble before.'

Tucker was torn between an eagerness to pin this on a non-Mason and a fear of provoking accusations of racial persecution. He said fearfully, 'Not a particularly prominent family, is it?'

'Quite prominent, I would say, sir. The father is well known and well respected in local circles. The lad working at the White Bull is Wasim Afzaal.'

Tucker's heart pounded anew. 'Not the son of—'

'Son of the Afzaal who owns the cotton mill and the supermarkets, yes, sir. He's the lad we let off with a caution after an attack on old Harry Alston's corner shop.'

Tucker closed his eyes for a moment, gathering his strength to direct his odious subordinate. 'Go carefully, for God's sake, Peach. You could stir up all sorts of adverse publicity for us here.'

'Yes, sir.' Peach did not seem to find the prospect as distressing as his chief did. 'But I don't think you should worry too much. We shall probably clear Afzaal of this fairly quickly. My guess is that our murderer will be a Mason.'

He left with a smile on that happy thought, carrying the

picture of Tommy Bloody Tucker's distressed face down the stairs with him to buoy him for the rest of the day.

DI Peach was wrong about one thing, however. Young Wasim Afzaal would loom much larger in this case than he currently thought.

Thirteen

It was like watching a stoat with a rabbit. You knew the rabbit had no chance, but some survival instinct would make it struggle until it died.

The rabbit being killed off by Percy Peach was a lad called Tom Cook, who worked in the kitchens at the White Bull. He seemed an innocent sort of lad, and Lucy Blake found herself wondering quite what he had done to deserve this.

Peach gave her the answer to that in his next phrase. 'Concealing information,' he said heavily across the table in the manager's office at the hotel. He made it sound as if the acned youth had killed several old ladies with a cleaver. 'Concealing information in a murder case. Oh dear, oh dear, oh dear!'

'I don't know what you mean by—'

'Don't make things worse for yourself, lad. Think before you speak. We'll get you a lawyer, if you think it would do you any good. Better if you told the truth, though, if you want my advice.'

Tom didn't, but it didn't seem the moment to say so. He looked up at the cornice round the high ceiling of the old room. He hadn't been in here since he'd been interviewed for his job in the kitchens. The manager would want to know why the police had singled him out for this special treatment. His own voice sounded to him like someone else's as he said, 'I told the truth to that constable who interviewed me. The one who took my statement. I was in the kitchen for the whole of the time he asked me about. I was there from eleven twenty until after midnight. Working most of the time.'

126

'Shifty, you were, PC Curtis said, and I have to agree with him. Shifty.' He relished the word, rolling it on his tongue as if savouring a fine wine.

Tom felt a fine sheen of sweat dampening his forehead, resisted a pressing urge to wipe it away with the back of his hand. 'I don't know why he should say that. I wasn't trying to conceal anything.'

'Really?' Peach gave him the smile that a hundred criminals could have warned him was a red light. 'Maybe you weren't. Just maybe. We'll reserve judgement on that, for the moment. But were you trying to add a little something to your version of things. You chefs like to add a little something, don't you? Liven up a dull dish. But you shouldn't try to liven up a dull story with the odd addition. Naughty, that would be. We wouldn't like it at all.'

Tom Cook wasn't a chef. He was on the bottom, very slippery rung of the sous-chef ladder. It didn't seem the moment to say so. 'I just said where I was between eleven twenty and midnight. I don't think I added anything.'

'Ah!' Peach pounced on the word like the stoat going for the rabbit's throat. 'You don't think. I don't like the sound of that word, "think". It denotes uncertainty to me. And we don't like uncertainty in our statements, do we, DS Blake? Especially in a murder inquiry. Get you into a lot of trouble, uncertainty can.'

Tom Cook swallowed. His Adam's apple leapt violently up and down the thin neck with the effort. 'If I said anything wrong, I'm sorry. I don't know what it would be.'

'Don't you, now? Well it's possible you said nothing wrong. I have to admit that. But what you said smells a bit to me, so we need confirmation. Or revision, of course, if you decide that's appropriate.' Having brought his victim to the point of capitulation, he gave him a broad beam. 'We mustn't lead you to say anything against your will, of course. Not just to please pleasant people like us. You mustn't do that.'

'No.'

'So can you just confirm for us what you said about one of your colleagues on the staff of the hotel?'

'Wasim?'

'Ah! You remember!' Peach seemed immensely pleased with himself and the miserable youth in front of him. 'Wasim Afzaal, that's the chap. I thought you might want to review your statement. In particular the bit about Wasim being with you for all of that time.'

'He wasn't.'

'Aaaah! But you said he was, in your statement to our uniformed officer.'

'Yes. I'm sorry.'

'I'm sure you are, now. Well. We shall have to see whether sorry is good enough, shan't we? What was our friend Mr Afzaal up to during that time?'

'I don't know. Nothing, as far as I know. He just asked me to say I was with him. So that you couldn't pick on him.'

Peach gave Cook a smile which didn't bode well for Afzaal. 'So why should we "pick on" the poor chap? Unless we found that he was trying to get someone to tell porkies for him, that is.'

'I don't know. He just said he was frightened you'd have it in for him. I suppose because he's . . . well . . .'

'Coloured?'

'Asian, I was going to say.'

'So you thought we'd persecute him?'

'Well, no, not really. But Wasim seemed to think that—'

'What he should have thought is that if he persuaded some silly sod to tell porkies on his behalf, he'd end up deep in shit. Up to his neck, in fact, whatever colour that neck might be.'

'Yes. He was foolish.'

'*Foolish*?' Peach was histrionically aghast at the weakness of the word. 'He was a bloody sight worse than foolish, lad. Unless he's a vicious murderer, trying to set up an alibi. In which case the misguided twat who helped him would be bloody mad, not foolish. Accessory after the fact, he'd be.'

Tom felt his feeble resistance slipping away. All he wanted

was to stop this man from talking. 'I'm sorry. He . . . he had a
bit of a hold over me. He'd supplied me with pot and threatened
to expose me. And he gave me some more when he asked me
to include him in my statement – just cannabis, mind.'

Peach sighed theatrically. 'First threats and then bribery, eh?
You'd better tell us everything you know. Make a clean breast
of it and throw yourself on our mercy, as you were taught at
school.'

Tom opened his mouth eagerly to comply with this, then
realized he had nothing to say. 'I . . . I've told you everything
I know.'

'What was your pot-pushing friend doing when he claimed
he was with you?'

'I don't know. Nothing, as far as I know.'

'Let's hope not, for your sake. Accessory after the fact.'
Peach savoured the repeated phrase as he gazed at the pale face
with its sheen of sweat. 'Piss off and make some omelettes, Mr
Cook. Don't leave the area without telling us.'

Sergeant Jack Chadwick was a contemporary of Peach's.
Twelve years earlier, when they had both been detective
constables, Jack had been shot in the shoulder after a bank
robbery. He had been a hero for a week, and a recipient of
a medal a few months later, but the incident had ended his
CID career.

Jack knew he was stuck at sergeant, but he was not resent-
ful: it could have been much worse. He was now the most
efficient scene-of-crime officer in the area. Percy Peach always
demanded Sergeant Chadwick and his team for serious crimes,
and Jack for his part knew how insistent his colleague had
been that he be retained in the service. There was a bond
between them which was never openly voiced, but Jack knew
that his interests would be preserved by Peach against the
incompetence of prats-in-office like Tommy Bloody Tucker.

He was at the Brunton police station with Percy now,
reporting on his investigation of the break-in at the home
of Eric Walsh during the night after the Irishman had been

murdered. 'Doesn't look like a burglary,' he said. 'There's not a lot of value in the place, but there's some silverware, very portable, which would normally have gone. Also quite a valuable carriage clock. Even a little cash in a kitchen drawer. All left behind.'

'Do we know precisely when entry was made?'

'No. Sometime during the early hours of Saturday, the ninth of November, is as precise as we can be. There was a neighbourhood party at the end house, which many residents of the road attended. People were leaving until about one a.m. No one saw anything happening at Walsh's house or any strange cars in the road before that time, so pretty certainly the break-in took place sometime between one and seven in the morning.'

'Method of entry?'

'No sign of forced entry. The lock is a Yale and well worn. All the same, my bet would be that chummy used a key.'

'Any clue as to what he came for, or whether he found it?' As usual with policemen, the criminal was male until events proved otherwise. It didn't mean they had ruled out a woman intruder; it was simply that in well over ninety per cent of crimes like this, the culprit was male.

Chadwick smiled grimly. As usual, it was impossible when it wasn't a straightforward burglary to know whether the intruder had found what he had come for and removed it or had drawn a blank. 'I think our man was after something he didn't want someone else – probably us – to find. It's impossible to say whether he found what he was looking for. He went through the filing cabinet and the desk in the room Walsh used as a study and may have removed documents from them. He turned out all the drawers in the bedrooms. He may or may not have found what he was looking for. I think the chaos indicates a certain desperation, so perhaps he didn't.'

'So he went through most of the house?'

'He did. And the way he did it suggests he knew there was no one in the house and that he wouldn't be disturbed. There's no hint that he went about things stealthily. Drawers are thrown open and things scattered about quite carelessly. He must have made quite a noise.'

Peach nodded slowly. Both of them knew what he was thinking before he voiced it. 'This suggests that he already knew that Eric Walsh was dead. Only a few hours after it happened.'

'It looks like it. That's what made me think he was looking for something that he didn't want us or some other third party to find in Walsh's house.'

'It also suggests that Walsh's death and the search of his house are directly connected. That it may even have been the murderer who went there, later in the night.'

Jack Chadwick nodded. 'You know more about your suspects than I do. But I'd be pretty certain that whoever went into that house knew that Eric Walsh was already dead.'

'I agree. And even if he didn't kill Walsh, he must presumably have been among the gathering at the White Bull on Friday night, to know that he was dead.'

'That would leave the staff of the hotel as well as those Masons and their wives who were there after eleven twenty, though. Still quite a number of people.'

'Too bloody many!' said Peach gloomily.

'There's no knowing whether they're connected with the break-in, but we found a couple of spots of blood on the step outside the house. We've taken a sample and the blood is fairly recent, but you can't be certain that that blood came from the person who'd illegally entered the house.'

'And you've no idea what was taken away?'

'For what it's worth, my opinion would be that chummy didn't find everything he wanted to remove from Walsh's house. I suspect he tried to delete things from the computer, but couldn't get at them.'

'What makes you think that?'

'You need passwords to get into files, so it wouldn't be easy. But there's a lot of evidence of frustration in the dining room of the house where we found the computer. It's a laptop – quite compact. But it had been flung on the floor quite violently. And the monitor had been smashed with a shoe. We've got a heel imprint on some of the glass. There's not much of it, but if you could provide us with the actual shoe we might try for a match.'

Peach shook his head in frustration. This wasn't going to help at this stage: no one would give him search warrants to collect shoes from all and sundry. It might help the lawyers to construct an eventual court case after they had made an arrest, that was all. Assuming they did make one. 'Is the computer still working?'

'It seems to be. I've passed it on to the boffins. They'll get into those files, given time.'

Peach sighed. 'Apart from the evidence of a break-in, did you find anything of interest in Walsh's house?'

'Various things which connected Eric Walsh to extreme Loyalist factions in Northern Ireland. But nothing which suggested that he was active in any recent terrorist activities. Walsh was a bigot who wouldn't concede a single inch to the Republicans, but there are plenty of those about.'

'And nothing else of interest?'

'We didn't have any very clear brief of what we should be looking for, of course. I brought some photographs from the top drawer of his bureau.' He reached into the briefcase at his feet and produced a carefully labelled folder.

Peach went methodically through the pile, taking care not to disturb the order in which they had been found. They were a series of snapshots of women, sometimes alone, sometimes with a smiling Eric Walsh. They looked like a collection of his conquests, preserved as much through vanity as sentiment.

But vanity has its uses in a murder case. The last and largest of the photographs, the one Chadwick had found on top of the pile, showed the dead man with his arm round the waist of a smiling Ros Whiteman.

'We meet again, Mr Afzaal,' said Peach.

'Yes. I can't think why,' said Wasim.

They were in the same office where they had seen Tom Cook

two hours earlier. The sous-chef had been sent home and they had taken the young Asian in here as soon as he arrived for his evening shift.

Peach lifted his expressive black eyebrows. 'Really?' He turned to Lucy Blake at his side. 'Mr Afzaal can't think why we should want to see him. Rather strange, that.'

'Very strange,' said DS Blake. She turned with relish to a blank page in her notebook and took the top off her slim gold ballpoint pen. She had the air of one who expected to make copious notes on an interesting subject.

There was no hint on the smooth olive features of the turmoil behind them. 'I made restitution to Harry Alston for the damage we did to his shop. I understood the incident was closed. If you're—'

'Nothing to do with that,' rapped Peach. 'This concerns events in this hotel. To be specific, the murder of one Eric Walsh last Friday night.'

'I can't help you with that, I'm afraid. I was here, of course, but I gave my statement to one of your officers along with my colleagues who were working that night. If you're singling me out for special treatment, I'd have to ask whether my racial background had—'

'You've singled yourself out for special treatment, lad. Doesn't matter whether you're black, pink, yellow or two-tone.' Peach inspected the man on the other side of the big managerial desk carefully, as if trying to decide which of these he might be.

'I gave a statement to your PC Curtis. I don't wish to alter anything in it, because it's correct.'

Peach wondered if Asians were better liars than native Lancastrians, or whether he just wasn't an expert at reading the signs. He had dealt with thousands of Asians by now, but he still found it difficult. 'I see. You're saying that you knew nothing about the killing of Eric Walsh.'

'I'm saying just that.' Wasim expected a challenge, but none came, and he filled the silence by saying, 'I didn't even know the man.'

He looked quickly from Peach to Blake to register their reactions, and Percy knew in that moment that he had told a lie. 'Then why did you bring pressure on a colleague of yours to change his statement? To add matter that was demonstrably false?'

Despite his dismay, Wasim kept his face calm. 'I suppose you mean Tom Cook.'

'You suppose that, do you? Are there other people you have persuaded to lie for you?'

'No, of course not.'

'There is no "of course" about it, Mr Afzaal. We have turned up one case where you have attempted to pervert the course of justice. For all we know, there may be others.'

'I wasn't attempting to pervert the course of justice. I was just trying to protect myself. I realize now that I may have been a little foolish.'

'Not a little, Mr Afzaal. Though perhaps you have not been foolish at all. Perhaps you had a lot to lose. Perhaps you had a serious crime to hide. The most serious of all.'

'Now look here, I—'

'No, you look here, lad. If you want a lawyer, get yourself one, and we'll continue this at the station. We'll arrest you and hold you for twenty-four hours whilst we determine whether there's enough material for a murder charge. It's up to you. I'm sure your father could provide you with a sharp brief.'

The mention of his father brought the first flash of panic to the brown eyes. 'I don't need a brief. I haven't done anything. I didn't do anything in those forty minutes you asked us about. But I couldn't prove that, and I panicked when I saw you come into the hotel to take charge of the case. I thought that as you'd seen me about Harry Alston only a few days earlier, you'd have it in for me. So I asked Tom Cook to say he'd been with me throughout those forty minutes.'

The words came in something of a rush, but he managed to deliver them quite smoothly. Too smoothly for Percy Peach, who said, 'No. You had something to hide. If you didn't go anywhere near Eric Walsh's car, you'd only to say so and

134

brazen it out. Whatever we thought, we couldn't have proved you wrong.'

'I was frightened. You don't realize how you can frighten ordinary, innocent people.'

Percy smiled. He did know. He frightened them all the time. And not just the innocent ones. 'What was your connection with Eric Walsh, Mr Afzaal?'

'I hadn't any connection. I was only working at the White Bull on a placement for my university course. I was there quite by chance.'

'And yet you thought it worthwhile to pressurize a witness into giving you an alibi. It doesn't add up.'

'I told you, I panicked. I thought you'd victimize me.'

Wasim looked from Peach's implacable face to the softer, female one beside it, hoping that he might find more understanding there. Lucy Blake looked up from her notes and said quietly, 'Did you make illegal entry into Eric Walsh's house later on that night?'

This time he was shaken. There was a hint of panic in his voice as he said too loudly, 'No! Of course I didn't. I was nowhere near Park Road on that night.'

Peach let his smile spread slowly beneath the shining bald pate, allowing Afzaal to realize the mistake he had made, savouring the moment when the fish had swum unexpectedly into his net. 'So you know where he lived. Unusual, that, for a man who claims not even to have met Eric Walsh.'

'I – I didn't say I hadn't met him. I said I didn't know him well.'

Percy glanced at DS Blake. 'Not what my notes say, sir. "Didn't even know the man", was the phrase, I think. And later Mr Afzaal reiterated that he "hadn't any connection".' She looked into the troubled young face. 'I expect you'll want to change that, now.'

'All right, I knew him a little, that's all. I was interested in his singing. I was trying to persuade my dad to employ him for one of his functions. And we were both bachelors. We had an interest in girls. We had the occasional drink

135

together, when I was home from university. That's all there was to it.'

It was desperately improvised stuff, and it sounded like it. Peach gave it his dismissive smile and said, 'But what was the real connection, Mr Afzaal?'

'There wasn't one. There was no more than that. I panicked because I thought if there was any connection at all you might put me in the frame for his murder.'

His face set like a mask on that, and though they pressed him, they got no more from him. He said eventually, 'I'm helping you voluntarily, as a good citizen should. Arrest me, if you think I'm not telling the truth.'

Peach smiled, concealing his anger. 'You know the law very well, as I might have expected. No, we won't arrest you. Not yet. We may come back to do that, after we've talked to other people. In the meantime, if you are as innocent as you claim, you would be well advised to come back voluntarily with the full facts. Good night, Mr Afzaal.'

Wasim went straight to the washroom and doused his face in cold water before he changed into his evening dress for the night's work. He could feel his pulse racing. But he didn't see how they could get him for this, if he kept cool and stubbornly silent.

Fourteen

Tuesday was going to be one of those November days when the clouds stayed low, and the light was so poor it was scarcely more than an interval between nights. Even the big, well-spaced houses in Brunton's best residential road looked drab in this light, as though huddling themselves against a hard winter ahead rather than looking back to the glories of summer.

There were dahlias still in bloom beside the drive of the Whitemans' house, but their petals were sodden with wetness and refusing to open, as if waiting for the mercy killing which would arrive with the first frost. Lucy Blake swung the Mondeo round the tree in front of the big double garage and left it pointing towards the gate. She had a feeling she might want to get away quickly after they had finished their business here.

Ros Whiteman looked more in control of herself now than when they had seen her two days ago, on the Sunday morning after Walsh's death. She managed a smile of welcome, whatever her real feelings were, and she moved with a swift grace as she led them through a hall and into the drawing room where they had seen her forty-eight hours earlier. 'I made some coffee,' she said. 'I know it's early in the day, but on a clammy morning like this I thought it might be welcome.'

Her hand was perfectly steady as she poured coffee and milk and handed them the cups, but there was a tiny, involuntary sigh of relief as she sat down in the armchair on the other side of the long coffee table. It seemed she had set herself some small test and acquitted herself satisfactorily. 'Have you made much progress?' she asked. 'Are you any nearer to arresting Eric's killer?'

Peach, who would sometimes hardly allow a person to think or to speak when he was on one of his tirades, could be completely silent when it suited his purpose. He had said not a word as the rituals of formal welcome and coffee had been conducted, allowing Lucy Blake to make the small, meaningless phrases of acknowledgement as he studied the lithe movements and pale face of Ros Whiteman for anything they had to offer him.

He looked into her face now for a moment before he spoke, as if he had been waiting for her to settle and give him her full attention. Then he gave her a small smile and said, 'You wouldn't expect me to discuss the details of our progress with you, Mrs Whiteman. But no, we haven't made an arrest and we don't yet know who killed Eric Walsh. Not for certain.'

She looked sharply at him on that last phrase, but the small smile was still there, teasing her, probing for any sign of nervousness in response to this enigmatic reply. 'I'll do whatever I can to recall that dreadful evening for you, of course. I feel rather more composed now than I did on Sunday. I suppose I was still suffering from delayed shock then. But I doubt if I can offer you much help.'

Peach was rather amused by these middle-class niceties, like the first modest bids at bridge as people tested the hands held around the table. But he could afford to be amused: he held all the aces in this deal. And it wasn't like bridge bidding at all: he didn't have to reveal what was in his hand until he chose to. He said unhurriedly, allowing the menace to come through in the words rather than in his manner, 'Oh, but I think you can be very helpful to us, Mrs Whiteman. Assuming that you're prepared to be more honest than on Sunday, of course.'

She looked at him sharply, and found his dark pupils staring unblinkingly at her. It was her gaze which eventually dropped to the carpet. She said dully, 'I don't know what you mean by that. I told you everything I know. I can't think who might have killed Mr Walsh.'

'I think it's time you were more honest with us about your relationship with the murder victim.'

There was a tense pause. Lucy Blake wondered what she would do if the woman went into angry denials or, much worse, hysterics. Ros Whiteman did neither of these things. Instead, she eventually said, 'You know about Eric and me, don't you?'

Peach was not going to reveal the limited extent of their knowledge. He nodded and said gravely, 'As you would expect, we always conduct a detailed search of the house of a murder victim. Among other things, there was a collection of photographs. This was one of them.'

He waited whilst Lucy Blake produced the photograph of Eric Walsh with his arm round the waist of the woman who now sat opposite her. She looked at it for a moment and said wistfully, 'He kept it, then. I remember that being taken.' Then, with sudden, surprising bitterness, she said, 'I expect there were others, weren't there? Other women, with Eric smiling beside them. Other trophies!'

Peach said, 'There were other photographs, yes. But this is the one which interests us at the moment. This is the one which brought us here today. This is the one you chose not to mention on Sunday.'

She gave him an acid smile. 'You can see why I didn't want my husband there when I spoke to you then.'

'You had been conducting a relationship with Mr Walsh, hadn't you?'

She grinned caustically at the formality of his words. 'We had an affair, if that's what you mean. I slept with Eric Walsh, yes. Repeatedly.' For a moment, it seemed she would venture on into coarser phrases. Lucy was aware of Peach's intense concentration at her side. He had a reputation for intensive grilling of people with information, but sometimes, as now, he used silence as much as aggression as a tool to secure revelations. In that quiet room, the tension stretched for long seconds before Ros Whiteman said, 'My husband doesn't know about this. I'd like it kept that way.'

Peach said, 'My guess is that that won't be possible.

139

We don't release confidences, even to spouses, unless the information has a bearing on the investigation. This time it may well do that. Especially since you chose to conceal the matter from us initially.'

'John knows nothing about Eric and me. If he had, he'd have—' She realized just in time where she was going and stopped abruptly.

Peach completed the thought grimly. 'He'd have killed him, you were going to say.'

'It's a figure of speech, no more. He'd have reacted violently, that's all. I don't blame him. And it may not be relevant to your inquiries, but I must tell you for my own sake that it's the only time I've strayed from the straight and narrow since our marriage.' She smiled; whether it was at the old-fashioned expression or her own protestation of fidelity was not clear.

Lucy Blake said quietly, 'Are you sure your husband didn't know about you and Eric Walsh?'

Ros Whiteman looked into the young, serious face beneath the lustrous red-brown hair. 'I understand why you ask. It would make him a suspect, wouldn't it? But no, John didn't know anything about Eric and me. And he would never have known, because it was over by the time Eric died.'

She looked from the sergeant to the inspector, seeking for the effect of her own bombshell, but they registered no more than mild surprise. It was Peach who said, 'Why did it finish?'

'Is this relevant?' She tried and failed to keep the anger out of her voice.

'I don't know. You'll need to tell us.'

She looked at him with a distaste which had no visible effect upon him. 'Very well. I found he'd been to bed with someone else. That he was two-timing me. I suppose there were a dozen women around who could have told me it would end like that. I knew all about his previous affairs, but I thought he was serious about me, that this time it would be different. He told me it would, almost in those words. Now I believe he'd probably told others that, before me.' She stared past them and out of the window at the grey leaves of a rhododendron beneath the louring sky, as if her spleen could make the dismal picture darker still.

Lucy Blake said quietly, 'Obviously it upset you, finishing it like that.'

She whirled on the young, earnest face, wanting suddenly to take out her frustration and fury, to damage this young, unlined flesh which knew so little and put queries of such banality. 'Of course it did! I don't make a habit of sleeping around, and I didn't go into the affair like a teenager. I thought we were serious and I was assured by Eric that he thought so too.' She looked past them and through the window again. 'It seemed serious at the time.'

Peach said, 'Serious enough to disrupt your life? Serious enough to consider a divorce?'

For a moment, it seemed again that her wrath would take over and she would refuse an answer. Her struggle for control was quite visible in the heave of her shoulders. Then she said in a monotone, 'Yes, I suppose so. We hadn't got round to discussing details, but that was the assumption. I suppose I should say that was *my* assumption.'

'How long did your association last?'

'From when I first slept with him? Five months. All but two days.'

Her reply combined the precision of a teenager in love for the first time with the bitter tone of mature disillusion: Juliet with Cleopatra, Peach thought. He reminded himself that a Cleopatra driven by passion could easily have committed murder. 'How did it end?'

'I told you, I found out he was sleeping with another woman. A younger woman, of course.' Pain as well as resentment flashed across the pale face.

'Forgive me, but you must see that this is relevant to a murder enquiry. Who was the woman involved?'

'I don't even know her name. Eric assured me that it wasn't serious.'

'Was she from the Masonic circle?'

She allowed herself a wan smile at the thought. 'No. She

was one of Eric's musical conquests. She was a member of the Brunton Light Operatic Society, I believe. According to him, it was "just a fling". That meant he took whatever he could get, wherever he found it.'

The acerbity hung in the room for a moment, like a cloud of living matter. Then Peach said, 'Did you kill Eric Walsh?'

She threw him a look of pure hatred, which disconcerted him not a jot. When emotion took over, whatever the passion behind it, people became less guarded, more vulnerable. Peach said, 'It's a fair question, when you've made no secret of how angry and humiliated you were – and still are – about the break-up of this relationship. You must see that.'

She breathed heavily for a moment, wanting to fling these persistent questioners out of her home and banish them forever, but realizing that she could not do that. When she had a measure of control, she said, 'Yes, it's a fair question. I didn't kill Eric. Given the opportunity, I think I might have done, immediately after I'd found out just how little I meant to him.'

Peach nodded. 'You had that opportunity, on Friday night. Anyone could have slipped out of that gathering and waited for Mr Walsh in his car. He was taken by surprise by someone sitting in the back seat; the manner of his killing means it could have been a woman just as easily as a man.'

She winced a fraction at the thought of the ruthless garrotting, of a man fighting for his life, of the neck she had caressed so intimately being ruptured. Then she said, 'It wasn't me. And I've no idea who it was. There were a lot of people there. It could have been any of them.'

'Indeed. Or even someone who had come into the car park from outside. But you are one of the people who had motive as well as opportunity.'

She looked at him evenly. 'Yes. But I didn't kill Eric. I told you on Sunday, I was with other people during the period you asked about, the time when Eric was murdered.'

'You also gave us to understand that you had no connection with the murder victim. You must accept that we now have to treat everything else you said then with a degree of scepticism.'

Ros Whiteman's sallow skin flushed beneath the glossy dark hair. She had not had her integrity questioned since she was a schoolgirl. 'I didn't kill him. And I've no idea who did.'

'You said your husband knew nothing of this affair with the dead man. Are you absolutely sure of that?'

She gave them a wan smile. 'Oh, yes. I'd know about it, if John had found out about me and Eric.'

Peach was looking at her as keenly as he had done throughout their exchanges, totally unembarrassed. It was part of being a detective, to observe people in the most trying of circumstances. Sometimes the most important part. He now said quietly, 'If Mr Whiteman had known, it would have given him a motive, wouldn't it?'

'I suppose it would. He wouldn't like to see me made a fool of. He would enjoy being seen as a cuckold and a fool himself even less. But he didn't know about Eric and me, so it doesn't arise.'

Percy Peach and Lucy Blake wondered as they left how much was left of the marriage which looked from the outside so secure. Would she take up the reins again and live out her life as though nothing had happened? Would John Whiteman remain forever unaware of the liaison which had threatened the fabric of his life?

Lucy Blake swung the police Mondeo carefully into the quiet road where some of the richest of middle-class Brunton lived out their lives. 'You see people's lives, in this job,' she said presently.

'More than you want to, sometimes,' said Peach unexpectedly. She glanced sideways, saw the strain on his face for the first time, and realized that he did not always relish the pressure he applied as much as he appeared to at the time. She had too much sense to make any comment.

Jack Chadwick was waiting for Peach when he arrived back

at the CID section of the Brunton police station. The scene-of-crime sergeant looked thoroughly discomfited. 'I've got the SOC findings from the car park of the White Bull,' he said. 'You should have had them earlier, but I took the team off to the victim's house when we found there'd been a break-in. We'd found nothing much in a quick survey of the car, and the break-in seemed more urgent.'

'You did the right thing,' said Percy. 'Used your initiative. The thing Tommy Bloody Tucker tells us we should have done whenever something unexpected turns up. Except that he doesn't hesitate to bollock us if we don't do everything by the book.'

'That's right. Well, he'll bollock me in due course over this.'

'Not unless it's pushed under his nose on a large plate, he won't. What the hell's bothering you, Jack?'

'Something I think you should have had earlier, that's all,' said Chadwick gloomily as he followed Peach and Blake into the inspector's office. 'Look, let me give you the findings in order. First, we've lifted various prints from the car, but I think we'll be lucky if there's anything useful.'

'So chummy wore gloves?'

'Almost certainly. There aren't many prints on the rear door of the car, but it had been opened recently by someone with gloves on. Pretty certainly your killer. It might argue that he or she came prepared for the killing.'

'It might. But it was a cold night in early November. Anyone could reasonably have been wearing gloves. This could just as easily have been an opportunist crime as a planned one.'

'Except for the murder weapon. Someone came there with a thin cord which was ideal for the job. We haven't found it, of course, but the PM report says that that is what was used.'

'It's still possible that anyone who saw the opportunity would have had a piece of cord or rope to hand. Lots of people have something like that amongst the rubbish in the boot of their cars. I have myself.'

Lucy Blake said, 'My mum has a piece of rope in the back

144

of her little car. She carries it as an emergency lead for the dog, in case she forgets the proper one. I have one in the back of my Corsa, for the same dog.'

'How did chummy get into the car?' said Peach.

'We're unlucky there. It's a vintage car: a Triumph Stag with the original locks. Very good for pulling the women, but not at all secure. In the days when Stags were manufactured, if you had a bunch of keys, you could get into most cars. Even if you hadn't got a key, it was easy to get in with a bit of wire and a minimum of know-how. I showed the Stag to our pet AA man. He thought he could get in within fifteen seconds, especially with such a worn lock on the driver's door.'

'Is that how the murderer got in?'

Chadwick shrugged. 'Impossible to say. There are minute scratches round the lock, and it's pretty certain someone has got in that way in the last year or two. But it could be Walsh himself, if he'd locked his keys inside, or an AA man, if one was called to help. It could even have been some previous break-in which had nothing to do with this crime.'

'Or it could have been someone with a key.'

Peach was thinking about Ros Whiteman, the elegant, embittered woman they had just left.

'Easily. As I said, security wasn't such a concern when they built Triumph Stags. Anyone with a selection of keys could probably have turned that lock. It's simple and it's well worn, which makes it even easier.'

It was also possible, thought Lucy Blake, that someone who had been close to Eric Walsh had had a duplicate key to his car, made with or without the dead owner's knowledge. Someone like Ros Whiteman. Or one of the other women he had disappointed in the past. Or some cuckolded husband or lover looking for revenge. Or . . . This didn't help a lot.

'So any vicious sod with a grain of nous could have got into that car.' Percy Peach summarized her thoughts with his usual vigour. 'So what else have you found to indicate who that vicious sod might be, Jack?'

'Not much. Forensics have been over that car like wasps

round a jam jar – they're still working on it now. They've sent stuff off to the labs, but it's my guess and theirs that they're not going to come up with much.'

'No prints that are useful, you said. Any fibres?'

'Quite a few from the driver's seat. Most of them have already been matched with clothing belonging to Walsh, as you might expect. More interesting ones from the front passenger seat. You may get a match with something worn by one of your suspects, in due course. I wouldn't count on it.'

'And from the seat behind the driver?'

All of them knew this was the key spot, the one where the murderer had crouched and waited for his prey. Or hers. Chadwick shook his head sadly. 'Very little. It looks as though your killer wore gloves throughout, as I said. Probably also an anorak or something similarly smooth, that wouldn't excite any notice on a cold November night. We've got a single navy nylon fibre, the kind that might come from an anorak. But there's nothing uncommon about it, and it didn't necessarily come from the killer's clothing.'

Peach nodded glumly. The forensic scientists look for an 'exchange' at the scene of a serious crime, where the criminal leaves behind something of himself or herself. It looked as though this time the residue was minimal. 'Anything from around the car?'

Jack Chadwick looked mortified, as he had when he had first come into the office. Embarrassment did not sit easily on his square, stolid face. 'We found various bits of paper, as you'd expect at the end of a pub car park. The lads bagged them up together. 'However . . .' He delved into his briefcase and produced a scrap of paper, no more than five centimetres by ten, which had been put in a protective polythene cover. 'This was quite near the Triumph Stag. Within two metres of the back seat where the murderer waited for Eric Walsh.'

Peach picked up the polythene envelope by its corner, studied the unremarkable-looking paper slip inside it, then passed it to Lucy Blake. 'It's a receipt for petrol.'

146

'Yes. Paid for by credit card. With the number of the credit card printed out beneath the price.'

'And you've traced it.'

'Yes. We couldn't do much over the English weekend, as usual. Then the banks put up the normal blank wall about confidentiality, but the suggestion that they might be obstructing a murder inquiry worked wonders.' Chadwick was relieved to draw attention to his persistence, which he saw as belated, because he hadn't seen the significance of this scrap of paper at first. In reality, as he said, he couldn't have achieved a result before Monday.

'So whose account was it?'

'The Master of the North Brunton Masonic Lodge. John Whiteman.'

Fifteen

The man was almost six feet tall, solidly built, running to a little fat in his fifties. He wore a dark grey suit and a maroon tie and looked just a little too large for his clothes. Most policemen would have placed him immediately as an ex-copper. Superintendent Thomas Bulstrode Tucker did not.

He said, 'You shouldn't really have been shown up here. I'm in charge of the CID section, you know. You should have seen someone on the ground floor.'

'I asked to see the officer in charge of the Eric Walsh murder case. I suppose the desk sergeant thought it might be important.'

Tucker looked at him suspiciously, searching for irony. But that heavy face beneath the thinning, sharply parted black hair didn't seem the frame for irony. The superintendent forced a smile and said, 'Well, it's not your fault, I suppose. And I am in charge of the case, of course I am. But it's my job to maintain an overview, you see. I have to keep a perspective on this and other important cases. To fit everything into the overall framework.'

The man recognized bullshit when he heard it. He hadn't spent twenty-seven years in the service without developing a nose for bullshit. He said, 'I understand that. Perhaps I should speak to someone in touch with the day-to-day development of the investigation.'

'The day-to-day development. That's just it!' Tucker seized on the phrase like manna in the desert. 'You'll need to see Inspector Peach. He's the man in charge of the day-to-day conduct of the case.' He picked up the internal phone. 'He's just gone out,' he said resentfully a moment later, as if Peach's exit represented a personal desertion. 'Should be back in about an hour.'

'I'll wait,' said his visitor.

'Downstairs, then,' said Superintendent Tucker decisively. He tried to look apologetic. 'I've got a meeting in a few minutes, you see.'

The dark-haired man went heavily down two flights of stairs, was directed to the canteen by a constable who recognized him as an ex-copper, and got himself a coffee. He read his newspaper and waited for his man with a patience developed over twenty-seven years. He reflected without rancour that the wanker upstairs hadn't even asked why he was here.

At the moment when Tucker's visitor was taking his first sip of coffee, Peach and Blake were being shown into John Whiteman's office at the back of the Victorian building which housed the family firm of solicitors.

'I've been trying to think of things which might help you to find your murderer,' Whiteman said as they sat down. 'I'm afraid I haven't been able to come up with much. I can give you the names of two or three women with whom I know Eric had . . . well, shall we say *associations*, but I'm afraid it's not a comprehensive list!' He sniggered self-consciously at his little joke. His normal day didn't allow a lot of opportunity for jokes.

Lucy Blake noted the names of three women, assuring him that their lives and the lives of those around them would not be disturbed more than was strictly necessary. Peach was silent throughout, observing the bearing of Whiteman rather than what he had to say. He waited until the solicitor was back behind his desk, looking expectantly from one to the other of his police visitors.

Then Peach said, 'We've been busy building up a picture of our murder victim. Eric Walsh was an Orangeman, dedicated to the preservation of the status quo in Northern Ireland. That seems to have been very important to him when he lived in

Belfast, but less so since he came to Lancashire. He had a small import-export business, which doesn't seem to account for everything in his bank account. But perhaps he didn't declare everything: import-export is notoriously difficult to pin down.'

He looked interrogatively at John Whiteman, who shook his head. 'It was always a bit of a mystery to members of the Lodge, how Eric earned his living. We thought he might have private means.'

Peach looked at him closely, then apparently accepted this. He went on, 'Walsh was a highly competent amateur baritone, active in various light operatic groups and in the Brunton Choral Society. Those are things which distinguish him from other members of your Masonic Lodge: we're always interested in the distinctive things about victims. The other thing obvious thing about Walsh is the stream of women he has left behind him, most of them disappointed when he moved on. You've just given us the names of three to add to those we have collected elsewhere.'

He paused, and Whiteman leapt in as he had hoped, to fill the silence. He smiled and said, 'I would never claim to have a comprehensive knowledge of Eric's dealings with the fair sex.'

'You know more about the way he behaved than us, never-theless – certainly more than we did two days ago. We now have quite a list of his conquests. Would you say the women were easy for him?'

'Easy? I don't quite know—'

'Habitual drawer-droppers, were they? Women out for a bit of nooky? Women who had a history of rumpety and—'

'No! That is a monstrous assumption to make! I should warn you that—'

'Question, not an assumption, Mr Whiteman. Just look-ing for information, that's all. You must see that it has a bearing on our investigation. Women who indulge in affairs habitually are less likely to behave violently when ditched, in our experience. Women for whom it's a serious affair, who thought it was going to develop into a permanent liaison, are more likely to go off the rails. If they have a husband or partner who is not used to such sexual cavortings, he's likely to react violently too. Sometimes to the affair itself; sometimes to the slur on his partner when she's cast aside and devastated.'

'I see your point. I don't think there was any need to couch it in the language you did.'

Got a reaction, though, didn't it, thought Percy. The regular features beneath the hair that was almost too perfectly groomed were flushed, and the fingers on the hands which were clasped together on the desk were now folding and unfolding as Whiteman tried to maintain his composure. Peach said, 'You haven't answered my question. Let me use more acceptable language. Do you think the women Walsh successfully bedded were habitually promiscuous?'

'I'm not qualified to say.'

'Even when you're trying to do your duty as a responsible citizen and help us with a murder inquiry?'

'I don't know. I've never thought about it.'

'You're the Master of the Lodge, Mr Whiteman. You must have acquired a knowledge of most of your members over the last twenty years. And of their partners, whether married or otherwise.'

'It's not the central part of our activities, to study the sexual proclivities of members.' He was fencing now, and all three of them knew it as his eyes dropped to the desk. Noticing the feverish movements of his fingers for the first time, he stilled them abruptly.

Peach smiled. 'I'm glad to hear it. But you know more about these things than you are telling me, nevertheless.'

Suddenly, Whiteman shouted, 'What do you want? A detailed account of all Walsh's women, and what he did to them in bed?'

Peach let the shout echo round the walls, allowed Whiteman to wonder how much the people in the outer offices had caught of their leader's loss of control. Then he said quietly, 'You knew all about your wife and Eric Walsh, Mr Whiteman, didn't you?'

For a moment, it looked as though Whiteman would hit his tormentor. Then he said, through a mouth that hardly opened, 'I don't know what you mean.'

'I think you do. I'm sorry I have to raise it. But as a lawyer you will see quite clearly that I must pursue these things when a man has been murdered.'

'That bloody man Walsh deserved to be murdered.' The voice which had been a shout was now scarcely audible.

'That may be your view as a husband, Mr Whiteman, and it is naturally of great interest to us. But as a lawyer you know perfectly well that every victim has the right to justice, that every suspicious death must be properly investigated.'

'All right, all right! Walsh was shagging my wife!' The word he had never used in public dropped harshly from his lips. 'You've dug up your nasty little bone. Now go away and bury it again.'

Peach was totally unruffled. 'Can't do that, I'm afraid, Mr Whiteman. Has to be investigated, you see. We have to make sure it has nothing to do with this death. Especially as it's information you chose to conceal from us. Especially as you've just voiced the opinion that Eric Walsh "deserved to be murdered".'

'Figure of speech. No more than that.'

'Perhaps. Remains to be seen, that.'

'Ros isn't promiscuous. She hadn't done anything like this before. That made it worse.' He sounded like a man pleading for understanding.

Peach wasn't interested in understanding the man's emotions. At this moment, he wanted only the truth, and he sensed an opportunity to get it. He said, 'So you took it hard when you found out about Eric Walsh and your wife. You're not the first husband to do that. Not even the first husband to murder the man involved.'

'I didn't kill Eric Walsh.'

'So who did?'

'I've no idea. But I'm telling you here and now that I didn't.'

'You'll need to convince us of that, having lied to us so comprehensively about what you knew.'

John Whiteman looked at that moment as if he would have liked to kill Percy Peach. Instead, he forced a smile and said, 'I'm enough of a lawyer to know that that isn't true. I don't have to prove anything. The burden of proof is on you. And you haven't a scrap of evidence.'

Peach gave him an answering, much broader smile. He liked a bit of resistance. Especially when he still had trump cards to play. 'You realize by now why we have been asking everyone about the forty minutes between eleven twenty and midnight last Friday. Eric Walsh was last seen alive at eleven twenty. His body was discovered in his car just before twelve o'clock.'

'I gathered that. Superintendent Tucker was taken out to see the body by the hotel staff at just after midnight.'

'So why did you lie about where you were in those forty minutes?'

Whiteman forced himself to take his time. They saw him swallow, an exaggerated movement which he obviously found quite difficult. He raised his right hand and caressed the becoming patch of grey at his temple, as if the touch could give him reassurance. 'I didn't lie. I don't know why on earth you should accuse me of that. I was surrounded by other members of the Lodge in the bar, chatting over the events of the evening. They were plenty of people around me. They'll confirm I was in the bar for the whole of that time.'

The words were definite enough, but the certainty leaked out of his voice as he proceeded, as if he spoke in hope rather than conviction. Peach looked at him coolly for a moment before he said, 'On the contrary, one person has already confirmed to us that you left the bar during that time.'

'Then he's mistaken.'

'On the contrary, the person concerned is quite certain.' He wasn't going to tell Whiteman at this stage that it was his wife who had said that he had been out of the bar. These two had quite enough to sort out as it was; Ros Whiteman was still under the impression that John knew nothing of her affair with Eric Walsh. 'I've no doubt we can get other witnesses to confirm this, if you insist you were there throughout that forty-minute period.'

Whiteman gave an unconvincing impression of giving the matter some thought, of remembrance dawning. 'If I left the bar at all, it was only for a few minutes. I must have gone to the gents' at some time after the formal part of the evening was concluded. We all did, I imagine.'

'A few minutes were quite long enough to kill Eric Walsh. A man you say you thought deserved to die.'

'I suppose that is so. But I didn't kill him. I went to the gents', as I told you.'

'What time was this?'

'I can't be sure. You don't think when you go for a pee that you have to record the time.'

'How long before Superintendent Tucker was summoned to see the body?'

'Ten minutes, quarter of an hour perhaps. Not more. There weren't too many of us left in the bar by the time I went.'

'About quarter to twelve, then. Have a conversation with anyone in the cloakroom, did you?'

'No, not that I recall.'

'Pity, that. It might confirm that you were actually where you claim to have been at that time. Important to do that, as you lied to us about it as long as you thought you might get away with it.'

'I didn't lie. It slipped my memory, that's all. You don't think you're going to be grilled about a visit to—'

'The cloakroom's the only place you went to whilst you were absent from the bar, is it? You didn't pop outside and garrotte the man who had bedded your wife?'

'Look, Inspector, you seem to be trying hard to be deliberately offensive. Perhaps I should remind you that I am on friendly terms with your superior officer at Brunton CID. And—'

'And perhaps I should remind you that you have lied consistently about both your knowledge and your conduct, until we forced you to be more honest. Quite how honest remains to be seen. I'm asking you again, did you go out to Eric Walsh's car whilst you were allegedly visiting the cloakroom at the White Bull? It's a simple enough question.'

'No. I didn't even go into the car park, let alone look for his car.'

'You're sticking to that?'

'I'm sticking to the truth, if that's what you're asking me.'

'Very well. DS Blake has something which might interest you. A receipt for a purchase of petrol.' Lucy Blake produced the small envelope of polythene with its innocuous-looking slip of paper. She displayed it to Whiteman, keeping it just out of his reach across the desk. He must not be allowed to damage what might eventually be a courtroom exhibit.

John Whiteman was genuinely puzzled. Like many another man before him, he had never studied the computer trivia which modern life threw up. He said, 'So it's a petrol receipt, if you say so. Am I supposed to be impressed?'

Peach studied him for a moment, decided that the man was still unaware of the significance of what Blake held. 'It's a receipt for petrol, paid for with a credit card. With the number of the credit card account included in the garage printout. Your account, Mr Whiteman.'

They watched him whilst a sick realization crept through his veins. He said dully, 'So it's a receipt given to me. Why are you claiming it has any significance?'

'Because of where it was found, Mr Whiteman. It was picked up beside the back door of the Triumph Stag in which Eric Walsh was murdered.'

There was a pause whilst they watched him suffer. Eventually he said, 'You could have planted this there.'

'If that's your defence, I'm sure the Crown prosecution service will be happy to take you on. I think the jury in a murder trial would be inclined to believe our scene-of-crime team.'

They could hear his breathing, heavy and uneven, before

155

he said, as though speaking to himself, 'It must have been in my pocket. I must have dropped it when I pulled out my gloves.'

'On Friday night?'

'Yes.'

'So you now admit you went out to that car.'

'Yes. But I didn't kill him.'

'In view of your persistent refusal to tell us the truth, you can expect us to treat that with—'

'He was dead when I got there.'

'Is this your latest fiction?'

'I went out to tell him what I thought of him. To tell him that I knew about him and Ros and I wanted him out of the Lodge and out of my sight. He was dead when I got there. Sitting with his head slumped forward.' Whiteman spoke in a dull monotone, like one recalling a nightmare. Or one reciting a statement prepared for just this situation.

'What time was this?'

'Ten to twelve. I looked at my watch as I went back inside the hotel.'

'You're sticking to this?'

'It's the truth, this time.'

'I seem to remember you saying that before.'

Whiteman flashed a look of hatred at this implacable opponent. 'You can see why I did that. You're going to say I killed him.'

Peach studied him coolly for a moment, waiting to see if there would be any further revelations. The head was hunched forward, the eyes cast down, and he knew Whiteman was not going to look at him again. He said, 'We'll need to get a formal statement from you, in due course. There is still time to change what you have said, when you have had time to reflect upon it.'

John Whiteman stayed looking at his desk as they left him, scarcely believing he was still there. He had expected the formal words of arrest.

Sixteen

Peach and the man in the dark suit eyed each other cautiously across the few feet of the inspector's small modern office. 'You say you were sent to me by the superintendent,' said Peach, more as accusation than question.

'Ay. The tosser upstairs who doesn't know his arse from his elbow,' said the man with distaste.

Peach leapt forward for a vigorous handshake. 'Detective Inspector Peach. Universally known round here as Percy. And the tosser upstairs is Detective Superintendent Tucker. Universally known round here as Tommy Bloody Tucker. That's on his good days.'

'Ian Graham. Until five years ago Detective Sergeant Graham.'

Peach nodded. 'It shows. But we all have our skeletons in the cupboard. You weren't round here, though.'

'No. North Riding CID. But I retired to Clitheroe. My wife comes from the Ribble Valley. And being retired, I don't have to watch my opinions any more. I can call a spade a spade. Or a tosser a tosser.'

Peach grinned, taking in the maroon tie, the white shirt, the shoes which shone as brightly as his own. He felt he knew the answer to his next question almost before he asked it. 'So what are you doing in retirement, Ian?'

'Private enquiry agency. Not my own. I work for someone else.' He said it defensively, wondering what reaction he would get. Working coppers do not usually take kindly to men working outside the system.

But Peach nodded equably enough. 'Better than being a glorified nightwatchman in a factory, I expect.'

Graham grinned ruefully. 'It's dull enough work, most of the time. Trapping petty fiddlers with their hands in the till, following randy husbands to chronicle their meetings with bits on the side. You spend a lot of your time sitting in a car. Occasionally we come across something a bit more interesting.'

'Which is why you're here now.'

'Which is why I'm here now.' Ian Graham grinned comfortably, happy to be on the same wavelength with a CID man after his unfortunate experience upstairs. 'Eric Walsh. Have you found who did for him yet?'

'No. We've lined up a few suspects.'

'I'm not surprised at that. He was a man who made enemies, Mr Walsh.'

'Were you one of them, Ian?' It was always as well to know where people were coming from when they spoke of dead people.

'No. We had what you might laughingly call a professional relationship. He was paying my firm to investigate the activities of someone else.'

Peach tried not to show the quickening of his interest. All good CID officers are hunters, and when they get an interesting scent, their noses react to it. 'And who was that?'

'Man called Adrian O'Connor. You know him?'

Peach nodded. 'I know him. We've questioned him in connection with Walsh's murder. Alongside a lot of other people who were around at the time, I have to say.'

Ian Graham nodded. 'I'm not saying he did it. And I'm afraid I've not come here to give you a murderer on a plate.'

Peach grinned. 'So why are you here?'

An answering grin, a grin of recognition between two professionals. 'Because I can't take it any further. Because I'd quickly be out of my depth if I tried. Because I'd need a full police murder team to help me. And because no one's going to pay me to take this any further. Eric Walsh was paying my fees. They stopped abruptly with his death. So did the investigation of Adrian O'Connor.'

'Fair enough. But what is there to take further?'

'Maybe nothing. Maybe a hell of a lot. All I can say is that when Eric Walsh was murdered, I thought immediately of Adrian O'Connor. I've nothing to offer which would give you a conviction in court. Nothing which directly connects him with Walsh's death. I just think you should follow up what I have found, that's all.'

Peach looked at him keenly, then nodded. When a murder isn't a simple domestic killing, there are usually people who come into police stations with wild accusations. Usually they are cranks, sometimes harmless, sometimes malignant. This man was a professional, acting as a professional should when events moved beyond his control. 'Right. Thanks for coming in. Let's have whatever you can give us about Adrian O'Connor.'

Graham took a deep breath, using what was plainly an orderly mind to deliver his material. 'First of all, I was employed by Eric Walsh. He asked me to check up on the activities of O'Connor. He wanted discreet probing, not an official stirring of muddy waters. There is a history to this, which you may or may not know.'

'We know O'Connor was questioned by the RUC in Belfast in 1988. In connection with an assault on a certain Dennis Walsh. Eric's brother. The RUC were pretty certain O'Connor was involved, but he got off with a caution. Dennis Walsh had been courting a Catholic girl: Kathleen O'Connor, Adrian's sister.'

Ian Graham nodded, impressed and slightly disappointed by what this sharp-eyed inspector already knew. 'That is substantially correct. I had the advantage of being able to speak to Eric Walsh about that, of course. I think the only thing I'd really argue with is your word "courting". Walsh didn't say so in so many words, but I think his brother was out to bed a Catholic girl and be on his way. I don't think he'd have stayed around to marry her, even if that had been possible. In the peculiar world of the troubles in Belfast, a Catholic harlot would have been a trophy for the Protestants to brandish.'

Peach nodded. 'Certainly Eric Walsh's subsequent record with women would imply that that was the family approach. He didn't stick around too long, once they dropped their drawers, our Eric. Perhaps Dennis was the same.'

'I think he was. I think the danger, and the idea of putting one over on the Catholics, were what appealed to the Walshes. Which would make O'Connor all the more bitter. Eric seems to have been the driving force behind these events. He was the elder brother, and the head of an active Loyalist cell in the powder keg which was Belfast at the time. He moved out pretty smartly after his brother was assaulted: perhaps he thought he'd be the next victim.'

'And fourteen years later, he decides to employ you to make discreet enquiries. Why?'

'Because he thought Adrian O'Connor had come to this area to pursue him. It's melodramatic, but in terms of Irish feuding, it's possible.'

'Entirely possible. What did you find?'

'I found that the Kathleen O'Connor who was involved with Walsh's brother had committed suicide. She took an overdose in 1989. I don't know whether it was connected with the Walsh episode of the previous year or not, but it seems likely. His sister's death would certainly make Adrian O'Connor bitter.'

'But surely it would have been more logical to pursue the younger brother, Dennis Walsh, who was the man directly involved?'

'Maybe they did. Dennis Walsh was shot dead at the beginning of 1990. He opened his door late in the evening of January seventeenth and was shot through the head at point-blank range. No one ever found out who did it.'

'But I suppose it looked like O'Connor or some agent of his.'

'Eric Walsh certainly thought so. And he felt that as head of the Walsh group at the time, he was also a target.'

'And if he hired you to investigate matters, I presume he felt he was still a target.'

'He did. Perhaps with some reason. Adrian O'Connor arrived in Brunton three and a half years ago. Out of the blue, as far as Eric Walsh was concerned. He then set about getting close to Walsh. Again, it's only Walsh who says that, and I imagine O'Connor would say the idea was ridiculous.'

'He already has said so, to us. Did you find anything to support Walsh's view that he was a target?'

'Nothing definite enough to warrant an arrest. Quite a lot of circumstantial stuff.'

'Such as?'

'The way O'Connor arrived here, for a start. He's an engineer, now working as an executive for the Shell Oil Company. I made a few enquiries in Manchester. He'd spent most of his Shell career in the Middle East and London. He applied for a transfer to the north-west, for "personal reasons". He turned down Cumbria and Cheshire, but accepted a job in Preston.'

'Couldn't it have been a normal promotion?'

'It wasn't that. He got no rise in salary and moved at the same grade. If you look at his bonuses, he probably took a small drop in salary to take the job in Preston. And he immediately bought a house not in Preston, but in Brunton.'

Peach pursed his lips. 'It's only ten miles away. But let's agree between ourselves that it represents fairly strong circumstantial evidence that he was looking to get near Walsh. Is there more?'

'A little. O'Connor hadn't been a Freemason at any time, nor shown any interest in the movement. Within six months of arriving in Brunton, he had managed to get himself into the Brunton Lodge. I've checked that with the man who introduced him to the Lodge. Eric Walsh thought it was all part of a plan to get nearer to him. He thought O'Connor enjoyed turning up wherever Eric went and watching him sweat. He did it with his singing engagements, not just with the Masons.'

'He might have been doing just that, of course. Watching him sweat and enjoying it. Persuading Walsh that he had designs on his life. He may not actually have killed him.'

'Exactly. Which is why I'm happy to pass all this on to you now. If someone else killed Eric Walsh, though, it would be quite a coincidence, when you have a man at hand who seems to have been threatening him. Was O'Connor anywhere near the scene of the crime?'

Peach frowned. 'He was near it all right, but not at the right time. He claims to have left the White Bull whilst Walsh was still alive, and it looks as if that's genuine. He was quite tightly parked and one of the hotel staff watched him go to make sure he didn't scrape anyone else. He confirms that O'Connor was off the premises by eleven fifteen last Friday night, when we know Walsh was still alive.'

'I suppose he could have got someone else to do his killing.'

'Indeed. But no one in the hotel spotted any strangers around. But a contract killer would have made it his business not to be seen. We shall need to have further words with Mr Adrian O'Connor.'

It is a common enough story. Loan sharks encourage people to take on impossible loans, at rates of interest which merely add to the problems. When the borrowers default on the repayments, they have to be taught a lesson: the loan shark may already have had his money and more back in interest, but it doesn't do to let the defaulters get away with anything. Bad for discipline, that is: other borrowers might be encouraged to default on their repayments, if the axe of retribution does not fall quickly.

In the murky world of the sharks, violence is never far away. Defaulters are dealt with quickly and firmly. Not by the shark himself, of course, but by his well-paid agents. A broken nose, the occasional broken arm; for repeat offenders, a serious beating-up. It is not personal, the victims are given to understand, but to discourage others from defaulting. The word gets round and other potential defaulters cringe and pay up.

That is the theory of the matter, and practice generally follows theory without many complications. But the muscle-men who work for loan sharks are not notable for their intelligence; they are employed for things other than brainpower. And occasionally their judgement lets them down and they overdo things. Instead of quietly limping away after having been taught a sharp lesson, their victims end up in hospital. The loan shark does not like this at all, for it excites police attention.

Lucy Blake smiled into the woman's face, trying to conceal how much its injuries disturbed her. There was a livid purple valley down one side of the features where the cheek had been pushed in and the skin seemed to have disappeared altogether. One eye was closed and the swollen lips were twisted into a permanent crooked smile. It was impossible to tell how old she was.

Lucy said gently, 'This should never have happened to you. Should never happen to anyone. We'll put them behind bars for you.'

The single eye looked not at her but at the high ceiling of the ward. 'Can't pay. They've done all this to me and I still can't pay.'

The voice was no more than a croak, but the despair which lay behind the words was more awful than their distorted sound. Lucy said, 'They won't do it again. With your help, we'll get them, Beth.' She'd no idea how, but her voice carried conviction: at that moment she was very determined.

'Are they all right?'

For an instant, Lucy struggled to understand. Then she said, 'The children are fine, Beth. They're in good hands. They'll come and see you when you feel a bit better.'

'Not now. Not like this.' It was the first animation she had shown, and the single eye turned for the first time to the earnest young face beside the bed. 'You're police, aren't you?'

Lucy smiled, doing her best to reassure. 'Yes. Detective Sergeant Blake, of Brunton CID. Lucy to you.'

Gratitude for a moment in that single eye, then alarm. 'I can't help you, love. They'll come back, you know. Get the kids.'

'They won't do that, Beth. They might threaten it, but they never attack kids. There's no point: kids don't have money.'

'Neither do I, but they did this to me. They've had all I get from the social, for the last three weeks. I had to try to feed the kids.'

Lucy fought down the rising tide of anger. This ruined creature was probably no older than her, possibly even younger. Sounding off would be a relief, but it wouldn't help anyone. She leaned forward, took the small hand lying on the blankets between hers, and said gently, 'Who were they, Beth, the men who did this? It's time for us to go after them.'

The voice from the damaged face said hopelessly, 'I don't know. Really I don't. I hadn't seen them before. Big men, with big fists.' A shudder ran through the slim form beneath the blankets.

Lucy was conscious of the nurse, hovering at the edge of the screen round the bed as she heard the exhaustion in the voice. She said desperately, 'We need to protect you and others like you, Beth. Whom did you borrow the money from in the first place?'

The seconds stretched agonizingly, until Lucy wondered whether the woman in the bed was refusing to answer or had lost consciousness. The single eye was closed now. The nurse was coming to the bedside to tell Lucy she must leave when the faint voice beside her said, 'Cartwright. Darren Cartwright.'

'It isn't very convenient, you know, all this.' Adrian O'Connor looked round his comfortable office, with its square of thick carpet on highly polished wood flooring, its four comfortable armchairs, its drinks cabinet in the corner, its prints of old Preston docks and 1930s adverts advising motorists with overcoats and cheerful smiles to 'Fill up with Shell' on the walls.

He didn't look inconvenienced, thought Percy Peach. Bit of a contrast with his own cramped office, this. He said unhurriedly, 'We've been looking into your background, Mr O'Connor. Not DS Blake or me personally, but members of our team.'

O'Connor, who had been standing and looking out of the window towards the estuary of the River Ribble after inviting them to sit down, sighed and kept his eyes on the wide expanse of water for a few seconds. Then he turned abruptly and came and sat in one of the armchairs opposite them. 'Is that news supposed to frighten me, Inspector?'

'That's up to you. It might give you food for thought.'

'I don't see why it should. I've no doubt you've turned up the startling news that I have links with the Irish Republican Movement in Ireland.'

'Irish Republican Army, Mr O'Connor. An illegal organization. A terrorist organization.'

Adrian smiled. He wasn't going to be intimidated by that. It was an old accusation, one which he had thrown back into the faces of worthier opponents than this stocky policeman and his beautiful sidekick. 'One man's terrorist is another's freedom fighter, Inspector Peach.'

'You've given money to them, these murderers who shoot men in front of their children and shatter the kneecaps of defenceless boys. You've taken an active part in their activities yourself, in the past.'

O'Connor lifted an eyebrow, finding the gestures he had practised in negotiations within the firm useful now in this other context. 'I doubt if you could prove that, Inspector. In any case, it's all a long time ago. We do things as young men we would not countenance later in life.' He was easy with himself and them, knowing that they had not really come here to talk about this.

Adrian remembered much tenser conversations with the Ulster police, years ago, when it was touch and go whether they would have to let him go free or not. This one, on his own comfortable ground, from the safety of his successful business life, was going to be much easier. 'I made no secret of my desire for a united Ireland when we last met. I'm not alone in those views: there are a good couple of million of us, I would suggest.'

Peach said, 'Your past activities may or may not have a bearing on this visit. Those who have acquired a taste for violence as young men often resort to it again much later, when they feel pressure.'

'I am not under pressure.'

'Why did you take this job, Mr O'Connor?'

The suddenness of Peach's question shook him, despite his determination to remain calm. 'That is surely irrelevant. It is certainly impertinent. My employment is none of your business.'

'You refuse to answer?'

'I refuse to discuss the details of my professional life with some jumped-up police inspector.'

Peach was delighted to hear his man rattled. He raised the arches of his black eyebrows expressively and said, 'It's not irrelevant. We have reason to believe that you took your present post for a particular reason.'

Adrian O'Connor forced himself to be calm, to give this bumptious man his most patronizing smile. 'It was a promotion. Even you must have had those, to become an inspector, so you should understand.'

'Our information is that it was not a promotion. We know that you turned down other situations in the north-west of England. That you took a slight drop in salary to come here.'

Adrian's anger burst out now. 'You know a damn sight too much, if you ask me! And if you've been using the resources of the police service to pry into my career with Shell, I can assure you you'll regret it very—'

'We don't reveal our sources, Mr O'Connor. I will tell you that there has been no police investigation of your background with the Shell Oil Company. Are you saying that what I have just said is incorrect?'

'I'm not going to comment on your assumptions.'

'We now believe that you came here for a particular reason.'

Adrian found that he didn't want them to put that reason into words. It would be one step nearer to disaster to hear it voiced a second time. He stood up and walked over to the window again, looking west at the glinting of the sun on the water as it moved towards its early setting. 'This is a pleasant part of the world to live in. You don't realize how beautiful the Ribble Valley is until you've been here. The image of Lancashire as all mills and industrial smoke is very far from the truth. But you know that, you two. You live in the area. Play golf at the North Lancashire Golf Club, in your case, Inspector.' He enjoyed displaying a little knowledge of his own.

Peach raised the black eyebrows a millimetre further than seemed possible. 'You're saying that you took this job to live in a pleasant environment?'

Adrian turned and returned with measured tread to sit in the armchair again. 'I've had a successful career with Shell. More successful than I ever envisaged when I started. When you get towards forty and you have a comfortable salary, you decide that there are more important things than money. I'd had enough of living in cities long ago, when I was in Belfast.'

Percy Peach smiled and looked at Lucy Blake. She said, 'We have reason to believe that you came to this area to get near to Eric Walsh.'

Adrian had known for the last few minutes that this would come, but to hear it stated in such calm tones by the smooth face beneath the fringe of red-brown hair was more unnerving than if it had come from Peach. He said, 'You made the same tiresome suggestion last time we met. I refuted it then and I do so again. I'm quite sure you're unable to substantiate your accusation.'

DS Blake gave him a small smile which lit up her young face, making what she said even more of a contrast. 'We don't have to substantiate it, Mr O'Connor. We are asking you whether it's true.'

'No, it isn't. Of course it isn't.'

167

'I see. It's the opinion of our source – which as Inspector Peach told you we cannot reveal – that you came to the area to be near Eric Walsh. That you went to concerts and other occasions where he sang just to get closer to him. That you took up Freemasonry and joined the North Brunton Lodge specifically because Mr Walsh was a member of that group. That you had a grudge against Mr Walsh which stemmed from the Walshes' association with your sister in Belfast in 1988 and her subsequent suicide. That you were determined to get even with Mr Walsh and were planning some violent retribution.'

Adrian was shaken by this cool recital from a young woman who had hardly spoken previously. He forced himself to be calm, tried to inject some conviction into his voice as he said, 'It's a pack of lies, that, from someone's fevered imagination. Perhaps from Eric Walsh himself. He had it coming to him, that man. I'm delighted it happened when it did!'

Despite his attempt at composure, he had almost yelled the last words about Walsh. It was undoubtedly a mistake, but he didn't see how they could make him pay for it.

Peach allowed the silence after his shout to stretch before he reminded him, 'You were at the Lodge Ladies' Night when this man died, Mr O'Connor.'

'And I left before he was killed. We established that at our last meeting, Inspector.'

'No, Mr O'Connor, we didn't establish it. You told us that it was so.'

'Are you now disputing that I left at eleven fifteen?'

'No. As a matter of fact, we have found one of the hotel staff who supports your story. He confirms that you asked him if the hotel clock in the reception area was right as you went out to your car. It was then ten past eleven.'

'Really? Well, I don't remember that, but no doubt it happened if you say it did.'

'Very fortunately for you, since it confirms your story.'

'Yes. I suppose you're now going to claim I bribed this worker at the White Bull to lie for me.'

'No. He seems genuine enough.'

'I'm glad to hear it.'

'We have also interviewed another hotel worker who watched you extricate your car from a tight space at eleven fifteen.'

Adrian tried hard not to smile. 'I didn't know that.'

'So who do you think killed this man you say deserved all he got?'

Adrian O'Connor had recovered his composure. He made himself take his time over his reply. They weren't going to arrest him, despite this stocky man's truculence. 'I'm happy to say I've no idea who killed Eric Walsh. And I hope you never catch him!'

Seventeen

The morning of Wednesday the fourteenth of November saw the first sharp frost of the winter. The grass was white in the fields and the public park as Peach drove to work. A brilliant sun burnished the autumn gold of the trees with new bright reds and oranges after the frost. It was altogether a wonderful morning to be alive. Unless, of course, you had a meeting with Superintendent Tommy Bloody Tucker as your first duty of the day.

Percy had had an interesting conversation with the forensic laboratory at Chorley before he left home, which meant that Tucker was in the station before him. As Peach climbed out of his police Mondeo, he saw malicious intent in the bright eyes of one of the station pigeons. Sure enough, within two seconds it defecated copiously and accurately on to the very middle of the windscreen of Superintendent Tucker's dark blue BMW. Peach turned back to his car and produced the last quarter of a bag of crisps. Even so plump a bird deserved a reward.

Perhaps today wasn't to be such a bad day after all.

Tucker was bright and cheerful when Peach had climbed the stairs to the penthouse office. 'Made an arrest yet, Percy?' he asked breezily.

'No, sir. You'll be the first to know when we do.' It was always a sign of danger when Tucker used his first name.

'You must be getting nearer after four days' work with a full murder team. It'll be a week since the murder come Friday night, you know. Most murders are solved during the first week. A high proportion of those where an arrest has not been made after a week remain unsolved.'

Tucker quoted the facts that every raw recruit knew as if they were his original thoughts. Master's degree in the blindin' bleedin' obvious, thought Percy. 'Yes, sir. I'm bearing that in mind. Let's hope we can produce something significant by Friday.'

'Yes. I'd expect that from a man who was twisting my arm to become a chief inspector.'

Percy took a deep breath and decided to ignore this. 'Looks odds-on it being one of your Masonic friends, sir.' He brightened visibly at the prospect.

Tucker frowned. 'I don't want you jumping to any conclusions, Peach.'

Percy hadn't lasted long as the preferred mode of address, then. 'They're proving to be a pretty devious lot, sir, your colleagues in the North Brunton Lodge, if you don't mind my saying so.'

'I do mind, Peach, unless you have very clear grounds for your views, which I don't believe you can have.'

Peach allowed himself the blandest of smiles before he warmed to the task. 'I'll start at the top: the Master of the Lodge, John Whiteman.'

'A man of shining reputation and impeccable judgement. I told you that when you brought up his name before.' Tucker leaned forward confidentially. 'I may tell you, in the strictest confidence, that I have reason to believe John will support my own claims for the Mastership in a year or two.'

'Impeccable judgement, then, as you say, sir. But that judgement seems to have failed him when it came to Eric Walsh.'

'I can't think that John Whiteman would be in any way involved in—'

'Of course, I should think it would affect your judgement if you found that your wife was dropping her drawers to the local Pavarotti. Never happened to me, more's the pity – I'd have waved a grateful goodbye to *my* wife. But once a man finds he's a cuckold, his judgement tends to fly out of the window, in my experience.'

171

Tucker was aghast. 'You're telling me that Ros Whiteman, the Master's lady, was conducting an affair with Eric Walsh? That is quite incred—'

'Dropping her drawers on a regular basis, sir, on her own admission. Amazing what goes on in Masonic circles.' He leaned towards his chief, as if struck by a sudden thought. 'I don't suppose you've had the benefit of the lady's favours, yourself, sir, have you? I seem to remember you being very taken with her when we last spoke. By Jove, but you're a dark horse! I can begin to see some point in all this Masonic stuff, if—'

'Peach! Your imagination is running riot! Not for the first time, I may say. Kindly confine yourself to information about whatever suspects you have been able to turn up.'

'Yes, sir. Well, there's the Whitemans, for a start.'

'Both of them? Surely it must have occurred even to your limited brain that if Ros Whiteman was conducting a relationship with Eric Walsh she was hardly likely to kill him?'

'Good point, that, sir. Very good. But the affair was all over. She found that Eric the nightingale had been removing the drawers from other women whilst swearing his allegiance to her. Very nasty. So was her reaction to this discovery. She's got to be a candidate for throttling the nightingale, sir. A woman could easily have done it, the post-mortem says. Or she could have employed someone else to do the dirty work for her.'

'A crime of passion, you mean? I suppose it's possible, if we accept your startling proposition that such a fragrant lady could be two-timing her husband.'

'Fragrant, sir? Yes, I like that word. Seem to remember you using it before about the lady. Didn't I recall a judge using it about another lady, in a different context? However, we haven't found anyone who saw Ros Whiteman with her hands round the victim's throat. Or anywhere else, for that matter. But we have caught her husband out in a few lies, sir. Your close friend John Whiteman, solicitor and Worshipful Master of the Lodge.'

'Not the Worshipful Master until he's finished his year of

office, strictly speaking, Peach. And not a close friend of mine. A man of high reputation and judgement was all I said.'

No rat could desert a sinking ship with more speed, thought Peach. 'Impeccable, sir, I think you said. Well, we've found him distinctly peccable. Pretended to us he knew nothing about his wife's affair, when in fact he knew all about it. Told us he had never left the bar of the White Bull between eleven twenty and twelve on Friday night, when in fact he had sneaked out for ten minutes during that key period.'

'John Whiteman was chatting with a group of us after the formal part of the evening was over. Who told you he left the bar during that time?'

'His wife, sir. She could be lying, of course, but I'm sure such a fragrant lady will be accurate. Besides, we've checked it with the hotel staff; they remember him going out of the bar.'

'Why did he leave?'

'He says to go to the gents' cloakroom.'

'The most obvious reason. And probably a genuine one.'

'Yes, sir. Except that he didn't just go there. He went out to Eric Walsh's Triumph Stag in the car park.'

'Good heavens! Are you sure of this?'

'Absolutely, sir. He's admitted it. But not at first. Only when he was forced into confessing it. The scene-of-crime boys found a credit card slip beside the car, which brooked no argument.'

The superintendent stared uncomprehendingly at his inspector. The Master of the Lodge a murderer? Tucker's world was collapsing about his ears. He said dully, 'Has he admitted to the murder?'

'No, sir. He says Eric Walsh was dead behind the wheel when he got there. That he went out there to have a frank exchange about his wife and found a stiff waiting. He would say that, sir, wouldn't he?'

Tucker stared bleakly at his desk for a moment, then decided reluctantly that he must support his team. 'Yes, he would. Have you arrested him?'

'No, sir, not yet. I'm letting him contemplate his situation. Seeing whether he'll come up with anything else. Same with his wife.' He shook his head dolefully, then brightened again. 'There are other suspects, you see, sir. Other dubious characters among your friends at the Lodge.'

'Others? But surely—'

'The killer is usually to be found among the victim's intimates, I remember you saying, sir. Very illuminating, we all thought it at the time.' Don't think you have a monopoly on the blindin' bleedin' obvious, Tommy Bloody Tucker. 'Eric Walsh was a single man, a Mason of long standing, who found many of his close friends – male friends anyway – among the Lodge members. So we have investigated those intimates in accordance with your advice, sir. And very revealing it's proved to be.'

Tucker said faintly, 'You don't mean you've found more . . . more . . .'

'More suspects, sir? Oh, yes. Some pretty devious characters amongst the members of your Lodge, sir. Surprising, really. But it wouldn't surprise you, sir, no doubt. Because you'd be well aware of my finding that a Freemason in this area is four times as likely to commit a serious crime as an ordinary citizen!' Peach inserted his favourite statistic with characteristic relish.

'I'm well aware of that claim of yours, because you shove it down my throat at every opportunity.'

'Sorry, sir. I expect I am a little too zealous at times. But I regard you as our mole planted within this dangerous organization. Careless of any danger to his person. Vigilant but unsuspected.' Peach contemplated this unlikely scenario for a moment, then shook his head at the wonder of it.

Tucker's jaw had dropped at the mention of danger. He said huskily, 'You're telling me you have found other suspects among the Lodge members?'

'Two more at the moment, sir. Making four in all, with the Whitemans.' He leaned towards the big desk, looked over his shoulder at the closed door, and said in a low

174

voice, 'There may be others whom we haven't turned up yet.'

Tucker closed his eyes and hoped that this wasn't happening. But when he opened them he found Peach still there, staring at him earnestly. Tucker had the sudden thought as he looked into those dark pupils that Rasputin would have looked just like this, if you took away the beard and the hair on the top of his head. The superintendent said, 'You'd better let me have your thoughts, however unlikely.'

'Keep you briefed, sir, as you say!' Peach's energy seemed to increase as his chief's bearing grew more sickly, as if he fed parasitically upon the other man's life-force. 'There's your friend Darren Cartwright, sir, for starters.'

'Not my friend, Peach.' Tucker's faint, automatic protestation came as though it was spoken through a blanket.

'Glad to hear it, sir. Cartwright Financial Services is straightforward enough. Offers advice with investments, helps people with capital to make even more money, that sort of thing. But we've suspected for some time that he was operating a seedy loan-shark business. Lending at high rates to desperate people and sending in the heavies when they default on payments. As always happens eventually, the heavies went too far and put a woman in hospital: young single mother trying to rear two children on her own. She's prepared to put the finger on your friend – sorry, your acquaintance – Darren Cartwright.'

'I'd never have thought it. He was always so polite to me at the Lodge nights.' Tucker contemplated this evidence of stainless character for a moment. 'But it doesn't make him a murderer, you know.'

'No, sir. You see the weakness in a case with your usual swift acumen, if I may say so. But there is more. Last week he was scared stiff about these threats on his life; this week he seems to have forgotten all about them. Curious, that.'

Tucker had been searching his battered brain for something he knew was there. Now he suddenly found it. 'But a man has to have opportunity as well as motive for murder. Darren

Cartwright didn't have the opportunity. He wasn't at the Ladies' Night last Friday.'

'Ahhh!' Peach drew out the syllable, then paused for a moment, allowing Tucker the delicious notion that he was disappointed. He was in fact elated, since Tucker seemed to have forgotten what he had told him earlier in the week about Cartwright. 'Strictly speaking, you are correct, sir. As Darren Cartwright was at pains to insist himself, he was not at the Ladies' Night. He was, however, at the White Bull on Friday night, as you may remember. He lied about it, but eventually he admitted he was there.'

'Why was he there?'

'Dropped in for a quiet drink, he said.'

Tucker digested this. 'That doesn't sound very likely, you know.'

'That's just what DS Blake and I thought, sir! Glad to have confirmation from the mind at the top, as always. First of all Cartwright tried to conceal his presence, then he said he had just dropped in for a drink. But it's not his local, sir. Nor is he in the habit of using the White Bull as a watering hole. We've now established that. Which makes his presence there last Friday night all the more interesting.'

'But was he there at the time when Eric Walsh was killed?'

'You go to the heart of the matter as usual, sir. And the answer to your question is most interesting. He says he wasn't. Says he left when last orders in the pub were called, that he was away before quarter past eleven. But we don't think he was. The public part of the hotel doesn't close until eleven thirty on Friday nights. If he was there when it closed, as he admitted to us he was, then he was around at the time when Walsh died.'

'You should question him again, you know. Press him hard about these things. And you could throw in all this stuff about the loan-sharking at the same time.'

The most annoying thing of all about practitioners of the blindin' bleedin' obvious was that they thought they were offering original insights, thought Percy Peach. He said tersely,

'Glad you think that, sir. I plan to see him again later today, with DS Blake.'

'You mustn't let the fact that he is a Freemason, and an acquaintance of mine, in any way affect your judgement. Press him hard.' Tucker stuck out his jaw in a belated assertion of leadership.

'Yes, sir.' Peach nodded several times, as if accepting an idea he would never have thought of himself. Then his face lit up with a happy inspiration. 'Should we try to lure him into a confession, sir? Get him off his guard? I could get DS Blake to flash a bit of gusset at him, let him think he was on to an easy thing, and allow her to persuade him into admissions. We could—'

'Nothing like that, Peach! Extracting information like that is as worthless as getting it from prisoners under duress, when it comes to a court of law. You must realize that.'

'No gusset, sir? Not even a quick flash to—'

'Nothing at all of that sort! Those are my express orders.'

Peach sighed histrionically. 'Very well, sir. There's another leading suspect among your Lodge friends, though. Adrian O'Connor.'

'He's no friend of mine, Peach! I distinctly remember telling you that earlier in the week. He's a Catholic, you know.'

Peach wondered again about his chief as a pillar of ecumenical Christianity. 'Yes, sir, we do know. And he and Eric Walsh go back a long way. They were involved in the sectarian violence of Belfast in the 1980s.'

Tucker thought for a moment, then nodded sagely. Sage nodding was one of the gestures he was good at: Peach sometimes wondered if he practised it in front of a mirror. 'This may very well be your man, you know.'

'Glad to hear such an objective view, sir. Walsh's Protestant brother seduced O'Connor's Catholic sister in 1988: a highly dangerous thing to do in the Shankill area at that or any other time.'

'Romeo and Juliet, eh?' Tucker was pleased to dredge up a literary reference to keep his underling in his place.

'Nothing like that, sir. It seems the Walshes weren't serious about the girl at all. She was to be a Catholic trophy to be brandished amidst the petrol bombs and the street violence. The girl committed suicide in 1989.'

'And you think Adrian O'Connor might have been pursuing revenge?'

Peach nodded. 'It's a long time later. But Walsh got out hastily after the IRA ambushed his brother and made a career for himself, initially in Europe, then over here. There's some evidence that O'Connor was pursuing him. He works for the Shell Oil Company, and he seems to have taken a post in this area principally to get near to Eric Walsh.'

'He hasn't been a member of the North Brunton Masonic Lodge for very long, you know.'

'Just over three years,' said Peach patiently. 'Did you see any evidence of animosity between O'Connor and Eric Walsh?'

Tucker frowned. 'He's a fairly low-key member, Adrian O'Connor. Doesn't say a lot. But he could well be your man. I remember him not applauding once, after Eric Walsh had sung.'

Peach didn't see that as the clinching piece of evidence in a dramatic murder trial, even in the hands of a trenchant QC. 'We're following up our earlier enquiries, sir. And you're right: O'Connor is a practising Catholic, a regular church attender.'

'Ahh!' Tucker sat back in his chair, feeling the pieces of the jigsaw falling into place, gratified by his key contributions as leader of the team.

Peach let him enjoy the moment for a few seconds before he said, 'There is one snag, though. Adrian O'Connor appears to have left the gathering some time before Eric Walsh was actually murdered.'

Tucker looked glum as the vision of an arrest melted from his fevered imagination. 'You mustn't just take his word for that, you know. He could be lying. Probe, Peach, probe!'

'I'm afraid his departure has been confirmed by two members of the hotel staff, sir, as well as his fellow Lodge members.

He seems to have driven away from the White Bull before eleven twenty.'

'Ahh!' This time the long syllable was filled with disappointment, not satisfaction. The superintendent gathered his remaining resources and said sternly, 'But have you just been ferreting around among members of the Lodge? Your preoccupation with Masonic crime is something of a fetish, Peach. It does you no credit, you know. It does not denote the objectivity I should be entitled to expect in a chief inspector.' He was pleased he had remembered to dangle the carrot again, after belabouring his man with the stick. Good man-management, that.

Peach was tempted to tell him to stick his promotion where monkeys put their nuts. But he resisted; he was getting better at resisting temptation, he thought. Perhaps his off-duty activities with Lucy Blake were relaxing his tensions: he made a note to redouble his efforts in that field. He said slowly, 'There is one other person who has been lying, sir. A member of the staff of the White Bull. He actually persuaded a member of the kitchen staff there to give us false information.'

'Ah! This is much more promising. This is a much more likely source of criminal violence.'

'Yes, sir. Would you like to interrogate the man yourself, sir?'

'No, no, I'm not suggesting that. You know I never like to interfere unless it is absolutely necessary. I wouldn't be putting your name forward for promotion unless I had absolute confidence in you.'

Unless it was absolutely essential if you are to secure the rank of chief superintendent for yourself, you mean, you old fraud. 'Yes, sir. Well, it's the young fellow I mentioned at our last meeting, sir. A man who was attending to your needs earlier in the evening, sir. One of the staff in the hotel.'

'So he was in touch with Eric Walsh at that time. And possibly before that time. And no doubt he had some real or imagined grievance against poor Eric which made him offer violence to the man.'

'Perhaps, sir. We haven't established that yet.'

'Then you must do so with all possible speed. I shan't interfere, but my feeling, based on years of experience with serious crime, is that this could well be your man. *Our* man, I should say.'

'You're not suggesting that I should manufacture evidence, sir?'

'No, no, Peach, of course I wouldn't suggest that. But there is nothing wrong with showing an appropriate zeal, is there?'

Peach allowed his puzzled frown to evaporate slowly. 'You're suggesting a bit of third degree, sir? The old light in the subject's face during the interview, the injury as he falls down the stairs to the cell! Right, sir, say no more. I didn't think we could get away with these things in the twenty-first century, but it's good to have a man at the helm who knows the way to get results and is prepared to take responsibility for it! Just wait till I tell the lads you've given the okay for—'

'Peach! I am suggesting no such thing. Put it out of your mind altogether. I'm simply suggesting that there are ways of interviewing young thugs to get what we want from them. Now, has this man got previous convictions?'

Peach sighed. Alzheimer's was a terrible thing in someone as young as Tucker. 'He smashed up old Harry Alston's corner shop only last week, sir, if you remember. And got away with a caution, on the condition that he make full retribution to the owner of the premises. Harry wouldn't bring charges, or we might have had the man behind bars. Except that some bloody JP would have told him to wash his hands and be a good boy.' A surge of genuine irritation broke through Peach's Tucker façade.

'Anything else against him?'

'He's been passing drugs, sir. The lad he tried to persuade to lie for him has had drugs from him. Only soft, as far as we can tell, but we could probably make a case against him as a pusher.'

'Then get out there and pressurize him. Lean on him. Get a confession of murder out of him, and we can wrap this up.'

'Yes, sir. Of course, we're not sure he actually killed Eric Walsh, as yet.'

'He's just the type of young thug who would do a thing like that. Probably over no more than a few quid or a petty argument. He shouldn't have been allowed to get away with that assault on old Harry Alston last week. What's this man's name again, by the way?'

Peach sighed. He'd seen sharper memories in homes for the elderly. 'Afzaal, sir.'

Consternation replaced confidence on Tucker's face with the speed of light. 'Afzaal?'

'Wasim Afzaal, sir. And if you remember, sir, you were most anxious last week that we should not bring a prosecution over the damage to Mr Alston and his shop.'

'This is a prominent Asian family, Peach. Public relations are most important at this time. I thought you said the man concerned was a member of the staff of the White Bull.'

'Yes, sir. Wasim Afzaal is currently working there as part of a three-month university industrial placement. I understand he's reading for a degree in hotel and catering, sir.'

'This man's father is a prominent member of our local community, Peach. We mustn't offend him. Any hint of racial prejudice will cause immense harm.'

Most of the prejudice in this bloody nick is right at the top, thought Percy. He said, 'I see, sir. Does that mean that I drop the investigation of young Wasim Afzaal as a murder suspect? Is he no longer in the frame?'

'No, of course I don't mean that. I never interfere, as you should know by now. But go easy. Tread the path with kid gloves.'

Peach wrinkled his brow with the effort of assimilating this. He said nothing for a moment, then shook his head violently, as if clearing it of some harmful gas. 'That's it, as far as major suspects go, sir. Five in the frame at the moment. Four Masons and a university student. I think we could regard Mrs

181

Whiteman as a Mason for this purpose.' His face lightened with a sudden thought. 'This rather neatly bears out my theory that a Freemason in this area is four times as likely to commit a serious crime as an ordinary citizen, doesn't it, sir?'

'Get about your business, Peach. I have things to do.' Tucker picked up the single sheet of paper on his desk and waved it vaguely through the air.

Glancing through the window on his way back down the stairs, Percy Peach noted that another pigeon had crapped copiously on Tucker's new BMW. It must surely be a happy omen for the rest of the day.

Eighteen

Jack Chadwick was waiting patiently in Peach's small office. He studied the inspector carefully when he returned: sometimes Peach's temper was not at its best after a session with Tucker.

Today was not one of those days. Peach began with a short diversion on whether it might be possible to train pigeons to defecate in patterns on particular vehicles, then said, 'You must have something for me, Jack, or you wouldn't be here. You're not one for wasting time on social chit-chat.'

'The computer buffs have been busy. They've managed to get into the files on Eric Walsh's computer.'

'I thought it had been wrecked by whoever broke into the house on the night of his murder.'

Chadwick gave the superior smile of those who recognize technological illiteracy. 'It was just the monitor that was smashed, Percy. The computer itself seemed more or less intact. I told you the boffins would probably get into it, eventually. But you can't just access what you want: you need passwords to get into the files. Don't ask me how they do it, but the lads who know seem able to get into anything, given enough time.'

'And what have they found?'

'Some distinctly interesting material. Some stuff about Loyalist groups in Northern Ireland, which is probably out of date, but we'll pass on the names to the right people. A short file on Adrian O'Connor and his associates: doesn't tell us much, I'm afraid, but it shows that Walsh was scared of him. It looks as if he wanted to make up some sort of dossier on him, perhaps to hand over to us. But there's nothing very damaging on it. The other interesting file contains some ladies' names which you and I would know. Strictly in a professional capacity, of course.'

'Local Toms?'

'Many of them are known prostitutes, yes. But there are some others who may sell it from time to time but haven't got convictions. Ladies who don't walk the streets but are available for sex discreetly – at the right price, of course. The top end of the market.'

'Eric Walsh was pimping?'

Chadwick shrugged. 'It'd be difficult to prove that now, as well as pointless. There's no evidence he took a cut from the women. Maybe he just charged the men for putting them in touch. Maybe he sold them the list. Or perhaps he just expected favours in return for access to his list of available totty. One thing's pretty certain: the information would be expensive. There are some highly middle-class ladies on his list, who certainly wouldn't sell themselves cheaply.'

Chadwick smiled happily, as he always did when he unearthed corruption among the bourgeoisie of East Lancashire.

Peach grinned at his colleague. 'It's no use trying to sell the names to me, Jack. I can't afford it and I'm not interested. It's an interesting sidelight on Eric the randy nightingale, but hardly relevant to his death.'

'It could be.' Sergeant Chadwick, whose virtues were thorough exploration of the mundane and meticulous attention to detail, enjoyed being enigmatic when the opportunity arose.

Peach played along with him and grinned. 'All right, Jack. Tell me how it's going to help.'

'There's another list. A list of men's names. Cross-referenced with the list of women. Some interesting local dignitaries are on it. There are one or two of Walsh's Masonic friends. And a name that I knew would interest you because it's already come into your investigation.'

Peach knew his line in this little cameo. 'And who would that be?'

'A certain Wasim Afzaal.'

Whilst Peach reviewed the situation with Tucker and gathered new snippets from Chadwick, John Whiteman, respected East Lancashire solicitor and Master of the North Brunton Masonic Lodge, was getting increasingly restless in the imposing Victorian building where he worked.

Conveyancing property was boring work at the best of times, and when you had become involved in a murder investigation, you had other and more important things pounding at your mind. At eleven o'clock, John gave up the unequal struggle and left the office.

He had no clear idea where he was going when he eased the big Jaguar on to Preston New Road and drove out of the town. He thought of going for an early drink in one of the big, soulless main-road pubs. But he was too well known a figure in the area; he was almost sure to meet someone he knew, and he knew now that casual conversation was not the diversion he sought.

Almost before he realized that he had decided on this course, he found himself driving into the familiar curving drive of his own large house.

At first, he thought that Ros was out. He wandered through the downstairs rooms of the house, calling her name uncertainly, wondering whether he was pleased with the solitude that her absence afforded him or disappointed that she was not here. Then he thought he heard a sound on the terrace behind the house, and when he went into the conservatory they had added two years earlier, she stood in the doorway, easing off the short wellington boots she wore for gardening. There was mud on her thick blue denims, a smudge of dirt on her cheek, a tiny twig caught in her tousled dark hair. She looked at once healthy, competent and vulnerable.

A wheelbarrow full of autumn refuse was behind her. He saw in curious, useless detail the yellowing tops of perennials which had finished flowering, the sodden stalks and blackened flowers of dahlias finished by last night's frost, a few early rose prunings. He smiled weakly at her. And then he heard himself saying ridiculously, 'You've been working hard in the garden, then.'

Ros said, 'Yes. It was a nice day for it, after the frost. There's still a bit of warmth in the sun.'

They were two polite strangers, greasing the wheels of an unexpected meeting with safe small talk. Both of them wondered if it would be like this forever. Whether forever would even include the other. She had told him last night about her affair with Eric Walsh, in acrid, staccato phrases. And he had told her that he had known about it, had known for a full week before Walsh's death.

She said, 'Do you want coffee?' She looked at the garden refuse piled high on the wheelbarrow, as though registering it for the first time, and said, 'I think I've earned a break.'

'I'll put the kettle on.' He was glad of the release from her presence, of the relief offered by the small, mundane physical activity of taking the electric jug to the tap, of putting teaspoonfuls of instant coffee into the familiar china mugs which seemed suddenly alien. He knew for the first time what that expression about being a stranger in one's own house meant.

He realized when he took the tray into the sitting room that she had been watching his movements through the open door of the kitchen, sitting on the edge of an armchair like a visitor who had called on a charity collection and been invited into a situation where she did not feel comfortable. She took the coffee, refused the biscuit, as both of them had known she would, and eased herself back into the chair with an awkward movement which both of them noticed.

They sipped coffee in a tense silence, neither of them looking at each other, both of them staring through the wide window at the borders where she had been working. She said eventually, 'We're not the first couple to have to contend with something like this. It's common enough, nowadays. One of the factors in modern marriages.'

He said, 'Yes. I didn't believe it would ever happen to

me, that's all.' He thought of the increasing divorce business which passed through the office nowadays, of the way it had emerged from a few exceptional instances to a feature which was perhaps the most important and lucrative aspect of their work in the thirty years he had worked in the family practice.

She said, 'It was the one and only time, you know.'

'So you say.' He let the bitterness hang in the simple phrase, the monosyllables sour in his mouth as he spoke them. He believed her, but to acknowledge that he did would have seemed like weakness. When she said nothing more in mitigation, he eventually heard himself saying, 'Anyway, he's dead now.'

Still they did not look at each other, but from the corner of his eye he was watching to see if she winced, if he could hurt her with the iteration of her lover's death. Instead, she turned upon him suddenly and said viciously, 'You're glad about that, aren't you? Well, let me tell you, so am I! I told you, it was all over between the two of us. I was just an easy lay for him.'

He was shaken by the vehemence of this sudden directness. Eventually he said lamely, 'I'm sorry.'

'You shouldn't be. It should be music in your ears. Stupid middle-aged woman gets out of her emotional depth. Thinks she can still find love but ends up with a quick fuck!'

She spat the obscenity that he had never heard from her before, and it cut into him more than all the frantic shouting of the night before. He caught something of the passion she had felt for the dead man, and with it he saw the dead embers of their own passion, of the love which had grown cold and died with the years of dullness. But he couldn't help himself or her, couldn't stretch out his arms to try to bring them together. He said flatly, 'I accept that you're glad he's dead. You sound as bitter as I did when I found out. But I had two people to loathe. I hated you as well as Eric.'

She knew she should ask him if he still felt that hatred for her, should allow him to put down the first stones of the bridge which might eventually bring them back together. But she didn't know whether she wanted that, even if it should be offered. So she said nothing.

Eventually John produced the small lie which would end this and get him out of the house. He said, 'I must go. I've people to see back at the office.'

Ros nodded bleakly, happy to accept that he would depart with no progress made, that he would regret that he had broken his normal habit by coming here at this time of the day.

John Whiteman drove down a country lane and parked in a spot by a quiet reach of the River Hodder, where he knew that his dead father had fished for trout sixty years ago as a young man. His wife at home had not moved from the chair where he had left her, staring at the familiar garden which had seemed a source of therapy but which was now a foreign tract.

Each was thinking not of the affair but of what had followed. Each was wondering at that moment whether the other had murdered the third party in this triangle, Eric Walsh.

Inspector Peach seated himself comfortably beside DS Blake on the sofa in Wasim Afzaal's flat. He looked round at the expensively framed prints of Constable and Turner, at the very English wallpaper and furnishings. It would have been rudeness in an ordinary visitor; in a detective it was no more than careful, professional observation. He savoured the young man's discomfort without acknowledging it and then said unhurriedly, 'Nice place you've got here.'

Wasim acknowledged the cliché with a wan smile. 'You didn't come here to inspect the décor, Inspector Peach.'

'No. We're here because you've been a bad lad again, young Wasim. Exactly how bad remains to be seen.'

'I don't know what you mean. If you're still on about that bloody murder, I've nothing more to tell you.'

Peach had long since ceased to be surprised by a Lancashire accent coming from a Pakistani face. This accent seemed stronger now than previously; perhaps that came with the young man's vehemence. Or perhaps he found it useful at his university to be one of the boys; sometimes it was the ostensibly liberal institutions which carried unconscious prejudice. The inspector studied Afzaal unhurriedly. The young man was in casual dress, but it was not standard university gear. He wore not jeans but trousers, immaculately creased. The shoes were Gucci, the dark green sweater had the Pringle logo. Peach said evenly, 'You're in trouble lad. We can do this at the station if you don't want to do it here.'

Wasim glanced from Peach's round, implacable face to the softer one beside him, betraying his uncertainty in the movement. He tried to sound truculent as he said, 'And what if I refuse to go?'

'Would look very bad from our point of view, wouldn't it, DS Blake? And we could arrest you on suspicion, if you forced us into it. Hold you for twenty-four hours for questioning. Of course, we'd like to avoid that, if possible, because word gets round about these things and starts all sorts of unwarranted rumours, but if you're telling us that's the only way you're going to—'

'All right. I'll be as helpful as I can. Though I can't see what I can possibly add to what I've already volunteered.'

Peach smiled. 'Funny word, that. "Volunteered". And in this case wholly inaccurate. Everything we've so far had from you we've had to drag out of you, lad. Told us a pack of lies to start with. Tried to pressurize another witness into lying on your behalf.' He stopped and blew a silent whistle through rounded lips while shaking his head sadly. 'Only hope all that doesn't have to come out in court. It wouldn't sound good for you, would it? Might give the jury in a murder trial an unfavourable initial impression of you.'

'I didn't kill Eric Walsh.'

Peach looked at Lucy Blake and grinned wickedly. She said to the increasingly uneasy young man in front of her, 'You'll need to convince us of that, Wasim. Especially in view of what DI Peach has just pointed out about your previous conduct with us.'

'I'm sorry about that. I shouldn't have tried to deceive you. I

189

was worried about my university course. And about my father. Fathers from our culture tend to have unrealistic expectations of their children. Mine is worse than most. He thinks the eldest son in the family should be a paragon of virtue.'

'Which this one ain't!' said Peach, who came back in delightedly, despite the fact that Wasim had been addressing his appeal to Lucy Blake. 'This is the third time I've seen you in just over a week, Mr Afzaal. On the first occasion, you and your companions had terrorized an elderly local shopkeeper and done serious damage to his premises and his stock. You got off with a caution and with making retribution for the damage you had caused.'

'Which we did, within twenty-four hours.'

Peach went on as if he had never been interrupted. 'On the second occasion, we found that you had tried to suborn a witness, which you denied until you were confronted with the evidence. You then came up with a cock and bull story about your connection with the murder victim. You said that you had been interested in the man's singing, that you had been trying to persuade your father to employ him at some of his functions.'

'I think I admitted at the time that that was rubbish.'

'You did, rather. Though not in so many words. You then said you used to have the occasional drink with Eric Walsh, that you shared a common interest in girls. Distinctly more promising, though you were still holding things back. It went a lot further than a common interest, didn't it?'

'I don't know what you mean by that. I've tried to be frank with you, and all you do is twist everything I say.'

Lucy Blake had her gold ballpoint pen poised over her notebook. So far she hadn't bothered with a single note. She now said quietly, 'The electronics wizards have been examining Mr Walsh's computer files, Wasim. It takes them a little time, but they usually manage to get into whatever system is used, eventually.'

He was clearly shaken. But after a pause, all he said was, 'Good for them. I can't see what relevance that has to me.'

She smiled at him, using her softness where Peach had been all aggression. 'Don't you, Wasim? I think you do. It would be much better if this came from you than from us, you know.'

He looked from her earnest, persuasive face to Peach's happy smile, wanting to talk but finding that denial was all that sprung to his lips. 'I don't know what you're getting at. I want to help, but I can't tell you what I don't know.'

Peach's smile widened. 'What blood group are you, Mr Afzaal?'

The question was so unexpected, appeared so much a diversion from the previous line of questioning, that Wasim replied quite readily, 'AB. Rhesus-negative, I think.'

'Is it really? Reasonably rare blood group, that.' Peach's voice hardened. 'Now, let me tell you an interesting fact, Mr Afzaal. We spoke to you last time we saw you about a break-in at Mr Walsh's house a few hours after he had been brutally murdered. Our scene-of-crime team found a sample of fresh blood on the doorstep of the house, which we assume came from the person who broke in. This morning I had a phone conversation with our forensic laboratory. The blood group of that sample was AB. Rhesus-negative.'

There was a pause in which the traffic outside seemed unnaturally loud, even through the double glazing of this modern flat. Afzaal said hopelessly, 'That isn't conclusive.'

'No. A significant addition to the evidence, though, isn't it? It's a fairly rare group, as I say, which is fortunate – but perhaps not fortunate for you. You broke into the house that night, didn't you?'

Another pause. Then Afzaal said dully, 'I didn't break in. I had a key.'

'And how did you come by that, from a man with whom you only had an occasional drink?'

Wasim stared at Peach's feet. The twinkle of the highly polished black leather seemed to be mocking him. 'He didn't give it to me. I took his keys from his coat pocket.'

'After you'd killed him.'

'No. After someone else had. Mr Davies, the head waiter at

the White Bull, came in and said that Eric had been murdered in his car. He went off to fetch Superintendent Tucker from the bar. I nipped out and took the key from Eric's pocket whilst Davies was fetching Mr Tucker.'

Lucy Blake saw her moment, saw that they must keep him talking now that he had begun. She said softly, 'Eric Walsh had some kind of hold over you, hadn't he, Wasim?'

He nodded, suddenly anxious to explain himself, to try to persuade them that he hadn't committed the worst crime of all. 'It's not complicated. I owed him money. Quite a lot of money. Eight thousand pounds and a few hundred in interest.'

She said, 'We know all about Eric Walsh's lists of women. He supplied you and others with names of women who were prepared to have sex and be paid for it, didn't he?'

'Yes. He didn't charge all that much for the information, I suppose. But it got me in debt to him. And . . . and he lent me money for my gambling. It got into the thousands quite quickly. I kept thinking I'd get it back the next night at the casino.'

He sounded bewildered, as if he couldn't understand why that hadn't happened. It was a tone they had heard often enough before from people with serious gambling debts: there was a curious, fatal innocence about their optimism.

Lucy shook her head, 'It doesn't happen like that. You must know that by now. Was Eric Walsh threatening you about the debt?'

'Not with violence.'

'What, then?'

This time it was Wasim Afzaal who shook his head, violently, as if he might thus clear it of all confusion. 'Nothing. He wouldn't have had me beaten up, Eric. That wasn't his style.'

Peach said harshly, 'You stole a dead man's keys and broke into his house in the hours after he was killed. At the moment, it looks to us as if it was you who tightened that cord around his neck. If you want to convince us you didn't kill Eric Walsh, you'd better start telling us the complete truth, not the snippets you want us to have.'

Wasim looked at Peach as if he would like to have killed him at that moment. The inspector's face did not change; his eyes remained unblinkingly on the delicate, mobile features of the man in the chair opposite him. Wasim eventually dropped his eyes and his slim shoulders at the same time. 'He was threatening to tell my father.'

'And that's all?'

'All! Have you any idea what it would have meant if he'd told my father about the women? About the gambling? About the debt I'd built up?'

Still Peach moved not a muscle. 'My guess is that he'd have paid off Eric Walsh.'

'Oh, he'd have paid, all right! To preserve the family name! To preserve his own honour as a prominent businessman in the town! And I'd have been finished. He'd have stopped my university course, put me to work as a shelf-stacker in his humblest shop, and looked to my younger brothers to take over his business empire. In his eyes, I'd have acquired all the vices of a dissolute Briton. He'd have put me to work in his shops, at the lowest level. If I'd have kept my nose clean for a few years, he might have arranged a low-grade marriage for me. Oh, yes, I would have had everything to look forward to!'

The only sound in the flat at the end of this bitter outburst was of Afzaal's uneven breathing. Lucy Blake said softly, 'I think you exaggerate a little for effect, Wasim.'

He had been shouting at Peach, but now he rounded on her. 'Have you any idea what it's like to belong to a Muslim family in England? Of course you haven't! Listen, to all intents and purposes, I'm British. I was born here, reared here, in English schools, with boys who'd never been outside England. I want to complete my university course and get a job in a hotel, to make my own way, like the other graduates. I *feel* English! I *am* English!'

Peach could have pointed out that he seemed to have taken the worst from the British culture, with his paid sex and his desperate gambling. Instead, he waited for the passionate outburst to end and then said quietly, 'I think we'd accept that. The trouble is, Mr Afzaal, that you've just given us an excellent account of why you might have killed Eric Walsh.'

Nineteen

Agnes Blake picked up the silver-framed photograph of Percy Peach, dusted it thoroughly, and put it carefully back on the sideboard beside that of her dead husband, positioning them carefully so that neither should have precedence.

It was the greatest compliment Percy could have had, thought Lucy Blake as she watched her mother's movements affectionately through the low doorway of the old cottage. There was many a man behind bars who would not have recognized this picture of Percy Peach. Agnes had found a photograph in the files of the *Lancashire Evening Telegraph* which showed a very different side of the man. This smile was not the hunter's smile which criminals knew so well. It was the happy, almost boyish, smile of a man at play, a man who returns to the schoolboy he thought was long left behind.

Peach was dressed in white and carried a cricket bat. He wore a red cap at a rakish angle, covering the familiar bald head. Even the name was different: the black letters inscribed beneath the photograph in Agnes Blake's careful hand read: 'DCS Peach, after making 53 off 48 balls against Haslingden, 1998.'

This must be about the only place where Percy was afforded his full and proper forenames of Denis Charles Scott. He had been named after the legendary Denis Compton, the 'gay cavalier of cricket', the favourite batsman of his dead father and, more surprisingly, of Agnes Blake. 'Percy' Peach was a name devised by a police service which loved alliteration. Few people nowadays understood the significance of Percy's initials; fewer still revelled in them as delightedly as the sixty-eight-year-old Mrs Blake.

Agnes turned to find that her daughter had been watching her in the contemplation of the two men in cricket clothing, Percy and her dead husband. Like most Lancashire women of her era, she was embarrassed to be caught indulging a moment of sentiment. So she said briskly, 'You shouldn't creep up on people like that, our Lucy. Your washing's dry and folded near the back door. Don't forget it when you go.'

Lucy understood exactly that she had caught the older woman off guard. She said, 'You really shouldn't be doing my washing any more, you know. I've got my own machine in the flat.'

'Ay, I know. But it'll save you a bit of time. You're always short of time, you working women.'

Lucy came into the room and looked at the photographs of her dead father and Percy, standing together in joint preeminence on the sideboard. 'I'm glad you took to Percy, Mum.'

'Your Dad would have liked him. It's a pity they never met.'

Lucy looked down at the older picture, of her father Bill, with a shy, exhausted smile, taken after he had taken 6 for 44 against Blackpool. 'The paper said that even Rohan Kanhai had to treat him with respect that day.' Lucy quoted the familiar words before her mother could come out with them, teasing the older woman in the affectionate way daughters have with mothers they love.

'Ay! Well, it's true enough, however much you like to mock your old mother. You two moved in with each other yet, then?'

'Mother!' Lucy was genuinely shocked. With the unconscious arrogance of youth, she believed that sex had only really begun when she discovered it. To have a parent mentioning your love life was really quite unnerving. 'No, we haven't! I have my own flat and Percy has his house.'

'You won't do better, you know. He's a good lad, is Percy,

even if he's a bit older than you. He won't let you down, you know.'

It should have warmed her, to hear such approbation of her choice from her mother. But she wasn't ready for such frankness. 'We're happy as we are, thank you,' she said primly.

'Ay. And meantime I get older, and still no grandchildren. Time you made an honest man of him!' She smiled at her own little joke, enjoyed reversing the usual cliché, and enjoyed discomfiting Lucy even more.

'It's not straightforward, Mum. Not in the police service. We work together, you see. You're not supposed to have serious relationships with people you work closely with.'

'Serious relationships!' Agnes sneered at this modern evasion. 'You're not supposed to sleep together, you mean. Have to conceal it from people higher up the ranks, do you?'

It was too near the mark for comfort. If Tommy Bloody Tucker had been more in touch, he'd have seen how things were and separated them months ago. 'We have to be discreet, sometimes, yes. But we like working together. I wouldn't like that to end.'

'Well, you'll have to make your mind up, won't you? Time a lass of your age was thinking of getting wed. High time, if you ask me! Time you got yourself out of that dangerous job. You could have been killed last year, without Percy!'

It was true enough: she had almost been killed by a man who was now locked away in Broadmoor, a former colleague. She didn't care to remember the details. 'That was quite exceptional, Mum. It won't happen again.'

Agnes sniffed dismissively. 'So you say. Anyway, it's time you two made it legal, if you ask me. You're right for each other.'

Lucy smiled fondly at the ageing, anxious face. 'It's nice to have parental approval, anyway. But things aren't always as straightforward as they seem to you, Mum.'

It was a picturesque run back to grimy Brunton on that frosty Thursday morning as she drove her bulbous blue Corsa over the wide sweep of the Ribble at Ribchester and through the vivid autumn colours. But Lucy saw little of the morning, for she was busy wondering whether her mother might not be right after all.

She would have liked to know what Percy Peach thought about the matter.

Darren Cartwright sent his secretary out for the morning to investigate a new source of office supplies. He didn't want her around when Peach came; she might hear things which she should not through the thin wall which divided her outer office from his room.

Within minutes of the inspector's arrival with DS Blake, Darren was glad of this precaution. Peach had grounds now to arrest Cartwright, if he decided to do so. He no longer felt any need to disguise his dislike of the man. 'We need information from you, Mr Cartwright. A frank and full discussion. Here or at the station, whichever you prefer.'

'I'll help you in any way I can; that goes without saying. But I really can't see how I'm—'

'You can start by telling me why you employed two men to beat up a young mother on Tuesday evening.'

Darren hadn't expected this. When Lucy Blake had made the appointment she had said on the phone that it was in connection with developments in the investigation of the murder of Eric Walsh, and Darren had prepared himself accordingly. To have his involvement in loan-sharking challenged head-on like this threw him completely off balance. He said, 'I really don't know which young mother or which men you're referring to. A case of mistaken identity, I'm sure.'

Peach looked at him with a cold smile, like a tiger preparing to capture its dinner. 'No mistake, Mr Cartwright. Mrs Kershaw is in hospital, but one of our officers is outside the ward, in case you get any ideas of further intimidation. And your two gorillas are presently helping us with our enquiries.'

That was rather an exaggeration, since the two men were sitting in separate cells and refusing to talk. But it was only a matter of time, in Percy's view: those buggers hadn't yet had the full frontal onslaught of Peach himself. He watched as Cartwright thrashed around in his net. 'Cartwright Financial Services is a respectable organization. There is no way in which—'

'Cartwright Financial Services may be just that. I'm sure that everything which goes through the books is dull but respectable. I can't say the same for your other activities.'

'Other activities? I really think—'

'Loan-sharking. The thing we touched on in our last meeting, Mr Cartwright. Lending at excessive rates of interest to poor desperate sods who can't see what they're letting themselves in for.' Percy found himself breathing hard; he was having to control the genuine anger which he knew got in the way of efficiency.

It was Lucy Blake who said evenly, 'We now know all about your less publicized activities, Mr Cartwright. We can provide chapter and verse, whenever it should be necessary. The CID at Brunton has been interested in you for some time, you see. There are others, as well as Mrs Kershaw, who will act as witnesses when these matters come to court.' She was anxious to protect the young mother from intimidation when she came out of hospital: if she were the only witness she could well be in danger.

The mention of court proceedings deflated Cartwright. He repeated the feeble mantra he had ready for these accusations. 'It's not against the law to lend money. You try to help people; if they get themselves into difficulties with repayments, that is their own fault.'

Peach was back in control of himself and the situation. 'That is something which may well be tested in court. I'm sure a jury would be interested in the rates of interest you charge and the terms of repayment demanded. What is clearly illegal is your method of enforcement. The violence you have ordered against Mrs Kershaw and others will probably merit a custodial sentence.' He grinned in anticipation of that happy outcome.

Cartwright's smile was sickly. 'My assistants are strictly forbidden to use violence in the collection of debts.'

'Not what they say, sunshine.'

'I emphasize to them in all my orders that they shouldn't use force. It's even down in writing.'

'Perhaps you should employ heavies who can read, then. They seemed to have a pretty clear idea of what their duty was. And it wasn't to behave gently.' Peach sighed. 'But we're not here about that, are we, DS Blake? Not today, anyway. Other CID officers are dealing with that.'

Darren tried hard not to look relieved. 'DS Blake said you had more questions to ask about Eric Walsh.'

'Yes. If we can pin a murder charge on you, loan-sharking will seem almost insignificant. Pity, that would be.'

'I didn't kill Eric Walsh.'

'Glad to hear it. But in view of the state of Mrs Kershaw and your previous pack of lies, you won't expect us to take that on trust.'

'I wasn't even there. I told you, I didn't go to—'

'When we first saw you last week, you were very worried about threats to your life. You were scared enough to be demanding police protection. When we saw you on Monday, you made no mention of this supposed threat to your very existence. Why the sudden change, Mr Cartwright?'

They could almost see the mind working beneath the carefully combed hair and the furrowed forehead. Cartwright apparently decided that in this at any rate honesty was the best policy. 'By Monday, I no longer felt under threat. It was Eric Walsh who was sending me those threatening letters.'

'You knew that at the time when you reported the letters to us? Wasting police time, were you?'

'No. Well, yes, I suppose I was, if I'm completely frank.'

'Much the best policy, Mr Cartwright. Even if it does have an air of novelty about it, for you.'

'Eric was trying to scare me.'

'And why would he want to do that, Mr Cartwright?'

'I owed him money. Not a huge sum, but we were in dispute about it.'

'Money for what?'

Cartwright looked at them sharply, trying to assess how much they knew. He failed. 'Eric was a great man for the women, you know. And he provided . . . well, certain services.'

'He provided lists of drawer-droppers. Women who were prepared to sell themselves.'

'Yes.' Darren Cartwright looked thoroughly miserable with the admission that he had to pay for sex. 'Eric Walsh charged for that information. I hadn't paid him. He was asking for more than we'd agreed. It wasn't a large sum, but it was a matter of principle.'

He looked nervously at Peach, who broke into a delighted grin. 'I was almost believing you, until you spoke about a matter of principle. I'd say you hardly know the meaning of the phrase.'

Cartwright made a weary attempt at protest. 'If you've just come here to be gratuitously insulting, then—'

'You weren't receiving death threats over a trifling sum. There was more than that involved. You said a couple of minutes ago that you were going to be completely frank.'

Darren had a hunted look now. They probably know all about this anyway, he thought. 'All right. He was blackmailing me. I'd made him a couple of payments, but he wanted more. More than I could possibly afford.'

'He knew about the loan-sharking?'

'Yes. He never called it that. He always spoke about the "unofficial aspect of your business empire". He had information about a bit of persuasion that went wrong, last year. Threatened to give it to you people.'

'He knew about the man who was roughed up so badly he lost an eye?'

'Yes. Your people tried to pin it on me at the time. They hadn't the evidence.'

'Wish I'd been given the case, sunshine. I've read the file: I reckon I'd have had you last year.'

Darren thought he probably would have, too. He tried hard to concentrate on what he had to say. 'Walsh was threatening

201

me to make me pay up. I came to you last week because I thought that might scare him off.'

'And when it didn't, you took the initiative yourself and garrotted him. Decisive, that.'

'I didn't kill Walsh.'

'You've just given us a full account of how convenient his death was for you.'

'But I didn't kill him. All right, I'm glad the bastard's dead, but as I told you on Monday, I wasn't around when he was killed.'

'You told us that, yes. Even at the time, we weren't inclined to believe you. And now that you've given us a motive . . .' Peach completed the thought with a shrug of his powerful shoulders.

'Look, you can't pin this on me. I told you, I went down to the centre of the town for a casual drink and happened to drift into the White Bull.'

'Which wasn't convincing, even at the first time of telling. You don't use the White Bull as a drinking place. You went there because you knew Eric Walsh was going to be there that night.'

Darren Cartwright stared wide-eyed at Peach for a moment. Suddenly both hands rose and ran themselves through his carefully arranged hair, leaving it comically askew; he looked down at the offending limbs as if they had moved without his command. 'All right, I knew it was the Lodge Ladies' Night and I knew Walsh would be there. I suppose I was hoping for a chance to reason with him, perhaps with some of our Masonic friends in attendance. I didn't get the chance. And I told you, I left before the time you said he was killed. I was away from the pub just after eleven, long before he died.'

'Wrong, Mr Cartwright. What you actually said was that you left shortly after last orders were called, when the public bar shut for the night. But the bar shuts at eleven thirty, not eleven, on Friday nights. On your own account, that puts your departure at around twenty to twelve. Eric Walsh was dead by then.'

Darren Cartwright stared past Peach and Blake towards the beautifully framed pictures of the Lake District on the walls of his office. But he did not see them. He said flatly, 'I thought I'd convinced you that I'd left by ten past eleven.'

Lucy Blake, sensing a confession, said softly, 'Are you telling us that you killed Eric Walsh, Mr Cartwright?'

In the same flat monotone, he said unconvincingly, 'No. I didn't kill him. I'm glad someone did, but it wasn't me.'

Peach stared at him for a moment. Then he said, 'There'll be plenty of time for us to look for the evidence. The officers in charge of that case will be arresting you in connection with the injuries suffered by Beth Kershaw. Don't leave the district, Mr Cartwright.'

Twenty

On Friday morning, Peach found Superintendent Thomas Bulstrode Tucker brimming with an excitement he could hardly suppress.

'It's not for myself that I'm pleased, of course,' he said unconvincingly. 'It's for the CID unit as a whole. And of course for you, Percy.'

'You've found out who killed Eric Walsh, sir? Well, that is certainly reason to congratulate yourself. Bears out what I tell the lads and lasses down the pecking order, that does. "You may think the chief just sits up there and takes the plaudits, you may think he rides on the backs of us people labouring away at the crime face, but he's up there thinking," I tell them. "Using his experience and his brainpower to guide us to a solution." So who killed the brawny Brunton baritone, sir?'

'Eh? Oh, that. I haven't discovered who murdered Eric Walsh. That's your job. And in the grander scale of things, it is a mere detail.' Tucker drew himself up to his full height and gazed out with Churchillian vision over a world of pygmies. 'I am speaking of our promotions, Percy. The elevation in our ranks which will enable us to take the CID section forward to new heights.'

'I see, sir. Do you want my report on the latest developments in the Walsh case?'

'Have you made an arrest?'

'No, sir.'

'Then I really don't think I can be bothered with the detail of the case, Percy. Not this morning.' He turned from his contemplation of the old cotton town through the wide

window of his penthouse office. 'You and I have bigger
fish to fry.'

'I see, sir. It's just that diligent work by the team on the
ground has thrown up an interesting detail, and I thought you
might like to be kept fully aware of what I planned—'

'Oh, I don't think so, not this morning.'

For once, Tucker could not bring himself to sit down behind
the big desk he normally saw as the symbol of his authority.
'You don't seem to see the significance of what I'm saying,
Percy. Oh, your preoccupation with solving the latest crime
on our patch is all very praiseworthy, I'm sure, in the normal
order of things. But one needs to stand back and take the wider
view sometimes. This is one of those occasions.' He set his chin
at his indomitable Churchillian angle again and turned back to
gaze out over his empire.

'Well, of course, you've always been good at the overview,
sir, whereas I have busied myself with the mundane—'

'Mundane!' Tucker seized upon the word with unusual
alacrity. 'That is the word for your attitude, I'm afraid,
Percy.'

Peach gave up. You couldn't taunt a man with his head so
high among the clouds. 'You have news, sir?'

'Indeed I have, Percy. Good news. The very best of news.'

'Is my research monograph on Masonic crime in the North-
West of England to be published, sir?'

Tucker gave him a thin smile. Not even Percy Peach was
going to spoil his morning. 'The news of our promotion board
is through, Percy. You could be back in uniform and no longer
under my direct command very soon, if you become a chief
inspector.' He could not suppress a smile of anticipation at
that prospect.

'I see, sir.'

'This time in a couple of weeks, I shall be chief superintendent.' He elevated his chin a fraction, gazing over the town's
few remaining mill chimneys to the clear blue sky and the
lofty heights beyond. He sighed a reluctant sigh and turned
back to the sordid reality of the man behind him. 'And you,

of course, will be a chief inspector, Percy. If you play your cards right.'

'Yes, sir. Do you think I should mention my research interests? I thought it might go down well, with all this emphasis on the need for a cerebral input in modern policing.'

'We must stick together, Percy. Support each other. I shall tell them what a splendid officer you have been, loyal and supportive. And I expect you, Percy, will wish to dwell upon the unswerving support you have always had from your leader. Not that I would wish in any way to colour your opinions, of course. That goes without saying.'

'I see, sir. Well, I shall be happy to enlarge upon the degree of support I and others have had from you.'

'The assistant chief constable will certainly be on the board, I understand. I don't know who else, as yet.'

'Will the chief constable be there, sir?'

'It's possible, I suppose, in a small force like ours. But I doubt it.'

'Pity, that. We don't get much opportunity to speak to the top brass. Tell them what we really think of the way things work. Show them that we have initiative and a capacity for original thinking.'

Tucker coughed nervously. 'Promotion boards are not the occasion for original thinking, Percy.' He inclined his head confidentially towards his inspector. 'It's my belief that if we play this carefully, our interviews will be little more than a formality. We need to stick together.' He forced a smile. 'For my part, I shall enlarge upon your splendid achievements.'

'And what shall I do, sir? After I've outlined the kind of support you give us, I mean.'

Tucker's smile died as abruptly as it had appeared. 'It's not for me to say. It should be obvious.'

Percy's round face displayed total puzzlement, then a dawning of enlightenment. 'I could talk about you, sir, couldn't I? Enlarge upon the role you play in our tight little organization.' He beamed happily, turning the full force of his happiness upon his chief. 'I feel much happier about it now, sir. I certainly shan't be lost for words!'

The romantic view of detection is that it is all about intuition. A brilliant individual – The Great Detective – spots something which no one else sees. His feel for the case and his huge intellect then enable him to make deductions which would elude ordinary mortals. Case solved.

The people who actually make arrests know that the reality is very different. Neither criminals nor policemen are quite as brilliant or original as fiction would have us believe. Most CID men would support Edison's definition of genius as one per cent inspiration and ninety-nine per cent perspiration. The old proverb that genius is an infinite capacity for taking pains might be even nearer the mark. Certainly when carelessness creeps in murderers get away with far more than they should, as the tragic instances of Sutcliffe, the Yorkshire Ripper, and Frederick West, the multiple killer of Gloucester, amply demonstrate.

The team working on the murder of Eric Walsh was diligent and careful, and it eventually turned up a key fact. It was a small item, insignificant to an outsider, but to the man in charge of the case, DI Peach, it was gold dust.

The numbers of a dozen cars belonging to people involved in the investigation had been issued to the uniformed men working on the case, with the instruction to check their whereabouts in the hours before and after the murder. There were inevitably many blind alleys, many recordings of vehicles which looked interesting but led nowhere.

Then one sighting in a small side street near the centre of the town, by a constable who was not even part of the murder team, caught and held Percy Peach's attention. It was one of several numbers recorded by a constable patrolling his town centre beat at night. He'd noticed the inside light was on as the driver's door was left ajar; the keys had been left in the ignition.

When he rejoined the real world after seeing Tucker, Peach

spoke to the constable concerned. He checked the detail, the one which Thomas Bulstrode Tucker had refused to hear, went over the times with the alert young officer, and called in Lucy Blake.

When he had briefed her and they had exchanged reactions, he said grimly, 'I don't want you to contact him at work. I think we should go round to his residence tonight. I don't want him to have any notice of this.'

Though it was only half past six, there was a winter darkness on this November night. There would be a frost again later. The stars shone white against a navy sky and there was no wind to shift clouds across the thin, bright crescent of the moon.

In a few hours, it would be exactly seven days since the murder of Eric Walsh; they were just within the week which Tommy Bloody Tucker had quoted so blandly as their deadline. Peach smiled sourly at that thought in the blackness as they got out of the car.

He was very focussed at times like this, thought Lucy Blake. She wished she could be as single-minded, shutting out all thoughts but the tactics for those moments before arrest as Percy did. Instead, she found herself saying nervously, 'Will he give us trouble, do you think?'

Percy nearly said that she wouldn't be here if he thought there was any danger to her precious person. But she wouldn't like that, not in these days of sexual equality; he wondered at the myriad sensitivities he was having to learn. He said, 'No, I don't anticipate any trouble. We could do with an admission from him.'

Lucy realized that he was tense; his clipped words came through the darkness, hushed with something very like stage fright. Except that this melodrama was for real. She said, 'He could be armed, I suppose.'

'He could have a weapon somewhere in the place. But if we arrive unannounced, he won't be any danger to us. He's not stupid: he'll know when the game's up.'

In his own very different way, he was as nervous as she was. Lucy found that curiously consoling.

The flat was part of a conversion in a fine old Victorian house, built into the side of a hill, with fine views to the west and the north. In the days of King Cotton and nineteenth-century electoral reform, the town's Member of Parliament had dwelt here, holding court to his newly enfranchised male constituents very much in the way of the old lord of the manor. Those days were long gone, as were the days of the low wages which had allowed a multitude of servants to maintain a comfortable life for the denizens of the house. But the spaciousness of the original building had allowed a conversion into six large and luxuriously appointed flats for the occupants of the twenty-first century.

Peach looked automatically to the north from the car park. He knew that in daylight there would be a fine view of the distant heights of Ingleborough and Pen-y-Ghent. Now they could see nothing but the vastness of the night sky and its multitude of uncaring stars. Not even the lower and much nearer bulk of Pendle Hill was visible now. There was only the gaunt black outline of the house against the winter sky; the only relief in this forbidding silhouette was the soft orange of lights behind curtained windows, which looked very small within the bulk of the high walls of the massive building.

They pressed the right bell among the names, and the answering voice, a little metallic through the speaker, said, 'Come up, Inspector, by all means,' with just the right inflection of surprise.

He was there when they walked out of the lift on the first floor, standing tall in the open doorway of the flat. Adrian O'Connor led the way inside and said, 'Friday night and the end of the week, for most of us. Can I offer the two of you a drink – alcoholic or otherwise, as you prefer?'

To Lucy Blake, this seemed entirely unreal. A murderer going through the social graces in an apartment the estate agents would surely have described as 'spacious and beautifully appointed'. There were three windows in the big sitting room, each of them with curtains hanging to the floor. There was a wide-screen television and a stack of high-fidelity equipment, gold-framed pictures on the wall, and two deep sofas, maroon against the softer red of the carpet. Yet, accustomed as she was to her own small flat and the low-ceilinged cottage where she had grown up, this seemed to her too perfect, too tidy, like a show flat rather than one which was lived in.

As if he read her thoughts, O'Connor said, 'This is a comfortable place. Very comfortable, as a matter of fact. But I'm not here all that often. I bought the fixtures and fittings with the place when I moved in.'

'Didn't intend to be here very long, perhaps?' said Peach.

O'Connor looked at him sharply. 'I've already been here three years. It just suited me to have the place ready-furnished. I'm a busy man, with a demanding job. I prefer to spend what leisure I have on other things.'

They were like two dogs circling each other, waiting to see who would make the first aggressive move in the fight they knew was coming, thought Lucy Blake. She sat down on the edge of the sofa, then watched the two men sit at the same time, lowering themselves to the seats as if moving in slow motion. Peach said, 'You told us your first pack of lies at the station, your second in your office. I thought you might like to be arrested in your home.'

If he intended to throw his man off balance, there was no visible sign that he had succeeded. Adrian O'Connor took his time, whatever frenzied brain activity was going on beneath his heavy crop of brown hair. Then he said, 'I presume you're referring to the murder of Eric Walsh. I've never made any secret of the fact that I didn't like the man: you know something of the history of that. Perhaps I should now reiterate that I didn't kill him.'

'I think you came to the area three years ago with the specific intention of harming Eric Walsh. Whether or not you intended to kill him at that time I'm not sure. It is in any case irrelevant now.'

'And why should I want to kill the man?' For the first time, the southern Irish brogue was apparent in his voice. 'If you're dragging up the old times when we were on opposite sides in Ireland back in the eighties, I'd say that we were both then young men and that since that time we'd learned—'

'Your sister committed suicide as a result of the Walshes' attentions! I can't speculate on how much weight a court will allot to that when it comes to a recommendation for mercy. I assume you know that there is a mandatory life sentence for murder.'

'I wasn't even around when Walsh was killed. I've already explained to you that I left the White Bull some time before he died.'

'Yes. You seemed from the start to have a very clear idea of the exact time when Eric Walsh died.'

'That's as may be. I told you when I left. And as it happens, you turned up a witness from the hotel staff who confirmed that time.'

'Maybe it wasn't "as it happens", Mr O'Connor. More probably it was a very deliberate act. I believe you took pains to ask the hotel waiter the time just so that he would be able to confirm to us later that you left at ten past eleven. You'd already told us that the clock in your car read eleven fifteen as you drove out, and you wear a watch. You hardly needed that waiter to tell you the time. But it planted your departure firmly in his mind.'

O'Connor smiled. 'Interesting to see the way a suspicious brain works. But the fact remains, I left well before Walsh was killed. And I have a witness who confirms it. Unless you choose to call him a liar as well.'

'On the contrary, we always listen to people with no axe to grind. And there was no need for your little ploy; as it happened, another member of the hotel staff watched you drive out because he was afraid you'd scrape someone's car. But we always proceed from facts. We can't afford to do anything else, when we decide to make an arrest.'

'And the facts tell you that I drove away from the White

Bull at a quarter past eleven last Friday night. Having been seen going out to my car at ten past eleven.'

Peach nodded. He did not volunteer any of his range of smiles: the situation was too serious for that. But his dark eyes never left his man's face. 'Agreed. However, it is the recording of your car in another place which is the most interesting fact.'

For the first time, Adrian O'Connor looked a little uncertain. 'I can't think where that might be. But surely the fact that my car was seen miles away from the White Bull can only confirm that I could not have killed Walsh. Or are you now trying to make out that I brought someone in to do the killing for me?'

Peach nodded to DS Blake, who said in a clear, even voice, 'No, Mr O'Connor, we are not. But nor was your car seen miles away from the White Bull. It was recorded by one of the constables on town centre patrol as having been parked in Albert Street at twenty to twelve. A side street approximately one hundred yards from the car park of the White Bull. You drove it away from there at just before midnight.'

O'Connor would have argued with Peach. Even if he had been beaten down, he would have blustered automatically. But this cool, seemingly dispassionate female voice carried a ring of doom in his ears. He said feebly, 'There must surely be some mistake.'

Peach said quietly, 'There is no mistake. You parked in the shadows of that quiet cul de sac and walked back to Eric Walsh's car in the car park of the White Bull. You waited in the back seat of the car until he came out to it and then killed an innocent man in cold blood.'

'Innocent? Eric Walsh was guilty as hell!' Whether by accident or design, Peach had found the word to trigger an outburst. 'You don't know what mayhem the Walshes caused in Belfast. And they defiled an innocent girl. Broke her mind and her spirit. Drove my poor sister Kathleen to suicide and to mortal damnation. And Eric was the head of the whole bunch of them! I swore I'd get him years ago. And sure, I told him just why he was dying as I tightened the cord around his neck!'

There was something medieval in his wildness as well as his theology. The Irish accent grew stronger throughout his outburst. He stopped, panting, interested only in the effects of his self-justification, in whether he had convinced his listeners that there was a kind of justice in this death.

Lucy Blake stepped forward and pronounced the words of arrest in a clear, even voice. O'Connor made no resistance, even when she concluded the familiar formula and slid the handcuffs around his wrists.

The young, fresh-faced uniformed men regarded him curiously when they took him out to the waiting patrol car. Their first murderer. And so normal-looking. A bloke in an expensive suit, with a good job and a flash car. A bloke who could afford to live in a place like this.

Peach and Blake went back into the flat. They found a bright, newly-cut key to Eric Walsh's Triumph Stag in an antique tobacco jar on the very centre of the mantelpiece. Adrian O'Connor had been as confident as that that he would not be caught. Or perhaps he had wished to preserve the key as a trophy of war, a kind of medal.

They spoke little to each other as they moved through the big rooms of the flat. There was the now familiar sense of anticlimax, the deflation of spirits that followed the high excitement of a murder arrest.

It was not until they were back in the car that Percy said, as if shutting the lid on something unpleasant, 'He'll plead guilty, I expect. Get a clever counsel to play up his sister's death as a mitigating circumstance. Blame ancient Ireland for his upbringing in a war of hate.'

'And Tommy Bloody Tucker will claim the credit for his arrest,' said Lucy Blake resentfully.

It took Percy Peach all of ten seconds to find consolation for that. 'At least the murderer was a Mason,' he said, with his first smile in an hour.

'I've no doubt you'll make something of that,' said Blake.

'And this time next week it will be *Chief* Superintendent Tommy Bloody Useless Tucker.'

'It's an imperfect world we live in,' said Lucy Blake with a contented smile.